The Days of Elijah

Book Two: Wormwood

Mark Goodwin

For information on preparing for natural or man-made disasters, visit the author's website, PrepperRecon.com

Technical information in the book is included to convey realism. The author shall not have liability or responsibility to any person or entity with respect to any loss or damage caused, or allegedly caused, directly or indirectly by the information contained in this book.

All of the characters, places, and incidents are products of the author's imagination or are used fictitiously. Any resemblance to actual people, places, or events is entirely coincidental.

Copyright © 2017 Goodwin America Corp.

All rights reserved. No part of this publication may be reproduced, stored in a retrieval system, or transmitted in any form or by any means without the prior written permission of the author, except by a reviewer who may quote short passages in a review.

ISBN: 1540357724
ISBN-13: 978-1540357724

DEDICATION

Whoso findeth a wife findeth a good thing, and obtaineth favour of the Lord.

Proverbs 18:22

To my beautiful bride. Thank you for your love and support. I love you forever.

ACKNOWLEDGMENTS

A most heartfelt note of appreciation to my wonderful wife and constant companion. Thank you for your patience, encouragement, and support.

I would like to thank my fantastic editing team, Catherine Goodwin, Ken and Jen Elswick, Jeff Markland, Frank Shackleford, Kris Van Wagenen, Sherrill Hesler, and Claudine Allison.

CHAPTER 1

And the Lord saith, Because they have forsaken my law which I set before them, and have not obeyed my voice, neither walked therein; But have walked after the imagination of their own heart, and after Baalim, which their fathers taught them: Therefore thus saith the Lord of hosts, the God of Israel; Behold, I will feed them, even this people, with wormwood, and give them water of gall to drink.

Jeremiah 9:13-15

Everett Carroll brushed the dirt off of the potatoes as he picked them up and placed them in the plastic bucket next to the one he was using as a stool. "The garden has certainly produced better than last year."

Courtney Carroll gently swung the hoe, digging up potatoes just ahead of where her husband was working. "Much better. The heavy snow last winter seemed to knock most of the volcanic ash out of the air. The pollution from the ash was like a constant haze blocking the sun and pretty much snuffed out any hope of a garden. I hated being cold and pinned up in the cabin because of the snow, but it's been nice having fresh vegetables. I was worried that the next round of judgments would begin and wipe out this year's crop."

Everett picked up the bucket he'd been sitting on and moved it further down the row. "They could start at any moment. It's been eighteen months since the Seventh Seal was opened. Saturday is Rosh Hashanah. I always get nervous around the Jewish holidays."

"That's right. The Seventh Seal was opened on Passover." Courtney leaned on the hoe as she paused for a short break. "But Rosh Hashanah is the Jewish New Year. It's a time of celebration. It seems out of character for God to send judgment on a day designated for celebration."

Everett crushed large clods of dirt to check for any small potatoes that might be hidden within. "I see your point, but I'm not too sure about that."

"Why?"

"Typically, in the Bible, times of celebration are sort of a reward for being obedient. In Isaiah, chapter one, God lays out his case against Judah. He says he hates their appointed feasts because they aren't obeying him. He goes so far as to call their sacrifices vain oblations."

"So you think God could start the next round of judgments on Rosh Hashanah?"

Everett shook his head. "I don't know. I hope not. But if the seven years began when Luz signed the treaty on the New Year's before last, we've got just over five years left. Sooner or later, the angels will unleash the Seven Trumpets and the Seven Vials of Wrath."

Courtney stared at the soil beneath her feet. "And woe to us poor souls who have to live through it."

Everett stood up and put his arm around her. "Heaven is on the other side. Once we get through the next few years, it's all downhill from there."

She placed one hand on the back of his neck. Her smile didn't look sincere. "Yeah, thanks."

Everett tried to stay positive. He forced a smile in return. The hope of glory gleamed bright in his heart, but the heavy cloud of concern over the immediate future was dark and ominous. "You're a good wife. Times are tough, but I'm blessed to have you to help me through."

She put her head on his shoulder. "You're so sweet. I love you, Everett."

The piercing sound of a whistle rang out from the direction of the house.

"That's the alarm. Come on, let's get to the house." Everett clutched the handle of the bucket containing the potatoes and abandoned the one on which he'd been sitting.

Courtney followed him, carrying the hoe in one

hand and drawing her pistol with the other. "I guess we have to be thankful for the good times we've had. This past year has been fairly peaceful."

Everett walked briskly toward the house. "Considering this is the Tribulation, you're right. We have to count our blessings."

Sarah was putting Cupcake, the rough-looking farm dog who also answered to Danger, in the house when they arrived.

Everett set the bucket down on the porch. "What's happening?"

Sarah handed him the field glasses and pointed toward the east. "Another chopper."

Everett held the binoculars to his eyes and peered out over the foothills. "Courtney, douse the fire in the rocket stove. It doesn't produce much smoke, but if they're using thermal, the stove will stand out like a ketchup stain on a white dress shirt."

Courtney quickly ran to put out the fire which Sarah had started so she could cook lunch.

Kevin came outside and stood on the porch. "Are they headed this way?"

"It's hard to say." Everett watched the helicopter for a few seconds then handed the field glasses to Kevin. "I'd say they're roughly three miles out."

Kevin peered through the glasses. "They're definitely making a surveillance run. My guess is that they're gathering information on how many survivors are in and around Woodstock."

Sarah crossed her arms. "I suppose that means they'll be setting up shop in Woodstock soon. Once that happens, they'll be flying patrols around here regularly."

Kevin handed the binoculars to Courtney when she returned from extinguishing the fire. "It was fun while it lasted."

Sarah stuck her hands in her back pockets. "No fire in the stove means cold lunch."

Courtney led the way back into the house. "That's the end of our chores for the day. I'm going to call Elijah on the radio and let him know there's a chopper in the area."

Everett followed her in. "Make it a short call. They're probably scanning the frequencies."

"I will." Courtney placed the binoculars on the kitchen counter and headed up the ladder to call Elijah on the handheld.

Kevin went into the bedroom and returned carrying a cardboard box. "This was the last case of MREs under the bed. We'll have to make a run out to the cave soon. We're running low on some staples as well. We need rice, sugar, cornmeal, toilet paper, and soap."

Everett opened the doors of the cupboards and looked inside. "Yeah. We need to get that done before the aerial patrols start getting closer to the cabin."

Kevin opened the case of MREs and took out four packages. "I haven't seen any patrols flying at night yet. Maybe we should go at sunset tomorrow."

Everett stared at the sparsely stocked shelves as he thought through the suggestion. "Then we'd have to drive back after dark. The roads are in really rough condition between here and the cave. Even with the headlights on, it would be a difficult path to navigate."

Sarah took a seat at the kitchen table. "If the Global Republic decides to start flying night patrols tomorrow, they'll spot you from miles away with your headlights on. It doesn't sound safe to me."

Kevin placed the box on the floor and sat down beside her. "So we drive out to the cave just before evening tomorrow. We load up the truck, sleep at the cave and drive back at first light on Saturday."

Everett closed the cupboard doors and pulled out his chair to sit down. "Rosh Hashanah starts at sundown tomorrow night. I think Elijah is planning a big meal."

Kevin began opening his MRE. "Then we go the day after. We've still got a few weeks' worth of supplies."

"We could go tonight." Everett sighed. "As long as there are no helicopters flying when we're ready to leave."

Sarah looked at Everett. "You think something is going to happen, don't you? You think the Trumpet Judgments are going to start on Rosh Hashanah."

"I didn't say that." Everett tore the top off of his MRE.

Sarah took the individual components out of her MRE and positioned them on the table. "But you didn't deny it. There must be some reason you're pushing to go get supplies before the holiday. Did Elijah say something to you?"

"No. Nothing at all." Everett looked over his shoulder to watch Courtney coming down the ladder. "It's just that the Seventh Seal was on Passover. I'd rather be prepared, in case something does happen."

Courtney tussled his hair as she sat down. "Don't be scaring everybody. The Seventh Seal marked the end of the Seal Judgments. We're waiting for the beginning of the Trumpet Judgments."

Everett bowed his head. "Let's bless the food so we can eat."

All of them held hands as Everett said a short prayer.

Kevin opened his pouch and began eating. "Everett is right. It would be better to be prepared. We've been eighteen months without a major catastrophic event. Sooner or later, the next wave of chaos will begin."

"Then we'll go tonight. We can drop Cupcake off at Elijah's on the way." Sarah continued eating.

Everett nodded. "It gets dark around 7:30 so we'll head out around 6:00, provided there are no chopper sightings."

"Should we bring anything?" Courtney asked.

Everett shook his head. "Just battle rifles, in case we step in a mess on the way. We've got sleeping bags and everything we need in the cave. It will be a good chance to stay there and identify anything we should have in the cave in case we have to bug out."

"I hope no one has found the cave," Sarah said.

"You guys didn't take Scratchy over there, did you?" Courtney inquired.

Everett shook his head. "No. When he helped us haul our supplies across the landslide area, we brought everything to the house."

Kevin said, "We figured bringing him to the house was the lesser of the two evils. A boulder crushed the F-150 on the other side of the landslide during the Great Quake, so we had no choice. We needed his van to ferry the goods to the landslide. He offered to help us hike the goods over, one backpack full at a time, to our side of the landslide. We couldn't very well make him wait on the other side."

"Scratchy isn't going to rob us." Everett smiled.

"Unless he gets desperate." Courtney crossed her arms. "He's opportunistic. And that bunch he runs with down in Winchester would best be described as *omnivores*."

Sarah pursed her lips and looked at Courtney. "Yeah, bears are pretty gentle unless they're hungry."

Kevin nodded. "Even so, they know we're heavily armed, and there's no easy way to get supplies out of here. The roads are blocked in both directions."

Later that afternoon, Everett stood on the porch with the binoculars. He scanned the skyline, looking for helicopters and listening for the sound of aircraft.

Courtney joined him. "Do you see anything?"

He lowered the field glasses. "No. The coast is clear. Tell everyone that we'll leave in about fifteen minutes."

"Roger that." She kissed him on the lips and went back inside.

Minutes later Everett and Kevin retrieved the ladder. Next, everyone loaded into the green Tennessee Wildlife Resource Agency truck which Kevin and Sarah had brought with them to the cabin. Kevin drove, making a brief stop at Elijah's.

Elijah came out to greet them. "You're early! The dinner isn't until tomorrow."

Courtney explained the trip out to the cave.

Sarah asked Elijah to keep Cupcake inside as he would be a sure sign of an occupied residence if a chopper spotted him.

Elijah nodded. "Of course I'll keep him. I suppose I should consider keeping the goats in the barn as well. They won't like that. But we're all making adjustments. They'll have to do their part. Be safe and go with the blessings of the Almighty."

Everyone waved goodbye to Elijah and continued toward the cave. Once they'd traveled as far as possible by truck, they parked near the mountain stream and followed the backwoods trail on foot. Everett held one end of the ladder while Kevin followed him with the other.

Courtney was the first to reach the opening of the cavern. "It doesn't look like anyone has disturbed the cave. In fact, it's really overgrown. If I didn't know what I was looking for, I'd never spot it."

Everett was close behind her. "Yeah, it's very well concealed."

Kevin began clearing away the brush which was growing around the opening. "We better keep moving. It will be dark soon. I'd like to get at least one load down to the truck before nightfall."

Sarah clicked on her flashlight and peered inside before crawling through the opening. "I don't see any signs of bears or snakes. I can deal with anything else we might run into."

"I don't want to see any bats either." Courtney followed her through the small hole.

Everett helped Courtney into the cave then fed the ladder to her so she could pull it through. "Nor badgers. You can shoot a bear, but a badger running at you at full speed is a hard target to hit." Everett crawled low to clear the overhanging tree roots.

"There's no badgers this far east." Kevin was the last one in the cave. He stood up and brushed off his knees.

"I've seen badgers in Virginia," Everett protested.

Kevin repositioned his ball cap on his head. "You saw a skunk."

Everett launched his defense. "I know the difference between a badger and a skunk. If I was a betting man . . ."

"If you were a betting man, you'd be losing money on this one brother, trust me." Kevin patted Everett on the back as they proceeded back toward the wall with the ladder.

They arrived at the rear wall of the large open room which they called the cathedral. Everett and Kevin positioned the ladder near the opening on the upper level. Everett climbed to the storage area and began lowering supplies with a rope.

Sarah called to him. "Bring down enough supplies for two trips. While you guys are taking the first load to the truck, I'll ferry the other load to the entrance. Remember that I can't haul buckets on the uneven trail with my prosthetic leg."

"Sure thing." He lowered several more boxes and buckets then came down the ladder.

By the time they'd returned to the cave from the first sortie, the forest was pitch black. It was a new moon and the stars by themselves offered little more than a soft glow in the sky above.

"No use trying to navigate back down to the truck. It's way too dark. Using flashlights would defeat our purpose of coming at night." Courtney gazed into the void of the woods.

"I'm not sure we want to bring more than one more load of stuff anyway. I know we want to make the most out of every trip because there's no gas, but it's only a few miles. We could hike over on foot if we had to." Everett led the way into the cave.

Kevin followed him inside. "It wouldn't be the first time."

Everett climbed the ladder and retrieved the sleeping bags.

Courtney caught them as he tossed them over the side. "Can you grab the radio? We're going to be pretty bored in here all night with minimal light."

"Sure. We've got cards also." Everett crawled back into the long corridor which they were using as a storage area.

"Good, grab those too," Courtney replied.

Everett collected the remainder of the items they needed to make camp in the cave and climbed back down the ladder. He handed the radio to Courtney.

She turned on the power and scrolled through the channels. "Static."

Everett shined his flashlight at the roof and the cave walls. "I guess no radio waves are traveling through the layers of rock above us. We need some wire so we can run an antenna to the entrance."

"Do we have any?" Sarah asked.

Everett thought through the inventory of the

supplies stashed overhead. "No."

"Good. We can put that on our list of things we need to bring out to the cave." Courtney unrolled her sleeping bag. "At least we have cards. Who's ready to get whipped at Spades?"

Kevin positioned his bag. "I guess you are. Whether we're playing boys against girls, or couples, you ain't on my team, so your odds of whipping anybody are slim."

"You're getting a little too cocky." Sarah laid out her bag and sat down Indian-style across from Courtney. "Girls against guys. You're going down, Kevin."

Everett removed the cards from the box and shuffled them. "We'll see about that."

The four friends played several rounds of cards. It had been a reliable source of distraction over the past few months, much of which had been spent cooped up indoors.

Courtney laid down a card. "We'd be lost in here without flashlights. If we ever had to move here permanently, we'd have to bring a solar setup."

Everett considered the gravity of her statement. "You're right. We have to have light in here. I hope we don't get into a situation where we don't have time to retrieve all the components for a solar generator."

Kevin tossed his card on the pile. "Pulling the panels off the roof and disconnecting everything takes time. Twenty or thirty minutes, at least. Between the coming judgments and having hell's henchmen hunting us down, I can imagine quite a few scenarios where we wouldn't have that much time to bug out."

Sarah laid her card on top and picked up the book. "Yeah, and I can't think of any situations where we would have to leave, yet still have an extra half hour to burn."

"So the question should be, is it worth living without the solar generator now, to make sure we have it later?" Courtney looked over her remaining cards.

Everett peered at his hand. "It would be an inconvenience, but we can always go back to taking our batteries up to Elijah's to recharge."

"Given the alternative of being stuck in a cave with no way to recharge our batteries, it sounds like a minuscule inconvenience," Courtney said.

Sarah grabbed her flashlight and turned it off. "Everybody, turn off your light. Let's see if that helps us make up our minds."

Courtney was first to follow suit. Everett and Kevin turned out their lights next. The darkness was heavy. It seemed to grow as the four of them sat silent for the next few seconds.

Everett opened his eyes wide and stared at the vacant black before his eyes. He turned his head toward the position where he remembered last seeing Courtney. He could see nothing. The heavy darkness seemed to empty out, to become hollow. At first, he felt the dark laying dense upon his eyes like an iron lid or a wall of lead, but he had a sinking sensation like all light had been drawn into a vacuum, leaving no trace of anything in its wake. Minutes later, the impression of the void became maddening. Everett was sure everyone else was feeling the same thing, but no one broke. His thumb pressed against the soft rubber cover which enveloped the switch of the flashlight. He pressed against it gently; enough to eliminate the slack, but not enough to actually turn the light on. Everett considered what utter darkness must consume the souls of men damned to hell. His sense of overwhelming dread was replaced by deep gratitude because God had shown him grace, and had given him a second chance. Even if he were to hit the light, and it not come back on, even if none of the lights came back on, this realm was temporary, and he could take whatever it had to throw at him, as long as he knew his eternity would be spent walking in the light of the Messiah.

Courtney finally cracked. She turned on her light. "Okay, that was crazy! Were you guys good being in the dark like that? Because it was about to freak me out."

Kevin laughed. "No, I was going to give it one more minute, and I was going to cave if no one else did."

"You're such a baby!" Sarah chided Kevin playfully.

Kevin shined his light on her hand. "Look at your knuckles! They're white! You were aching to turn on your light. You just couldn't stand being the one who folded first."

"Whatever!" Sarah switched the light to her other hand and worked her fingers to get the circulation going.

Everett chuckled. "I guess we have a consensus. We'll bring the solar generator out to the cave."

The next morning, the team woke up early. Everyone rolled up their sleeping bags and tossed them up to Everett who quickly stowed them in the corridor above the cathedral.

Everett descended and laid the ladder down on its side. "Let's stash this nearby."

Kevin grabbed one side to carry the ladder out of the cave. "Okay. We can cover it with leaves for now. I'm sure we'll be back in the next day or two with the solar components. We can find a better hiding place for it then."

Once they had hidden the ladder, everyone slung their rifles over their backs and Everett, Courtney, and Kevin each grabbed a box or a bucket of supplies as they exited the cave. The sun was just beginning to peek over the foothills in the east when they reached the truck. The rays of sunlight immediately began to break the morning chill. Kevin started the truck, and the team headed back toward the cabin.

Sarah leaned forward from the back seat and pointed toward the east. "Chopper!"

Everett shook his head in disgust. "Wow! I've never seen them out so early before. I hope this isn't going to become an everyday occurrence."

Kevin gunned the engine. "Maybe we can get home before he gets close enough to spot us."

Courtney leaned forward from the rear. "No way. He's coming this way. Pull off the road and into that clump of trees. Elijah's place is on the other side of that hill. We can leave the truck here and walk over to Elijah's. We'll have visual cover from the forest the whole way."

Kevin looked at Everett. "What do you think?"

Everett nodded. "She's right. We'll come back and get the truck when the chopper is gone. He'll have to refuel after a while."

Kevin pulled the truck deep beneath the cover of the trees and cut the engine.

Everett looked at the temperature gauge. "The engine didn't get very hot, but maybe we should pop the hood to let out as much heat as possible, in case they're using thermal."

The team grabbed their weapons and exited the vehicle quickly. Kevin called to Sarah and Courtney, "You guys get going. Stay spread out. We're easier to spot if we're all clumped up."

The girls took off at a quick pace over the hill. Everett and Kevin popped the hood, locked the doors, and then trailed behind, maintaining a ten-to-twenty-yard distance between themselves.

Elijah held the door open as Everett and Kevin reached the porch. "Come in, come in, hurry!"

Everett smiled at the old prophet. "Thanks. We're trying to evade being seen by that chopper."

"Courtney told me. This patrol is a most unwelcome development. Most unwelcome, indeed." Elijah turned the knob on his gas stove and struck a match. "We'll have some coffee, and perhaps the threat will pass."

Courtney looked at the stove. "You still have gas?"

"I've used the wood stove to cook as much as possible, conserving the gas for such a time as this." Elijah set an old percolator on the burner. "But we'll be in a terrible predicament if we can't use wood to heat our homes this winter because we're trying to avoid being spotted by the Global Republic. The weather is turning cold already. I should guess it was in the mid-forties this morning."

Everett looked at the gas stove, the hot pot on the burner, then up at the cabin loft above them. He hoped the pot wouldn't generate enough heat to be seen through the loft floor and the ceiling above. He dismissed the concern quickly. If the chopper got close enough to see the pot, it would likely pick up on their body heat anyway. He looked at his HK rifle propped up in the corner and calculated his movements if he were to need it.

Sarah sat down at Elijah's kitchen table. "Do you mind if we listen to the radio? We couldn't get any reception in the cave last night. I like to keep up on the propaganda."

Courtney took a seat next to her. "Especially when we're being hunted down by helicopters."

"Certainly." Elijah extended the telescoping antenna and turned on the small battery operated radio.

A female Global Republic reporter with a thick British accent was speaking. ". . . Two lanes of Interstate 95 are now open from Miami to the previous Canadian border in Maine, making it the first fully functional interstate in North America since the Great Quake. Road crews have not yet reconstructed overpasses and exits, but the Department of Transportation has cleared the fallen debris from I-95. Most bridges on the primary north-south artery are one lane only, requiring vehicles to stop and let oncoming traffic pass before proceeding. All interstates are open only to Global Republic vehicles at this time so traffic is well controlled.

"Interstate 70 now has one lane open from Baltimore to Denver. Mondays, Wednesdays, and Fridays are being used by the GR for westbound traffic, while Tuesdays, Thursdays, and Saturdays are for eastbound traffic. Sundays are reserved exclusively for road construction crews.

"Department of Transportation officials have stated that they will focus on reopening one lane of Interstate 20 between I-95 and Dallas, before adding a second lane to I-70.

"Currently, there are no plans to build or repair roadways on the west coast of North America as the death toll from Vancouver to Southern California is estimated at above ninety-five percent. The Global Republic estimates that the quake and subsequent tsunamis killed roughly seventy percent of the population on the west coast. The other twenty-five percent died in the aftermath. The following weeks and months left the area in complete chaos, without food, water, sanitation or security. Unfortunately, the GR was overwhelmed by the magnitude of the disaster and unable to respond.

"Cities like Atlanta, Miami, and New York did not fare much better, although the GR was able to get some relief to those metropolitan areas within two months of the quake.

"We can say that New Atlantis is up and running. His High and Most Prepotent Majesty Angelo Luz has moved into his new home which was built on the site of the old White House. The Palace was constructed to withstand severe natural and man-made disasters as the Watchers have communicated that this current period of upheaval may present further challenges to the planet."

Elijah laughed and held one finger in the air. "Now there's the understatement of the year!"

The reporter continued, "The neo-classical architectural style of the palace itself has integrated Egyptian elements fluidly with Greek and Roman influences. It is remarkably reminiscent of the previous White House. In the front lawn sits an exact replica of the new Temple in Jerusalem. The GR constructed the model as an olive branch to followers of Jewish and Christian mythology.

"In a speech last week, GR Press Secretary Athaliah Jennings stated that re-establishing order, communications, transportation, food distribution, and power across North America would remain as the Global Republic's highest priority. She relayed His High and Most Prepotent Majesty's deep and passionate desire to see the world put back together so we can continue our global journey forward.

"Perhaps the biggest news of the day is that the Global Republic will begin its first televised broadcast next week. The highly-anticipated programming will debut with public news and information. Programming will be broadcast over the airways via digital, satellite, and even analog signals. Many survivors of the quakes have access to older television sets that can receive a signal via rabbit ears or external antennae, but have not yet been able to obtain satellite receiving equipment.

"One of the first broadcasts will be a televised tour of New Atlantis. His High and Most Prepotent Majesty believes this will inspire citizens of the global community, providing a ray of hope, and motivating people toward a cooperative spirit. With electric power, internet, sanitation, security, grocery stores, and entertainment, the city has become the first to totally rebound from the disaster. New Atlantis is fully functional and ready to lead the planet back to complete recovery from the quakes which toppled societies all around the globe.

"In somewhat more somber news, His High and Most Prepotent Majesty has decreed that those refusing to take the pledge to the Global Republic or receive their Mark implants can no longer be tolerated. He has declared these rebels to be enemies of the state. They will have public trials where they will be offered one last opportunity to be part of the new society. Those who decline His High and Most Prepotent Majesty's grace are to be executed immediately after their trials. Execution is to be by guillotine and will be televised. The means of dispatch may sound barbaric for such a civilized world order as the Global Republic, but it is also a sign of His Majesty's grace. It is his hope that the brutality and publicity of these sacrifices will encourage other holdouts to join the fold.

"In international news, Minister of the Americas Richard Clay will be visiting Secretary of the Chinese and Russian Alliance Chenglie Chau in

Beijing. The two officials hope to mend relations between the Global Republic and the East. Minister Clay stated that he believes reconciliation will replace the hostility that was so prevalent between the two super powers prior to the global earthquakes."

Sarah looked at the other people sitting around the table. "Beheading? Is she serious?"

"Indeed, she is, child." Elijah put his hand on her arm and looked at her compassionately.

Everett swallowed hard as he thought about undergoing the gruesome form of execution himself. "I guess I'm more motivated to not be taken alive now."

Kevin raised his eyebrows. "Yeah. Death by guillotine makes taking a bullet sound relatively pleasant."

Courtney shivered and curled her lip in revolt at the conversation. "I really wish we'd listened to Ken and Lisa. And you, Elijah."

Elijah smiled at her. "The Lord will get you through. He'll give you the courage and the grace to face whatever Angelo Luz has to throw at you. You are a child of God now. That's what is important."

Everett felt the same way Courtney did. He wished he could go back in time, listen to the wisdom of John Jones, follow the advice of Ken and Lisa, and escape this land of horror and tragedy by being caught up in the rapture. But he couldn't, so there was no use dreaming about it. Everett stood up and walked out to the porch. He listened for the helicopter. He looked out between the trees.

"Nothing. It's gone." He hurried back inside. "Guys, I think the chopper is gone. We've got to take our window of opportunity. Elijah, thanks for letting us lay low and thanks for the coffee. We'll be back tonight for dinner if the coast is clear. Also, we've decided to take our solar setup out to the cave, so we may need to recharge some batteries here from time to time. If you don't mind, that is."

Elijah waved his hand in the air. "Nonsense, I won't hear of it. You'll take my solar panels out to the cave."

Everett chuckled as he walked out the door. "We can't do that, Elijah. They were all your panels in the first place. We can't let you be up here with no electricity after you planned so diligently."

"Don't argue with a prophet of God!" Elijah's face was stern.

Everett was sure he was joking, yet it sent a chill up his spine. He decided not to press the issue. "Okay, thank you." Everett gave the old man a look of sincere gratitude. "Again."

Everett led the way over the hill to the truck. Minutes later, they were back at the cabin. The remainder of the day was spent unloading the supplies and stowing them away.

CHAPTER 2

And ye shall seek me, and find me, when ye shall search for me with all your heart.

Jeremiah 29:13

Everett breathed a sigh of relief as he stood on the porch of his cabin and watched the sunset Saturday night. "Rosh Hashanah is over. No sign that the next wave of judgments have begun. I guess we're in the clear." He mumbled to himself, "For now, anyways."

Courtney walked outside to join him. She zipped up her jacket. "It's chilly out here!"

"Yeah, but the air is crisp, fresh." Everett took a deep breath. "The leaves will be changing soon. I love this time of year."

She smiled at him. "You're awfully chipper. You

haven't said much all day. In fact, you weren't very talkative at Elijah's last night."

"I know. It was supposed to be a celebration; a new year and all that. I felt bad. Elijah put so much effort into dinner. It was great, but I have this sense of dread at every Jewish holiday."

She snuggled up close to him. "Well, you can breathe easy for a while."

He snickered. "Yeah, for a few days. Yom Kippur starts next Sunday."

"Remind me again, what's that one for?"

"The Day of Atonement. Jews fast that day as an act of atonement for their sins."

"Oh." Courtney furrowed her brow. "So I guess that one really has you worried, huh?"

"Yep," Everett replied. "In the context of the Great Tribulation, the Day of Atonement has something of an ominous ring. Wouldn't you agree?"

She nodded slowly. "So Seven Trumpets. We've got more earthquakes. Hail, blood, and fire falling from the sky. A giant comet that's going to poison the water. Do you think it's spread out or all at once?"

Everett shook his head. "I don't know. I wouldn't even know which one to wish for. Both scenarios present a unique set of complications."

She turned to face him. "You just came out of your funk, and now I've got you all bummed out again. Let's talk about something else."

"Sounds good." Everett smiled.

"Do you want to go play cards with Kevin and Sarah?"

"Not really."

"Then do you want to go to bed?"

"It's too early to go to sleep."

She leaned in to kiss him. "I didn't say anything about sleeping."

He smiled and gave her another kiss.

Sunday morning Everett awoke to the sound of Kevin's voice yelling.

"Everett, gear up and get down here as fast as you can. We've got company coming our way!"

Everett sprang out of bed, putting on his pants and then grabbing his HK rifle. He stepped into his boots and took his jacket which was hanging from a nail in one of the low rafters. He quickly retrieved three extra magazines from the safe, sticking them into various pockets and started down the ladder.

Courtney got out of bed and swiftly put on her jeans then pulled a sweater over her head. "What's happening?"

Everett paused briefly on the steps of the ladder. "I don't know. Maybe the GR chopper picked us up on thermal. Call Elijah on the radio and tell him there's trouble. You and Sarah take up positions from inside. Kevin and I will try to flank them."

"Be safe!" She grabbed her Mini 14 and followed him down the stairs.

"What have we got?" Everett found Kevin near the front door, AK-47 in hand, wearing a chest rig with several magazines.

"Motorcycles. Probably dirt bikes." Kevin opened the front door as he listened.

"We'll take a position up by the rock and the

girls can hold the cabin. What do you think?" Everett could hear the sound getting closer.

"I don't think we have time to get up the hill. We'll have to all stay inside." Kevin closed the door and opened the front window. "Sarah, Courtney. Open the back windows so you can shoot out. But stay back and find cover."

Sarah called out from the back bedroom. "Roger!"

Everett switched off the safety and stayed low in the corner of the room. He listened as the sound of motorbikes drew near. He could see three dirt bikes turn into the drive. All three riders had motocross helmets and were armed with battle rifles slung across their backs. They certainly didn't look like they were affiliated with the Global Republic. The riders pulled into the yard and cut their engines.

"Get your hands up! You've got three seconds to state your business before we unleash holy hell on you!" Everett screamed.

The three riders raised their hands. The one in the front was huge. He put one finger in the air and slowly moved his other hand to remove the helmet.

Everett whispered to Kevin, "I've got the big guy. You watch the other two."

"Got it," Kevin replied.

Everett kept his front sight trained on the man's chest. He'd fired the HK enough to know exactly how much slack was in the trigger, and he had his finger ready to fire.

The big man removed his helmet. "You folks are mighty jumpy."

Everett immediately recognized the voice and the

long beard. "Tommy?"

"We come in peace." Tommy lowered his kickstand and slowly stepped off the bike.

Everett slowly lowered his weapon. He trusted Tommy, but not that much. "Who is that with you?"

The other two riders removed their helmets and Tommy introduced them. "This here is Preacher; well, his name is Roy Thomas, but we all call him Preacher. The other fella is Devin. He used to be the bartender at the Gray Fox. You might have met him before."

Devin and Roy each slowly removed their helmets.

"Reckon it'd be alright if we come in and chat for a spell?" Tommy asked.

Everett looked at Kevin before accepting. "Sure. But if you don't mind, I think we'd feel better if you left your rifles by your bikes, at least until our hearts stop pounding."

Tommy looked annoyed. "That ain't too neighborly, but I guess I understand. We wouldn't have dropped by unannounced if I'd had your number."

Everett walked to the door and opened it. "Wouldn't have done you any good. I forgot to pay my phone bill."

Tommy chuckled and shook Everett's hand as he walked in the door. "How y'all been?"

"Jumpy." Everett winked. "GR helicopters have been flying over the past few days."

"Yep. The good ol' days of the government being as confused as a fruit fly in a bowl of wax bananas are long gone." Tommy unzipped his jacket.

Courtney and Sarah cautiously emerged from the back bedroom carrying their rifles.

Elijah let himself in through the front door. He was carrying his old double-barrel shotgun. "I assume everything is okay."

"Yes. But thanks for coming down." Everett introduced Elijah, Courtney, and Sarah to Tommy and his boys.

Courtney smiled politely but kept her hands on her weapon. "It's a pleasure to meet you."

Sarah took her rifle to the bedroom and returned. "Can I offer you some coffee?"

"That would be real nice, thank you." Tommy smiled and returned his attention to Everett. "The GR has set up shop in Winchester. We were getting along pretty well without them. Now they've come along with their what's-yours-is-mine notion. That ain't settin' well. They're helpin' themselves to whatever they see fit to take. The old government did the same thing, but they'd leave a man enough to feed his family. Not this lot. They don't leave you with nothing but a grumblin' belly."

Everett smiled. "You seem like you'd perfected your skills of evading the previous government."

Tommy chuckled. "I did. I reckon I still manage to stay out of sight and out of mind with this group of swindlers as well. But my business, and thereby my well-being, depend on the common folk being free to do as they please. I also see their liberty and prosperity as being something of a responsibility on my part."

"Sort of an unconventional statesman. I

understand. Go on." Everett was enjoying Tommy's dissertation.

Tommy proceeded. "Well, we figure it'd be best to hit this bunch now before tyranny takes root. From what I gather, they're still having a rough time of it and I expect there'd be a limit to how much time and resources they want to expend on little old Winchester."

Kevin nodded. "Sounds good, but what does that have to do with us?"

"You'd be beneficiaries of our toil. Them choppers you've been seein' down around Woodstock, they're flying out of Winchester. If we run them out of our town, your problem goes away."

Everett motioned toward the couch and the chairs. "Please, everyone have a seat. We'll bring in some chairs from the kitchen. So what are you asking us for?"

Tommy took a seat in the recliner. "We'd like you to fight with us."

Everett sighed as he walked to the kitchen to grab a couple of chairs. He returned, sat in one of the chairs and thought about how to decline the request.

Kevin took a seat in one of the chairs and looked at Everett. "Maybe we could make a donation to the cause."

Everett nodded and turned his attention toward Tommy. "We could probably scrounge up some food and ammo. Would that help?"

Tommy dropped his head. "Lloyd was so sure that we'd be able to count on you boys to be in the fight."

A sharp pang of guilt hit Everett in his stomach. He didn't want to be a coward, but this was a losing battle. "Tommy, you're talking about taking on the anti-Christ. I know you don't put much stock in the Bible, but we do. And according to the way we read it, this guy, Luz, he has been granted a free pass for the next five and a half years. There is no stopping him."

Tommy raked his fingers through his long hair. "I believe the good book. I'm not coming at this thing without considering what it says. Preacher, why don't you tell these folks what you told me."

Everett turned to Roy, the man they called Preacher. He looked nothing like a preacher. His hair was long on top, but cut above the collar. It was growing thin and had less gray than his beard which was little more than a week's worth of stubble. He had bad skin. His face was pitted, probably from chronic acne at a younger age. His jeans were old, and he wore a quilted-lined red plaid shirt for a jacket. Everett remembered what Lloyd had told him about Roy being a heavy drinker up until the Rapture.

Preacher sat up on the couch. "I've been a student of the Bible since I was a kid. Unfortunately, I wasn't too big on the whole repentance thing. At least not until now. But I'm getting off the subject. About the Global Republic. It's true, according to the Bible, they've been given a time to reign. But, Luz is still subject to the chaos and confusion that comes via the Judgments. You saw what a setback they had from the quake."

Everett shook his head. "So your plan is to kick the bully in the shin and run away, hoping that a meteor will fall on his head before he can catch you? That's a little overly optimistic, don't you think?"

Devin, the bartender from the Gray Fox, was younger than Tommy and Preacher. Everett figured him to be closest to his own age; late twenties, most likely. He had short dark hair, and he was tall and fit.

Devin smirked. "You're oversimplifying it. The Global Republic hasn't fully recovered from the quake. They're still vulnerable. If we can keep their heads spinning until the next round of cataclysms, we might have a chance. Otherwise, we're dead anyway. I don't know if you guys got the memo, but they're going to be televising mass beheadings of anyone who won't take the Mark. Once the GR gets a foothold in Winchester, they'll be all through these mountains. And if you guys don't take the Mark, you'll all get your fifteen seconds of fame by being decapitated on global television. Sure, we might get gunned down. But at least we'll die with dignity."

Everett grunted his displeasure at the situation. "Elijah, what do you think?"

Elijah put his hand in the air. "No. I have told you before. I will not always be with you. You must learn to hear from God yourself!"

Everett shrugged. "I pray and read my Bible every morning. Most of the time, I feel like he gives me the wisdom to make the right decisions. But this is a little perplexing. Isn't it okay to ask a man of

God for council?"

Elijah softened his tone. "It is. But you have to learn to seek God. To hear from him. To know his will."

"And how do we do that?" Courtney asked.

"You fast. You put aside food for a day or two, maybe three. You turn down the volume on your flesh and instead, you feed your spirit with God's Word, with prayer, with worship. As your flesh grows weak, your spirit grows strong. Like a radio when you get it in tune, and the static starts to disappear, you hear more clearly. And that is what you need, to be in tune with God. To hear his voice clearly, without the static of the flesh."

Kevin exhaled deeply and looked at Everett.

Everett was sure Kevin was thinking just what he was thinking. The old man was asking them not to eat. The one small pleasure they had in life, and Elijah was asking them to give it up. Everett turned to Tommy. "Can we get back to you in a few days?"

Tommy stood up. He seemed to understand that Everett couldn't give him an answer right away. "I reckon that'll have to be alright. I don't have much of a choice. Stewart has a radio set up in his basement. We don't use it much because we figure the GR is probably listening in. But we'll come up with a code and a time. We're planning to hit them a week from Thursday. Can you give me an answer by this Friday? That'd give me plenty of time to work you into the plan."

Everett nodded. "We'll call you this Thursday at 11:00 AM. If we say we're going to the dance, then you can count us in."

Tommy smiled. "And by us, you mean you and Kevin?"

Everett looked around the room before answering.

Courtney shook her head. "No. If Everett goes, I go. I have no desire to sit around here by myself and worry."

"Ditto," Sarah said.

Elijah sighed. "If the sheep wander away, the shepherd must also go. Provided I'm not given other instructions, that is."

Everett stood to shake Tommy's hand. "Do you know what frequency we should use to call Stewart?"

Tommy turned to Preacher. "Do you know?"

Preacher shook his head. "No, but you can give us a frequency, and we'll make sure we're tuned in at the right time. I know the handle he's been using is Mountain Saint. They used to all go by call signals, but radio etiquette has evolved along with everything else."

Everett found a pen and paper and wrote down a frequency and a handle. "If something comes up, and you can't get to the radio at that time, we'll try back the next day at 11:00 AM. As a matter of fact, we'll make sure we're listening every day at 11:00 in case you need to get in contact with us."

Tommy and his crew said their goodbyes. They retrieved their weapons, placed their helmets on their heads, and rode away on the dirt bikes.

Everett was not looking forward to learning his new spiritual discipline, but he trusted that it would work.

Everett, Courtney, Kevin, and Sarah all fasted the following day. The four of them gathered around the kitchen table and prayed that God would give them a definite answer. They asked that God would confirm the answer by putting them all at peace with the decision. Everett spent extra time reading the Bible, praying, and seeking God Monday morning. Afterward, he felt slow and tired, but there were chores to do, so he kept going.

At Sundown on Monday, Kevin and Sarah broke their fast. Everett and Courtney continued. Everett was famished, but he was determined to stick it out until he'd heard from God.

When Everett woke up on Tuesday, he wasn't quite so hungry as he'd felt the day before. He felt a bit dizzy, but he felt stronger and more energetic than the prior day. He continued reading the Word, seeking God and praying. He and Courtney sat on the front porch and prayed as the sun set that evening. They still had not heard from God.

Courtney held Everett's hand. "You know, maybe God doesn't work like that all the time. I'm sure Elijah meant well. And I'm sure it's a good thing to do once in a while. Maybe the fact that we haven't heard anything means that we're not supposed to do anything. Perhaps it's God's way of telling us to sit this one out."

Everett stared at the colors of the sunset in the sky across the foothills. He sighed. "We both heard from God when we went on the quest to confront Luz. You remember that, right? It wasn't just our imaginations. We both heard the same thing, from two different Bible verses. God was really speaking to us, individually. You still believe that, right?"

She smiled. "I do believe it. And yes, he was speaking to us. There's no doubt about it. Maybe he still will. We weren't fasting that time. Come on, let's get something to eat. We'll keep reading our Bibles and listening for an answer."

The thought of food sounded fantastic. Everett was certainly hungry. But, he felt an urge from inside to press on, to dig a little deeper. He looked up at Courtney. "You go ahead. I'm going to stick it out for one more night."

"Are you sure?" Courtney stood up, looking at him compassionately.

"Yeah, I'm sure." He nodded with a smile.

"Okay. I love you, Everett Carroll." She went inside.

Wednesday morning, Everett woke up from a peculiar dream. As soon as his eyes opened, the details of the dream faded like a vapor, but he knew he'd been in the presence of God as he slept. Right away, he felt an urge to open his Bible to Deuteronomy. He quickly took it from atop the bucket next to his bed. Everett scrambled to find Deuteronomy. He flipped through the front pages, stopping on Deuteronomy chapter seven. When he arrived at the second verse, he read it aloud softly, so not to wake Courtney. "And when the Lord thy God shall deliver them before thee; thou shalt smite them, and utterly destroy them; thou shalt make no covenant with them, nor shew mercy unto them."

He continued reading silently until he came to

verse twenty-three. "But the Lord thy God shall deliver them unto thee, and shall destroy them with a mighty destruction until they be destroyed."

Courtney rolled over and smiled. "What did you say?"

"Oh, I was reading. Sorry to wake you."

"Reading what?" She sat up to look at the Bible.

"Deuteronomy seven. This whole chapter is about God delivering the enemies of Israel into their hands, and about how he would protect them."

"Can I see?"

Everett handed her the Bible.

She read over the chapter. "So is this our answer?"

"Yeah. I think so."

She nodded. "I think you're right."

Everett got up and put on his clothes. "I'll tell Kevin and Sarah. I want to have Elijah over and run it by him before we decide to give Tommy a definite answer."

"Sounds good. You can invite him over for breakfast. I'm sure you're ready to eat."

Everett bent down to kiss her. "You're right about that!"

CHAPTER 3

And I saw the seven angels which stood
before God; and to them were given seven
trumpets. And another angel came and stood
at the altar, having a golden censer; and
there was given unto him much incense, that
he should offer it with the prayers of all
saints upon the golden altar which was
before the throne. And the smoke of the
incense, which came with the prayers of the
saints, ascended up before God out of the
angel's hand. And the angel took the censer,
and filled it with fire of the altar, and cast it
into the earth: and there were voices, and
thunderings, and lightnings, and an
earthquake. And the seven angels which had
the seven trumpets prepared themselves to

sound. The first angel sounded, and there followed hail and fire mingled with blood, and they were cast upon the earth: and the third part of trees was burnt up, and all green grass was burnt up.

Revelation 8:2-7

Early the next Sunday evening, Everett stood on Elijah's porch. He watched the clouds rolling in from the east. They were black and ominous. He could hear the low rumblings of thunder and see lightning inside the distant clouds. Everett walked inside where no one else seemed concerned.

Sarah picked at some of the food which Elijah had laid out on his kitchen counter. "I thought you were supposed to fast on Yom Kippur."

Elijah shrugged. "You're welcome to fast if you like. But Yom Kippur is the Day of Atonement. Your sins were atoned for, once and for all, by the sacrifice of Messiah. Paul says to the church in Galatia, 'This only would I learn of you, Received ye the Spirit by the works of the law, or by the hearing of faith? Are ye so foolish? Having begun in the Spirit, are ye now made perfect by the flesh?'

"When you try to be made right by the law, you are no longer putting your faith in the blood of Messiah. It is admirable to want to please God, but it is important to remember that no man is justified by the law in the sight of God. The just shall live by faith."

Sarah put more food on her plate. "I never learned that growing up. I always thought you had to abide by the rule book to please God."

Elijah smiled. "He does require repentance. And he has given us directions on how to live godly lives, but it is now a free life in the Spirit, not one that must adhere to the precepts of the Old Covenant."

Everett pointed toward the front window. "Everyone should go look out toward the east. The sky is turning black. I hate to be melodramatic, but it looks downright apocalyptic. Yom Kippur starts at sunset, and I have a really bad feeling."

Kevin walked out onto the porch first. Everett, Elijah, and the girls followed him.

"What's the next shoe to drop?" Sarah stood behind Kevin as if she were spooked by the menacing sky.

Everett pulled Courtney close. "The Seven Trumpets. Preceded by thunder, lightning, and an earthquake."

"And what happens with the first trumpet?" Sarah asked.

"Fire burns up a third of the trees on earth." Everett's voice was somber.

Kevin turned to Everett. "Should we maybe load up some critical gear and move it to the cave?"

Everett thought about the suggestion. "The only problem is the quake. When the angel throws the burning censer to earth, we get another shaker. I wouldn't want to be trapped in the cave when that happens. Nor would I want all of our gear to be in there. It could take a while to dig it out."

Courtney said, "Why don't we get everything loaded up. Then if we get the thunder, lightning, and a quake from the censer being thrown to earth, we can move the gear to the cave right after."

"Will we have a window between the censer and the first trumpet?" Sarah asked.

Everett looked at Elijah. "What do you think?"

"I didn't get a better schedule than you did. I have exactly the same book. There is a sentence in between the censer and the trumpet being sounded. 'And the seven angels which had the seven trumpets prepared themselves to sound.' Now, does it take the angels five minutes to prepare or five weeks to prepare? Your guess is as good as mine."

Everett looked at Kevin, Courtney, and Sarah, who were waiting for him to give the command. "Okay, we'll load up and move to the cave as soon as the quake comes. Elijah, sorry to ruin your dinner. Will you be coming with us?"

"Of course I'm coming. And dinner isn't ruined. We'll eat it at the cave. Also, I'll be bringing Samson and Delilah."

"Who's that?" Courtney looked curious.

"My two favorite goats. I can't stand to leave them behind. They won't be much of a bother."

Sarah pursed her lips. "Two goats, a cat, and a dog in a cave. At least we won't be bored."

"We'll load up the truck and come back to your place to wait out the quake. Maybe we'll still get to enjoy your nice dinner." Everett smiled at Elijah as he led the way to the vehicle.

Everett delegated jobs to everyone on the way home. "Courtney, get our guns, ammo, some clothes, and valuables out of the loft. Kevin, get your guns and ammo. Sarah, you're in charge of getting Danger and Sox ready to roll. I'll unhook the ham radio and get it packed."

When they pulled into the drive, everyone exited the vehicle and darted into action.

Everett could hear the thunder getting closer as he quickly disconnected the radio. His first move was to unplug the antenna. The last thing he wanted was to have it struck by lightning. That wouldn't be healthy for himself nor the radio. Everett secured the components of the radio in large plastic bins, wrapping them in towels to protect them from the bumpy ride to the cave.

Kevin walked into the back bedroom, where Everett was working, to retrieve another load of military ammunition cans. "Anything that's not waterproof, I'm stuffing into trash bags to protect it in case it rains, but you mentioned fire falling from the sky. Hefty contractor bags are high-quality trash bags, but I doubt they'll offer much protection if it starts raining fire."

"Hmm." Everett grimaced. "What if we pull a few panels of the metal roofing off of the back storage shed?"

Kevin nodded. "That might buy us some time."

The team completed their preparations, loaded the truck, and drove back to Elijah's.

Everett got out of the passenger's side of the truck to find Elijah loading his old pickup. "Need some help?"

Elijah looked around. "I think I've got everything I need. The goats will ride in the cab of the truck with me."

Everett looked at the various boxes and bins in the back of Elijah's old truck. "We put sheet metal from the roof over the back of our truck. If you want to pull a few panels off the top of your smoke house, I'll give you a hand."

Elijah nodded. "That might be wise."

A gust of wind swept through suddenly, stirring up a cloud of dust and leaves. Danger began barking and whining.

Sarah covered her eyes with one hand and held the leash tight with the other. "Elijah, can we take the animals inside?"

"Yes, yes. Go ahead." Elijah turned to Everett. "We should move quickly."

Courtney carried Sox in the makeshift carrier and followed Sarah into the house.

Kevin assisted Everett and Elijah in removing a couple panels from the smoke house. The wind grew stronger, blowing dust and debris. Everett and Kevin stood on ladders to remove the first panel, handing it down to Elijah to carry to the truck. As they removed the second panel, a violent gust grabbed it and whipped it out of their hands. The metal sheet blew across the backyard, stopping only when it reached two trees, which it could not fit through.

Everett checked his hands for cuts, then looked at Kevin who had been holding the other end. "Are you okay?" He had to speak loudly to be heard over the wind.

Kevin held up his palm, revealing a small trickle of blood. "I got a scratch, but I'll be okay," he yelled.

"You go inside and take care of that cut. Elijah and I will get the rogue panel and secure it to the truck. When was your last tetanus shot?"

Kevin folded his ladder and laid it on the ground so it wouldn't blow away. "Not long ago. I got one back when the economy started melting down. I figured things might get bad. Of course, I never guessed anything like this would happen."

"Okay, get that cleaned up. We'll see you inside." Everett helped Elijah get the sheet of metal roofing to the bed of the old pickup. They used a combination of bungee cords and ratchet straps to secure the panel over Elijah's belongings. Next, they retrieved the runaway panel and secured it to the bed of the truck as well.

Elijah led the way into the house. "Come, come, Everett. The sky is growing darker."

Everett looked at his watch. It was 6:30. Sunset was more than a half hour away, but it was already pitch black outside. As Everett walked inside, he had to fight the wind to close the door.

A loud clap of thunder broke out, rattling the windows and shaking the entire house. Danger, who was next to Sarah, barked and whined.

"It's okay, Cupcake. It's just thunder." Sarah petted him and tried to console him.

Courtney sat at Elijah's table, where a single candle glowed. She held the raccoon trap being used as a cat carrier for Sox, in her lap. "Elijah, do you have a towel? I think if I cover the cage, Sox might not be so afraid."

"Yes, yes. Let me get that for you." Elijah lit two

more candles to further dispel the darkness. He carried one with him as he left the kitchen.

Kevin emerged from the bathroom with a bandage on his hand. "Sounds like it's getting nasty out there."

A bright flash of lightning preceded another loud roar of thunder, which rattled the dishes inside Elijah's cupboards, and left a trailer of vibrations for several seconds.

Elijah returned with the towel. He gently covered the cage and whispered to Sox. "You are in very capable hands. I'm certain Courtney will take good care of you."

"Could we turn on the radio?" Sarah asked.

"Yes, yes." He picked up the small radio from the kitchen counter and turned it on.

The radio came to life. ". . . severe thunderstorm warning. The Global Republic is asking everyone within listening distance of this station to seek shelter. Listeners are urged to stay away from windows as gusts of up to 70 miles per hour have been reported. Additionally, golf-ball-sized hailstones have been reported in the New Atlantis metropolitan area. With the heavy winds, the hail becomes more dangerous as it can break windows and potentially injure those inside, vehicles, homes, and buildings.

"No tornadoes have been reported yet, but conditions are favorable for their formation. If you have a basement or interior room, that is the best place for you to shelter."

Kevin crossed his arms and looked at Everett. "Golf-ball-sized hail. If they're getting it in DC, it's headed this way. We can't drive in that. It could break out the windshield. Do you think we should head to the cave now?"

Everett threw his hands in the air. "We've still got a quake coming. I'd rather take my chances driving in hail than risk being buried alive in the cave. Elijah, what do you think?"

Elijah opened the plastic containers in which he'd placed the leftovers. "I think we should eat. Everything is cold, but it still tastes wonderful."

Courtney peeked under the towel to look at Sox. "How can you eat with such a horrible storm coming?"

Elijah made himself a small plate of food and sat next to her. "The LORD is my rock, and my fortress, and my deliverer; my God, my strength, in whom I will trust; my buckler, and the horn of my salvation, and my high tower. Of whom or of what shall I be afraid?"

Courtney looked perplexed; as if she didn't know if that was a rhetorical question or if Elijah expected a response. Either way, she didn't answer.

Everett envied the faith of the prophet. He wanted to be like Elijah, but he just wasn't there yet. He did find some comfort in being near the old man with the storm raging outside. At least until the hail began to pound the metal roof.

Samson and Delilah, the two goats who were tied up near the front door, bleated their protest to the noisy clamor from above.

At first, the hail sounded like large raindrops, but

Everett could hear larger pieces of hail hit the metal roof. The wind howled outside the small cabin with the wretched voice of some fiendish thing from another realm. Soon, the sound of hail pounding the roof was deafening. Everett could still hear Danger barking over the booming roar, but the radio was drowned out completely. He stood close to Courtney's chair with his hand on her shoulder.

Elijah sat at the table, eating his food as if nothing out of the ordinary were happening. Everyone else, including the pets, appeared to be on pins and needles. The storm raged on for several minutes. Lightning periodically lit up the inside of Elijah's home like a strobe light. Thunder shook the walls and the very foundation of the little cabin. The sound of the hail beating against the metal roof ebbed and flowed in waves. Just as the hail sounded like it might let up, another assault of the large ice stones would batter the roof. Two of Elijah's front windows were cracked from the hail, but none were completely smashed out. Everett doubted that the trucks had faired so well.

Finally, the hail subsided. Everett nervously waited to see if the storm would send one last volley of ice to pummel the roof. He glanced at his watch. "7:30. Yom Kippur has begun."

Courtney looked up at him. "Is the storm over with?"

He ran his fingers across the back of her neck. "I hope so."

Kevin walked cautiously toward the door. "I didn't feel any quake."

Sarah held Danger's leash tightly as she and the

dog followed Kevin to the door. "The house was shaking from the thunder. How would we even know if there was an earthquake?"

Everett looked at Elijah who was still eating. He decided to get a bit himself. He took a piece of Elijah's homemade pita bread and spread some of his herbed hummus on it. Everett sprinkled a few sliced black olives from the can on the counter then took his snack out on the porch where Kevin, Sarah, and Danger stood looking out over the mountains. "How are the windshields?"

Kevin walked out into the yard and shined his flashlight from vehicle to vehicle. "Elijah's has two small cracks. One in the middle and the other on the passenger's side. Ours has three holes, all surrounded by spider web cracks. We'll either have to kick out the windshield or stick our heads out the window to drive." Kevin shined the light down toward the ground which was white with hail.

Everett could hear the ice crunching beneath Kevin's feet with each step. "Be careful. That's probably slippery."

No sooner had Everett issued the warning than Kevin's foot slipped on the balls of hail. He caught himself before falling. Kevin walked with care, keeping one hand on the truck as he made his way back to the porch.

The wind grew quiet. The thunder and lightning ceased. Everett finished his snack as he peered into the dark sky.

Courtney joined them on the porch. "Is it over?"

Everett was hesitant to respond. "For now."

"That was unconvincing," Sarah said.

Everett snickered. "If I had more conviction, I'd sell it a little harder."

The silence was soon replaced with a gentle patter of rain falling on the metal roof. Everett listened closely to see if he could hear any signs that the storm was returning. He heard nothing but the hypnotic rhythm of the light droplets coming down.

Sarah sat down in the old rocking chair on Elijah's porch. "It sounds so peaceful compared to the hail."

"Yeah, I could go to sleep listening to this." Courtney stuck her hand out from beneath the cover of the roof to let the soft rain fall in her palm.

Against his better judgment, Everett allowed himself to breathe a sigh of relief. He let the muscles in his face relax and tilted his neck to the side. The tension was fading away.

"Ahhh!" Courtney yelled.

Everett was immediately raptured out of his easy state by Courtney's piercing scream. "What is it?" He sprang back to attention.

Her hand and wrist were covered in blood. She continued to scream as she held her bloody hand toward Everett.

"What happened? How did you cut yourself?" He quickly took off his shirt and wrapped her hand. He wiped off the blood and inspected her wrist for an injury. He found no cuts.

Courtney regained her composure. "It's not my blood. It's the rain. It's raining blood!"

Everett turned to see Kevin shining his light out into the yard. Only seconds ago, the ground had been clean, clear crystals of white, but now it was dark crimson. The yard was covered in blood, like the floor of a slaughterhouse.

Elijah came outside. "The First Trumpet has sounded. We should go to the cave. We should go now."

Kevin stood near Sarah. "I'm not sure we can drive in this. The roads are slick with ice from the hail and our windshield is busted out. We wouldn't be able to see to drive at night, even if it weren't raining blood."

"Better to drive when it's raining blood than when it's raining fire." Elijah clapped his hands. "Come now, let us go while we can."

Sarah stood up. "Now there's a man who knows how to put things into perspective."

Elijah looked at Everett. "I've got a shirt that you may wear. I'll blow out the candles and bring it to you. After that, we must go."

"Thanks." Everett waited for Elijah to return with the shirt.

"I'll be right back." Courtney went inside to retrieve the cat carrier.

Elijah returned with the shirt. "I'll take the lead to the cave. My windshield wipers work very well. We'll travel slowly to be safe. I'll tap my brakes two times when we approach any areas of the roads which were heavily damaged by the great quake. If you see my lights flash twice, you'll know to be careful."

"Got it," Kevin replied.

"Do you have an umbrella?" Sarah sounded hopeful.

"Sorry, child." Elijah shook his head as he

watched the steady stream of blood rolling off the edge of the roof, over the porch. Then, he stuck his index finger in the air. "Aha! What about trash bags? We could make ponchos!"

"Brilliant idea!" Sarah exclaimed.

Elijah quickly went back inside and retrieved large black trash bags for everyone. They all made small openings for their faces and put them over their heads.

Everett looked at Courtney. "On three. I'll run to the back-passenger door and open it for you. You follow me with Sox. Once you're in, I'll close your door and get in."

Kevin looked at Sarah. "Same plan, but driver's side."

"Roger." Sarah nodded.

Everett and Courtney executed their plan without incident.

Next, Kevin ran to the door and opened it for Sarah and Danger. Danger wouldn't budge.

"Cupcake! Come on!" Sarah tugged his leash. "He won't walk in the blood."

Kevin yelled, "Just carry him! Come on!"

Sarah grabbed Danger and hoisted him to the vehicle. Kevin closed the back door and got into the truck.

Everett felt sorry for Elijah as he watched him wrestle to get the two goats in the cab of the other truck. "It would be funny if it weren't raining blood."

Courtney tore the trash bag off of herself and dried her face with her shirt. The few drops of blood that had landed on her face while she got in the vehicle left red stains smeared across her light blue shirt. "Nothing about any of this is funny."

Finally, Elijah was in the truck with the goats. He started his truck and pulled out of the drive. Kevin stayed close behind Elijah.

Sarah said, "Courtney, we still have to hike up the hill from the creek to get to the cave. How are you going to get your poncho back on?"

Courtney let out a loud groan of disgust. "I wasn't thinking. I just wanted to get that blood off of me. This day can't get any worse."

Everett grimaced as the words left her mouth. He wasn't superstitious, but somehow, he knew she'd regret saying that. He looked through a spot of the passenger's side windshield that wasn't smashed. He peered over the cab of Elijah's truck in front of them just in time to see the tiniest solitary flare falling to the ground in the distance. "I think it just got worse."

Courtney leaned over the front seat. "Why?"

Everett spotted a second flame descending from the sky. "Look." He pointed toward the distant ember. Even through the shattered windshield, it was easily identifiable as fire.

"Fire?" Courtney sounded exasperated. "It's raining fire?"

Kevin huffed and shook his head. "Elijah better get a move on or this truck is going to turn into a Dutch oven."

With each pass of the wiper blades, small bits of blood were pushed through the holes in the windshield. The wipers left only a brief moment of visibility to see through clear areas of the cracked glass before it was again glazed in blood.

Everett tensed up as a fist-sized flame landed on the hood of the truck. He watched as it burned for several seconds before going out. He looked up to see branches of a nearby tree ablaze. Small fires were burning at sporadic locations, out in the forest floor, on either side of the road.

Elijah tapped his brakes twice and proceeded very slowly.

Everett pointed out the road hazard as Elijah's truck passed over it. "Major split down the center of the road. We better follow him and stay to the left."

Kevin nodded. "I hope he picks up the pace or it's not going to matter. We've still got to hike up the hill with all of this gear."

"We've got gear in the cave. The important thing is that we get there alive." Everett tried to focus on the road in between swipes of the windshield wiper blades.

Minutes later, they arrived at the creek. Elijah slowly drove his truck into the shallow creek.

Everett rolled down the window and called out to him. "I don't think you'll be able to drive back out of there."

Elijah looked out his window to call back. "We'll worry about being stuck in a creek if the truck survives the fire. But if the tires catch fire, the gas tank will blow."

Everett lifted one eyebrow. "Stuck in a creek doesn't sound so bad."

Kevin looked at Everett. "Do you think we should stick this one in the creek also?"

Everett looked around. "I don't see any other

places to drive in. Access is blocked by trees in either direction."

Keven pointed toward the water. "Ask Elijah to drive further up the creek if he can. We'll pull in behind him."

Everett made the request and Elijah complied.

Everett turned to Courtney. "You take my poncho. I'm going to be covered in blood anyway."

"No, I can't. I'm the idiot who ripped up my poncho."

Everett pulled the trash bag over his head. "I insist. You and Sarah, just get the animals up to the cave, and we'll worry about hauling the gear."

Sarah looked at Kevin. "Is that okay with you?"

He smiled at her. "Yeah. Courtney, could you try to lead Elijah's goats up the hill with you?"

"Sure. Thanks, guys." Courtney slipped Everett's trash bag over her head.

The trail which followed the creek was well lit by the multiple fires now burning around the forest. Smoke was beginning to fill the air. The sizzle of blood running down a nearby tree into a smoldering tuft of dried leaves sounded wicked.

Everett, Kevin, and Elijah helped the girls and the animals wade through the knee-high water and up onto the trail. The girls headed toward the cave, with the goats bleating and Danger whining in protest of being made to walk through the steady drizzle of blood and fire.

Kevin wiped the blood off of his forehead before it could run into his eyes. "If we could only move one item, I'd say it should be the ham radio."

Everett nodded. "I've got it broken down into

three boxes. Let's get it up the hill and see what we're dealing with in terms of fire. Then we can decide if we have time to haul another load."

Elijah squeegeed blood off his face with his finger. "Yes. Let's do that. The fire is very spread out, for now. It's not so hot that it is a major danger just yet."

Everett pulled the plastic bins containing the ham radio components, handing one to each of his companions. He took his box and started up the hill. "Our biggest concern is the smoke. If we come back down, maybe we should wear face masks."

"I've got bandanas in my duffle." Kevin stayed close behind Everett. "We can wet them in the creek."

Everett kept moving up the hill. "The creek water is full of blood."

"They'll be bloody anyway by the time we reach the cave," Kevin said.

The three men reached the cave opening and fed the boxes through to the girls who were waiting inside.

Elijah surveyed the fires around the forest. "It is getting worse, but the fires are still small. I agree with Kevin. We should wet the bandanas in the creek and use those for face masks."

Everett peeked in the cave. "We'll be right back."

"Be safe!" Courtney called from inside.

They made their way down the hill to the trail which ran alongside the creek. Elijah looked at the bloody water flowing below them. "This bloodthirsty generation of sorcerers, necromancers, and vampires. It is blood they have thirsted for and it is blood that Jehovah has given them to drink."

Everett looked all around. The trees, the leaves, and the rocks on the ground, everything was covered in blood. Fire continued to fall from the sky. Often times it would land in a puddle of blood and quickly be extinguished. In other instances, it would find just the right spot, on a dead tree branch or a pile of dried pine needles, and a flame would catch in the surrounding forest debris. From where he stood, he could easily count more than fifty individual small fires. Most, only the size of a small campfire, but a few were quickly growing beyond the size of a raging barn fire.

The three men hastily retrieved the bandanas and wet them in the creek to use as face masks. They gathered another load of their belongings from the trucks and headed back up the trail.

The fire and smoke were growing, but Everett felt they could make at least one more run. "I think we should try to pull off one more sortie."

On the way back down the hill, Elijah pointed to a flame which had just fallen from the sky into a puddle of blood. The blaze quickly sputtered out into a fading vapor of steam and smoke. "As long as the blood is falling, we have some protection from the fire."

Everett stopped walking for just a moment as he considered the old prophet's words. He muttered to himself, "The blood, it's protecting us from the fire. Just as the blood of Jesus has protected us from the eternal fire. Just as the blood smeared on the door posts of the Israelites protected them from the plagues in Egypt." Up until this moment, Everett had thought the landscape of blood and fire to be hellish in its entirety. But now, he saw the blood in a whole new light. It protected them. Suddenly, it didn't bother him so much.

The blood inhibited the spreading of the fire enough for the three men to collect all of their belongings from the two trucks. Everett breathed a sigh of relief once they safely reached the inside of the cave. "Hey!" He smiled at Courtney who had cleaned most of the blood off of herself.

"You're safe!" She winked. "Don't be mad if I don't kiss you."

He chuckled. "Please don't. I feel about as gross as I've ever felt."

She looked at him with compassion. "We managed to get fairly clean with just one gallon of water each. We left our bloody clothes wrapped up in the trash bags. We'll wash them out in the creek after the fire burns over. How is that looking anyway?"

"It's burning. Smoke is everywhere. We could barely breathe on that last trip. The blood kept the fire from spreading too fast, but now we've got several large areas, over an acre wide each, burning out of control. It won't be long until the whole forest is one raging inferno."

Sarah was nearby. "How long will it take to burn itself out?"

Kevin shrugged. "Maybe a day. No more than two. At least not for our immediate area. Of course, it all depends on how it spreads. If it's raining fire all across the mountains, the whole thing could burn itself out in a couple days. If not, and it has to spread progressively, it could take weeks before all the smoke clears."

Everett, Kevin, and Elijah cleaned themselves up in much the same manner used by the girls. Not knowing how long they'd be stuck inside the cave, they were stingy with the use of water. The water left in the buckets after their cat baths was used by Sarah and Elijah to clean up Danger and the goats. Fortunately for Sox, Courtney had managed to keep him from getting blood anywhere on him. She'd kept the towel over him and kept his cage close to her body as she scurried up the trail to the cave.

No one was hungry, so they pulled out the sleeping bags and got ready for bed.

Everett was tired. The day had been both mentally and physically exhausting. He felt happy to be safe in the shelter of the great cavern and glad to see the day drawing to a close. The air inside the cave was crisp and clear, but he could still smell the faintest scent of the fiery forest infused with the aroma of seared blood. He shined his light toward the ceiling of the grand cavernous room they called the cathedral. A vague current of smoke flowed from the direction of the cave entrance to the upper-level corridor where they stored their supplies. Everett whispered to himself. "It looks like we have air flow coming in from outside. But I wonder where it's going?" He was tired. Much too tired to be tracking down the terminal point of the air flow inside a cave. "I'll keep an eye on it when I wake up from time to time. If the smoke gets bad, I'll go close off the entrance, but it doesn't seem to be a problem. For now, I've got to get some rest."

CHAPTER 4

And the second angel sounded, and as it were a great mountain burning with fire was cast into the sea: and the third part of the sea became blood; And the third part of the creatures which were in the sea, and had life, died; and the third part of the ships were destroyed.

Revelation 8:8-9

Everett woke up to the soft massage of Sox who was purring while he pushed one paw against Everett's head and then the other. Everett switched on his flashlight to find Sox lying across the top of the sleeping bag, with his tail and hind legs tucked inside. Sox seemed to enjoy the close company of humans more so in the winter than in the warmer months. With the constant fifty-four degrees inside the cave, he would be quite the snuggle bug during their stay.

"Good morning Sox." Everett turned over and gave the feline a rough scratch beneath the chin. Everett emerged from the comfort of the sleeping bag and quickly put on his jacket. He tried to be quiet as he began climbing the ladder in search of some freeze-dried breakfast items. He found instant coffee and instant oatmeal. Neither would be good cold. He pulled several cans of Sterno and a folding stove out of one of the bins. "I don't suppose we'll ever need it more than we do now."

Everett stuck everything in a small backpack and gently descended the ladder. Once he had the Sterno lit, he turned off his flashlight to conserve the batteries. Everett warmed water in a metal canteen cup which nestled onto the bottom of one of the canteens he'd found when he first moved to John Jones' cabin.

Courtney was the next person to awaken. She layered on her clothing to stay warm and came to sit by Everett. "How did you sleep?" She whispered.

"Good. I was out like a light as soon as I closed my eyes."

"You were tired." Courtney sat with her body next to his to conserve warmth.

"And you?"

She nodded. "I slept okay. I dreamt about the blood and fire. It had me tossing and turning part of the night."

The two of them quietly enjoyed a packet of

oatmeal together and shared the cup of coffee. Soon the cavern was a buzz with flashlight beams reflecting off of the ceiling and walls.

Sarah came to sit next to Courtney and Everett. She was eating a granola bar. "Do you think the fire is still burning?"

"Yep." Everett nodded.

"You sound confident about that. What makes you so sure?" She took another bite of her breakfast bar.

Everett directed the beam of his flashlight toward the ceiling which revealed the steady stream of smoke trailing across the room.

"Hmm." Sarah finished chewing. "We've got air flow. Do you think it's enough for us to build a fire inside here without burning up all of our oxygen?"

Everett shrugged. "I don't know. Today probably wouldn't be a good day to run an experiment."

Kevin came to sit near the group. "I think we could get away with it, as long as we kept the fire small and burn it near the back wall. The air flow should act like a chimney and pull the smoke right out the corridor. But I agree with Everett. We don't want to try it when we can't leave the cave in the event that it doesn't work out."

After breakfast, Everett climbed back up into the storage corridor to find the spool of wire they'd brought for an antenna. He unrolled the wire and affixed one end to the telescoping antenna he'd removed from the AM/FM radio. The other end, he attached to the radio. As Everett carried the antenna toward the opening of the cave, the scent of smoke and burnt blood grew stronger. He could feel the heat from the fires still burning outside. The momentary warmth was a welcome sensation. Everett positioned the antenna outside of the opening and returned to the cathedral.

"Still burning, I assume." Elijah sat quietly sipping his tea and reading his Bible near the area with the low ceiling.

"Yes. Still burning." Everett looked at Elijah's old Bible. "Will we bother you if we check for some news updates?"

"Not at all." Elijah closed the weathered old book and followed Everett over to where the others were waiting.

Everett clicked on the small radio and set the frequency to the local GR affiliate.

The reporter was relaying the latest announcement with a dramatic sense of urgency. "If you are just tuning in, we remind you that if you live along the east coast of the Americas, you must seek higher ground immediately! Cumbre Vieja, a volcano on the island of La Palma, began erupting early this morning. One hour ago, the entire western face of the mountain collapsed into the Atlantic Ocean. The earth and rock which slid into the ocean have triggered a mega tsunami. The initial wave of the tsunami is expected to strike the shores of North, Central, and South America in the next six to seven hours. The wave height may be as high as one hundred feet and inundation may be as much as ten miles inland.

"Venezuela, Guyana, and the Eastern Caribbean islands are expected to be the first to experience the massive wall of water which originated in the Canary Islands."

"It's a good day to be in a cave on top of a mountain," Sarah said.

Everett nodded. "And a bad day for the beach."

Kevin turned to Everett. "Ten miles of inundation. I don't suppose that is a threat to New Atlantis."

Courtney shook her head. "No. DC is fifty miles from the coast. However, a hundred-foot wave is bound to back up into the Potomac. They'll get some serious flooding, but don't count on Luz being swept out to sea."

The reporter continued. "The Global Republic wishes to impress upon its citizens that the probability of surviving the tsunami in a coastal area is near zero. Minister of the Americas Richard Clay has issued a directive to the Global Republic Emergency Management Agency to begin setting up relief camps directly to the west of the I-95 corridor. He promises that anyone who can get west of the interstate will be provided with food, shelter, medical attention, and security. The GREMA relief camps will be set up in all major population centers. I know it is difficult to abandon your home and belongings, especially in this tumultuous age, but those things can be replaced.

"Minister Clay is asking global citizens to voluntarily restrict consumption of food rations as the already-fragile infrastructure is likely to be even more strained in the days and weeks following the tsunami. With Guayaquil, Ecuador having the only fully functioning seaport on the Pacific coast of the Americas, the continents will be severely troubled if major Atlantic seaports are taken offline. Repairs of the damage caused by the Great Quake on the port in Balboa, Panama are eighty- percent complete, but it is unclear what setbacks may be caused by the mega tsunami.

Initial reports are just coming in regarding the devastation caused by the island collapse of La Palma and the subsequent wave. All ships around the Canary Islands are thought to be lost. Likewise, all cargo vessels near Morocco's Port of Casablanca were capsized and most all shipping containers in the yard were swept out to sea. Similar conditions are being reported in Tangier, Gibraltar, and Lisbon where wave heights exceeded 120 feet.

Courtney put her hand on Everett's neck. "Two years ago, if you would have told me I'd be sitting in a cave, hiding out from blood and fire raining from the sky and saying, *it could be worse*, I'd have said you're crazy."

Everett kissed her on the head, but said nothing. He knew she was only trying to keep her emotional head above water by making light of the subject, but he couldn't laugh this one off. The seriousness of the event hit him as he considered the tremendous loss of life along the coasts of Africa and Europe. He knew their Christian brothers and sisters in those regions had just met a terrible end. And the pain was only beginning. The loss of provisions in the ports, the destruction of critical infrastructure in the way of seaports and refineries meant that many more would die of starvation and want.

The Global Republic reporter briefly paused from covering the tsunami to talk about the blood and fire which had rained down across the Americas. "No official statement has been issued by the GR as to what may have been the cause of the atmospheric anomalies which resulted in the thick red liquid coming from the sky, followed by fire falling like rain. However, scientists are certain that the red rain, which many citizens described as blood, was caused by a buildup of air pollutants over many decades. Likewise, the fire is also thought to be from those same pollutants catching ablaze. Nevertheless, they have yet to identify what could have caused the spontaneous combustion of the pollutants in the air.

"The GR Department of Health and Human Services has issued a ban on drinking water from lakes, stream, and rivers. The effects of the crimson-colored pollutants on humans and animals are unknown at this time. Health administrators are urging citizens to avoid all contact with the polluted water and drink only stored water or water that is coming from a deep underground source such as a well, aquifer, or spring. No estimate has been given as to when we can expect the phenomenon to dissipate."

Everett and the others continued to listen to the news updates on the approaching tsunami for the remainder of the day. Besides eating, playing cards, and sleeping, there was little else to pass the time.

Everett awoke the next morning and quickly made his way to the opening of the cave. As he headed toward the exit, he directed his flashlight toward the roof of the cave. "No smoke. Maybe the fire has burned out," he whispered softly to himself.

When he reached the cave entrance, he found Elijah sitting outside on a rock, reading his Bible in the morning light. "Good morning, Elijah."

The prophet glanced up only for a moment. "Good morning."

Everett surveyed the surrounding mountains. The landscape was black and charred. Smoke wafted up from the ruins of the forest. Very few of the burned-out trees had limbs. None had leaves. Most were little more than charcoal stumps. The blood was gone. So was everything else. The earth itself had served as an altar upon which God had provided his own blood sacrifice for a burnt offering. The inhabitants of the earth had rejected the atoning sacrifice of the blood shed by the Messiah, so in its stead, God had laid creation upon a consuming fire.

Elijah looked up from his Bible. "A third part of the trees and all of the grass were taken in this judgment. The Atlantic has turned to blood. All the creatures of the forest have been taken as well as all living things in the Atlantic."

Everett listened to the old man. Chills ran up his spine as he looked upon the destruction. The world had been laid waste, and there were still years to go before the end would come. Everett looked up at the sky. It was gray with smoke. Bits of white ash fell like snow from above.

Elijah stood. "Let's get the others. We should see what is left."

Everett nodded. "Judging from what I'm seeing, I don't have very high expectations."

Elijah led the way back into the cave. "Yes, but you never know what small mercy the Almighty may have granted us. The least little thing could be a tremendous blessing in such a world as this."

Everett and Elijah reached the cathedral.

Courtney was rolling up her sleeping bag. "Is the fire burned out?"

"Yeah." Everett sighed.

Kevin and Sarah were still in their sleeping bags but they were awake.

"What does it look like out there?" Sarah asked.

Everett shook his head. "Another planet. I don't know. More like the ancient ruins of something that used to be a planet. The sky is gray, the earth is black, and there's nothing but smoke and ash swirling around in between."

Courtney sighed. "I don't even want to see it."

Everett looked at Kevin. "Elijah wants us to go check out the damage."

"That sounds futile." Kevin sat up.

Everett said, "You're probably right. You and Sarah can stay here with the animals and keep watch if you don't want to go. Somebody has to stand guard over the cave anyway."

Kevin stroked his beard. "Sure you guys will be okay?"

"I'm sure. I can't imagine any threats would have survived that catastrophe," Everett said.

"Take rifles anyway. And be safe. There's probably a lot of smoldering trees and limbs that could come tumbling down with no warning," Kevin replied.

"Thanks." Everett grabbed his HK and waved as he, Courtney, and Elijah headed toward the exit.

Courtney immediately tied a handkerchief around her face to filter the residual smoke when she came out of the cave. "It's awful."

Everett nodded and followed Elijah down the hill toward the creek.

As they made their way down the incline, Elijah pointed toward the stream. "The water is still tainted, but it appears to be clearer than it was Sunday night."

Everett looked down at the brook. The water was muddied with ash and soot. It had a deep red tint. "So you think it will clear up?"

"Perhaps." Elijah continued along the path toward the trucks.

Courtney pointed ahead. "There's a burned-out tree trunk laying across Kevin's truck."

Everett picked up the pace so he could get a better view of Elijah's truck. He couldn't see any apparent damage, other than the cracked glass and dents from the hail. He was the first to arrive at the vehicle. Burnt twigs and small limbs which had been swept downstream by the creek were lodged against the bottom of the truck and were damming up the flow. Everett walked out into the water and began clearing away some of the debris so the water could move past. Ash and soot covered the vehicle. He wiped the window off with his hand and looked inside. "No fire damage inside the cab."

Elijah waded out to the truck and got inside. The engine cranked right up. The old man rolled down the window and looked out to Everett. "It still runs."

Everett examined the banks of the creek. Elijah's truck was blocked by Kevin's, which wasn't going anywhere anytime soon. Most of the brush that had blocked the banks before had burned away, but the banks were too steep to drive out of. "We'll have to dig out that bank and form a ramp."

Courtney stood at the water's edge. "I'll run back to the cave and get a couple of shovels."

"Be safe!" Elijah cut the engine.

Everett and Elijah cleaned the glass of the old truck with an old rag and water from the creek while they waited for Courtney to return.

Once she was back, the three of them took turns working on the bank of the creek so the truck could pull out of the water. The project was completed after about an hour and Everett guided Elijah as he drove up out of the brook.

"Get in. Let's see if there is anything left of our homes." Elijah waved for Courtney and Everett to get inside the vehicle.

The two of them laid the shovels in the bed of the truck. They climbed in the cab, and the three of them headed over the mountain to the location of their former homes. Elijah drove slowly, being careful of the rough roads caused by the Great Quake. As they pulled around the curve near his cabin, the old man sighed. "Dear, dear. There's my chimney."

Courtney was sitting in the middle. She put her hand on Elijah's arm. "I'm so sorry, Elijah."

"Yes, well, this world is not our home." The tone of his voice betrayed his attempt to stay positive.

"Look." Everett pointed. "Your old potbelly stove is still there."

Courtney's voice was excited. "Your barn! It's still standing!"

Elijah pulled into his drive and drove up to the small barn. It was darkened by smoke and soot, but it was still standing, indeed. Elijah got out and raced to the doors. The sound of goats bleating rang out from inside. Elijah opened the doors. Several chickens and the remainder of his goats came out. "Look at the lot of you." The old man laughed. His jolly disposition soon faded. "No matter. They haven't anything to eat. Perhaps it would have been more merciful had they not survived."

Everett furrowed his brow. He scanned the scenes of destruction all around. "Elijah. Nothing survived the fire. Every tree, every bush, all the animals of the forest, they're all gone. Don't you think these animals being alive is a miracle?"

Elijah inspected the goats, one at a time. "Perhaps."

Everett asked, "Then don't you think God could provide something for them to eat?"

Courtney chimed in. "Yeah, would he save the chickens and the goats, just to let them starve to death?"

"We shall see." Elijah seemed to be discouraged by the entire situation. "Let's drive down the mountain and see what has become of your home."

As they were getting back in the truck Elijah said, "You know, sometimes faith is being able to accept the tribulation of this world. If you expect God to be your genie in the bottle, you'll be sorely disappointed."

"But you were on the mountain with Jesus." Everett looked out the window at the forsaken moonscape. "I guess I expected you to be more . . ."

"Optimistic?" Elijah slowed down to cross a deep crevice in the roadway. "Let me ask you something. What is the first thing you remember from your childhood?"

Even coming from Elijah, Everett thought this line of questioning to be rather curious. "Hmm. I remember a birthday cake. I was really young. My parents were still together. I must have been three, maybe four."

Elijah asked, "What was the icing on the cake? What kind of cake was it? How many candles did it have?"

Everett shook his head. "I don't know. It's a very vague memory."

"Okay then. Now you know the clarity of my memories from the other side of the veil. I am a man, just like you. Yes, God speaks to me. Very directly at times. But at other times, he is silent. Don't assume I have a crystal ball. And as for the prophets, many have suffered greatly. They were stoned, they were sawn asunder, were tempted, were slain with the sword: they wandered about in sheepskins and goatskins; being destitute, afflicted, tormented; they wandered in deserts, and in mountains, and in dens and caves of the earth. So, am I optimistic? Yes, for my eternal reward, indeed, I am. But for this world, pardon me if I am somewhat apprehensive from time to time."

Courtney winked. "You've always had a little trouble with that, though. Right?"

"What do you mean by that?" Elijah asked.

"In the Bible, after you killed the prophets of Baal. Jezebel threatened you. You got a little apprehensive," she said.

Elijah scowled. "Do not think it such an honor to have your mistakes recorded in the one book preordained to withstand the winds of eternity."

Courtney put her hand over her mouth. "Elijah, no! I didn't mean to insult you. I'm so sorry."

"You are forgiven. Let us speak no more of it." His face still held a surly expression.

Everett's heart sank as they pulled into the drive where his cabin had been. "It's gone." He opened the door and walked by the burned-out shells of the Camaro and the BMW. Both were sitting on the ground as the tires had been completely incinerated.

"Smoke and ash." Courtney followed Everett out of the truck. "There's nothing left."

Everett groaned.

Elijah came and put his hand on his shoulder. "Sometimes faith is being able to accept the tribulation of this world."

Everett stood staring at the ash heap where the cabin had been. His home had been destroyed as a child, by divorce. Then, he'd moved on and made his own home, at his apartment in Ashburn. That home had been destroyed by the collapse. He'd moved on again. He'd married Courtney. Over the past three years, they'd made a home out of the cabin. And once again, his home was gone.

Courtney buried her head in his shoulder to cry. He held her tight. Everett turned to Elijah. "But what about the curses of Egypt?"

"What about them?" Elijah asked.

"God separated Goshen from Egypt. The plagues that devastated Egypt had no effect on the Israelites living in Goshen, just a few miles away. Couldn't God spare us from all this calamity that he's pouring out on the earth?"

Elijah looked at both of them with compassion. "He has already made his separation between Goshen and Egypt. His children were caught up in the disappearances. You were given a second chance. Your souls have been spared from eternal judgment. You must be grateful for that. But for this time of tribulation, you will have to endure. I am sorry."

Everett kicked a smoldering piece of wood near where the cabin had stood. He looked across the ashes to see if he could recognize anything. The chimney still stood, and the safe was lying face down. Nothing else looked the least bit familiar. "I guess we should get back. We can't salvage anything."

When they returned to the cave, Kevin and Sarah were setting up the solar panels, near the mouth of the cave and positioning the battery bank, charge controller, and inverter just inside.

Kevin looked Everett in the eyes. "Nothing left, huh?"

"Elijah's barn. The goats and chickens survived," Everett looked at the folding ladder which was standing alone on top of the hill above the cave entrance. "What's going on with that?"

Kevin pointed to the antenna sitting atop the highest rung of the ladder. "I've got the radio set up." He glanced at his watch. "I'm going to try to make contact with Tommy at 11:00."

Everett nodded. He had little expectation of them still being alive, much less having communications capabilities. "It's worth a try I guess."

Sarah handed a wire to Kevin. "Anytime the panels are out charging, someone has to be on the lookout for choppers. A reflective surface up against the charred landscape will be visible from miles away, given the angle. The same goes for the ladder and antenna. Of course, we'll only have that out when we're trying to communicate."

Everett nodded. "It would be good to have some camouflage that we could throw over top of the solar panels in case we had to hide them in a hurry."

"We've got some extra sheets." Courtney crossed her arms. "But I don't know what colors we have to choose from."

Everett helped Kevin get one of the panels positioned toward the sun. "Good idea. Any color would be better than shiny silver."

Elijah pulled his pocket watch out. "It is five minutes before 11:00. Perhaps we should begin trying to reach your friends."

"Okay." Everett went inside the cave to find the radio. The area where Kevin set the components up had less than three feet of overhead clearance. The team didn't have enough cord and cable to run the radio all the way back to the cathedral.

Kevin followed him in and reclined into a comfortable position near the radio and switched on the unit.

Everett pressed the mic button.

Courtney and Sarah gathered around to listen. "This is Undertow calling Mountain Saint."

Everett looked at his watch. "We'll give them a couple minutes then I'll try again."

At 11:00 AM on the nose, Everett repeated his call. "This is Undertow calling Mountain Saint. Come in Mountain Saint."

"This is Mountain Saint. Go ahead Undertow."

Everett was surprised to hear Stewart's voice. "I'm glad to hear you're still alive."

"We were prepared for the blood and fire. Preacher warned us what would happen."

"And what about our friends? Did everyone make it?"

"We're all accounted for. A couple of the folks had some smoke inhalation issues, but most of that seems to be clearing itself up. Hold on, someone wants to talk to you."

Tommy's distinctly low voice came over the radio. "I must say, I didn't know if I'd ever hear from you boys again. But I'm glad you're still alive. Did you all make it?"

Everett replied, "We're all still here. I guess it's safe to say the dance is canceled."

"No, sir. We're getting everything ready as we speak."

"Oh?" Everett was sure the GR compound in

Winchester was taken out by the fire. He wasn't sure how to ask for further clarification without giving up the code.

Tommy continued. "I reckon the fellas over at the dance hall must have had some idea about what was comin'. The dance hall sure ain't what it used to be, but it's still standing. We all feel obliged to go over there and give them a hand if you know what I mean.

Everett knew precisely what he meant. By *give them a hand*, Tommy meant to finish them off while they were still struggling to get organized. "Yeah. I do."

"And you understand the wisdom of helping them out right away. They're in a mess over yonder. They sure could use some good ol' mountain TLC about now."

"So the Dance is still on schedule?" Everett asked.

"If we could help them out getting the dance hall ready the day before it would be even better. Y'all get on over here that mornin' early. I'll have Lloyd pick you up about 8:00 AM. Be rested up and make sure you bring your clothes for the dance."

Everett kept his finger off the mic button. He looked to Kevin, Courtney, and Sarah. "The original plan was for Thursday. If he is going to attack a day early, that means tomorrow. Can we be ready to roll out?"

Courtney looked at Sarah. "We'll have to cancel our luncheon."

Sarah laughed. "Stop it."

Kevin nodded. "Tell him we'll be there."

Everett keyed the mic. "We're looking forward to it."

"Alrighty. I'll see ya then." Tommy shut his radio off as evidenced by a short burst of static on Everett's end.

CHAPTER 5

And such as do wickedly against the covenant shall he corrupt by flatteries: but the people that do know their God shall be strong, and do exploits. And they that understand among the people shall instruct many: yet they shall fall by the sword, and by flame, by captivity, and by spoil, many days.

Daniel 11:32-33

Wednesday morning, Everett led the way across the landslide area to the open road where Lloyd was to pick them up at 8:00. He wore a tactical vest full of spare magazines and a small pack which contained several essential items. Like everyone else on the team, he carried one of the AR-15s which Kevin had brought to the cave, rather than his HK. They had all drilled with the standardized rifle over the previous eighteen months so he felt confident he would be able to use it efficiently in a combat situation. Being able to share magazines and ammunition made them all stronger as a team. Everett glanced up at the sky. "It looks like rain."

Courtney followed close behind him. "That will make a real mess. Ash and mud."

Elijah was behind Sarah, who trailed Courtney by several yards. "We need the rain to wash the blood out of the streams. Perhaps it will stimulate new growth in the forest."

Kevin was the rear guard at the back of the line. "Rain is good hunting weather. It helps to obscure our movements visually as well as audibly. It's not comfortable to fight in, but if I'm hitting a compound full of trained men, I'd rather be wet from rain than from my own blood."

Everett chuckled. "When you put it like that."

The first drops of rain began to fall, just as they reached the pickup location on the opposite side of the landslide.

Sarah dug her military poncho out of her pack. "I hope Scratchy is on time."

Everett glanced at his watch as he put his own poncho on. "He'll be here. And by the way, he only answers to Lloyd. Scratchy is the moniker Courtney gave him before we'd been formally introduced."

Courtney tucked her rifle under her poncho. "I still like Scratchy better."

Kevin found a large rock to sit on while he

waited. "Elijah, how were the animals back at your barn doing this morning?"

Elijah pulled the drawstring to the hood of his poncho as the drizzling rain fell steadily. "They were thirsty. I'm sure they're doing better now that the rain is falling. Water from the roof flows into a rain catcher gutter and runs into a larger steel trough. I brought them a bag of deer corn from the cave. It was supposed to be for us to eat, but I simply can't stand to watch them starve. Besides, I couldn't possibly have more than a few months left here. I won't be taking my supplies with me when I leave."

Courtney came to sit by Elijah. "Don't say that."

He stuck his hand out from beneath his poncho and put it on her arm. "It is true, child. In the book of Daniel, we read of the seventy weeks. Each prophetic week represents a seven-year period. The final week began with Angelo Luz's treaty of the nations. It has been two years and ten months since. According to the way I read the book of Revelation, I am to prophesy in Jerusalem for three and a half years. At most, I will be here for another eight months."

"Still, I don't like to talk about you leaving." Courtney looked down toward the ground where rain drops were running off her poncho and mixing with the ash.

Elijah turned back to Kevin. "Some of the deer corn, I spread around my old garden plot. It's more than four years old, so I don't know if it will germinate. Even if it does, it's that genetically modified corn, so it may not produce. But, as long as a stalk grows, the goats and the chickens will eat it."

"I thought you bought all heirloom stuff." Everett looked curiously at Elijah.

"For my seeds, I did. Deer corn wasn't available as heirloom seed. In fact, when I bought it, it was illegal to plant deer corn. The company had a patent on the genetic modifications."

"I'm sure it's still illegal." Sarah repositioned herself on the rock next to Kevin. "It's just that Luz probably holds all the patents."

Kevin chuckled. "I wouldn't be surprised if it germinates and produces. They engineered that stuff to grow on concrete. I'm just not sure I'd want to eat it."

Everett rolled his eyes. "We've got less than four and a half years till the end of time. The amount of harm Frankenfood can do to your body is limited at this point."

Courtney stood up and pointed down the road. "There's Scratchy's van!"

Kevin got up from the rock he'd been sitting on. "Everyone spread out. Safety off and rifles at a low ready until we confirm that it is definitely Scratchy . . . I mean Lloyd, and that everything is going according to plan. We have to remember that this is officially the Apocalypse, and we must remain cautious."

Everett kept his rifle beneath his poncho but switched off the safety as the white van approached. He walked away from the group, positioning himself on the driver's side of the van.

Lloyd drove up and rolled down his window.

"Y'all getting wet out here?"

Everett looked inside the van to see who else was with him. "Only because you're late," he said with a wink.

"It's a quarter after. That's pretty darn good time considerin' the shape these roads is in. Y'all get on in here."

Everett nodded to the rest of the group and motioned for them to come to the van. He slid the side door open and held it while Courtney, Sarah, Elijah, and finally Kevin got in. Everett closed the door and got into the passenger's side with Lloyd. "It's good to see you."

Lloyd slowly maneuvered the van to turn around on the busted up pavement. "It's good to be seen, especially times being what they are."

Everett kept his eyes on the road to help Lloyd spot obstacles and hazardous cracks in the asphalt. "Did your home survive the fire?"

Lloyd shook his head. "It's gone. Tommy's compound faired a little better. Stewart's too. Tommy had some of his boys come in with front-end loaders and clear out fire breaks all around his property. He piled dirt up against the walls of the barn. Nearly as high as the roofline. He did the same thing to his house and to Stew's house. His house and the barn had metal roofs. Stew had shingles, but they spread a half inch of dirt on top of his roof.

"I was over to Stewart's the night it all started. The blood soaked into the dirt making it heavier. We could hear the trusses creakin'. We was afraid the dang roof was gonna cave in, but in the end, it held. We got up there first thing the next mornin' and cleared that mess off his roof."

Kevin stuck his head between the two front seats from the rear of the van. "How many guys are going with us?"

Lloyd shrugged. "I couldn't tell ya. There's me, Devin, Tommy, Preacher, and Stew, of course. Then Tommy's got several of the boys with their families stayin' out in the barn. There might be ten or fifteen fightin' age men over there. And Stew's cousin, little Joe."

"I thought we were talking about a much larger force." Kevin frowned.

Lloyd nodded. "There was about fifty of 'em or so. Bunch of 'em didn't make it. 'Course the fellas over to the GR compound got thinned out too. Ain't near so many of them either."

Everett huffed. "How many?"

"Tommy says way less'n a hunard."

Everett blew out a deep breath as a sign of his disgust. "If a hunard is anything like a hundred, we're way outnumbered."

"Less'n a hunard," Lloyd clarified. "Y'all hang on, we've got a good bump comin' up here."

The van jolted as it went over a major crevice in the pavement. Everett steadied himself by putting both hands firmly on the dashboard. "How much less?"

"Might be eighty or ninety of 'em, I reckon."

Everett gritted his teeth. "Lloyd. We're talking about twenty people or so on our team. This is suicide!"

"Tommy's a been dealin' with big government

numbers his whole life. It ain't about numbers. It's about leverage."

"And what's our leverage in this particular instance?" Everett's brow was heavily furrowed.

Lloyd swerved hard to narrowly avoid a missing section of road. "Heck, I don't know. Leverage is some big city word Tommy uses. I figured you boys would know what it meant."

Everett put his palm on his forehead. "Leverage is a mechanism that allows you to use a smaller amount of effort to do a larger amount of work than you could perform without that particular mechanism."

"Yeah, that makes sense then," Lloyd agreed.

"So what is it? I mean, what's the mechanism we're going to use?" Kevin quizzed.

"Hmm." Lloyd seemed to be thinking. "Could a surprise attack be leverage?"

Everett clinched his jaw as he turned to Kevin. "He doesn't know."

The trip which would take less than an hour prior to the Great Quake took nearly two and a half hours due to the poor conditions of the roadways.

Lloyd pulled past Tommy's house and drove toward the barn. Everett remembered how quaint Tommy's farmhouse had been. Now, it had dirt piled up on three sides of it, making it look like a bunker. He muttered to himself, "At least he still has a house."

The barn was surrounded on three sides by dirt mounds as well. The front entrance was fortified by a series of trucks, cars, and farm equipment which appeared to be situated to deter a frontal attack by a vehicle. The obstacles could also function as defensive firing positions if need be.

Lloyd got out of the van. "Y'all stretch your legs. I'll run up to the house and fetch Tommy."

Everett opened the sliding door for the others. "What do you guys think?"

"I don't like it." Kevin stepped out and helped Sarah to her feet.

Courtney pulled the hood of her poncho back over her head as it was still drizzling. "Elijah, what do you think? And don't tell me to pray about it. We did that, and we think we're doing what God wants."

"Then you have your answer." The old man got out of the van and walked toward the barn.

Courtney began to protest. "Yeah, but . . ."

Elijah shook his finger in the air. "Ah ah ah! Just because the circumstances have changed doesn't mean that God has."

Lloyd soon returned with Tommy. Tommy waved upon his approach. "Y'all get on in the barn and dry off."

The others headed toward the door to let themselves in, but Everett waited. He shook Tommy's hand. "I'm glad you guys survived the fire."

Tommy's eyes looked sincere. "Glad to see you're okay, too."

Everett walked next to the tall man. "What time are you planning to hit the compound?"

"I was going to leave it up to you boys." Tommy followed the others into the barn and closed the door.

Everett pulled the hood of his poncho off of his head. "Wait. So you don't have a plan?"

Tommy pointed to Kevin. "Weren't you in the military?"

"Yes. Sarah and I both were."

Tommy stuck his hands in his front pockets. "Lloyd said you told him you were in law enforcement for a spell also."

"That's right. We both worked for the sheriff's department."

Tommy turned and led the way back through the barn. "Then you two have more training in this sort of thing than anyone else."

Kevin walked quickly to keep up with Tommy. "I can't throw together an operation like this in a couple hours. It takes reconnaissance, planning, training; it takes time."

Everett listened as he walked past the people living in the barn. Ropes were tied between beams with various colored sheets hanging from them. The sheets appeared to partition off small rooms for the individual families. Men with their wives and children sat upon mattresses. They all offered a wave or a smile as Everett and the others passed by. Some of the families had boxes and furniture; tables and chairs. Others had nothing but a rug or blanket on the dirt floor. But all of them had guns. All of them were alive. All of them had chosen the hard path of saying no to the Global Republic. Everett wondered which of them had refused the Mark for the sake of Christ, and which had turned it down because they were patriots, rebels, or just preferred the underworld, like Tommy.

Tommy took them in the back of the barn to an area walled off with studs and drywall. The space had a poured concrete floor. He lit four kerosene lanterns which illuminated the room. "This was our office when we had the Gray Fox in the barn."

"What is a gray fox?" Courtney asked.

Tommy smiled. "It was a little waterin' hole we ran for the boys."

"Oh yeah. Your speakeasy. Kevin and Everett told us about it." Courtney found a chair and took a seat.

Tommy set one of the lanterns on a large table in the middle of the room. It had a smattering of wood blocks with assorted labels. "We've done as much recon on the location as we could. One of the fellas put this model together. It might not be perfect scale, but it'll give you an idea of how the place is laid out."

Kevin looked at the blocks. "This is Shenandoah University?"

"Yep. You been there?" Tommy asked.

Kevin looked back at Elijah and Everett. "We passed by there once, on our way to New Atlantis. The only thing the GR had set up at the time was a census station and a small relief distribution center. You had to take the Mark to get assistance, of course."

Everett looked the model over. The wood blocks representing buildings sat upon a sheet of cardboard from a broken-down box. Streets were drawn on the cardboard with a thick black marker and labeled. His finger followed along a path. "When we did our drive by, we came down University here then turned on Shockley and followed it through the underpass. This area was all wooded, right?"

Tommy smiled. "It was, but it's nothin' but charcoal now."

Kevin brushed his beard with his hand. "The census station would have been in this large building. And the relief center was set up in this parking lot on the other side of University Drive."

Tommy nodded. "Yep. That's about how they had it set up. But all these buildings are burned-out shells now. They're brick buildings, but they had flat roofs, and the fire burned straight through the rubberized coatings. The GR boys have moved back to these three buildings on the southeast corner of the campus. I reckon they put sand or something on those three roofs that proved to be a better fire retardant. These two buildings were dormitories. And this one was the dining facility. We figured they're using the dorms for living quarters, and the dining hall is their operations center."

Courtney put her finger on her lip as if she were in thought. "Tommy, Lloyd, do you have an estimate of how many survivors are left in Winchester?"

Lloyd replied, "Some. I can't say how many. Might be a thousand, might be five thousand. There's a good many brick houses and brick buildings with metal roofs. Most all them survived the fire lest they was in a heavily wooded area."

Courtney looked over the model. "Do you think the majority of the GR's supplies are in the dining hall?"

"Maybe," Tommy replied. "We can divvy up the

loot after the raid, but we have to live through it first."

"That's not really why I asked." Courtney turned to Everett. "Do they know where we used to work?"

"No. It never came up," Everett answered.

Tommy looked Everett in the eyes. "She's done got me curious now."

"We worked in intelligence." Everett continued to look over the small wood blocks on the table.

"You mean like CIA, NSA, that sort of thing?" Tommy's face had a curious smile.

Everett nodded. "Yeah. Something like that."

"Well, which one?" Tommy sounded excited.

"Both. I worked at the CIA, as an analyst. I wasn't a spy or anything. Courtney worked for a company that subcontracted for NSA."

Tommy turned to Lloyd. "You don't hear that every day. Did you know about all of this?"

Lloyd shook his head. "Nope, but I spect that's how they knew to get their tails out of the city when they did."

Tommy chuckled. "I expect it was. But what does all this have to do with our little exploit here? Why are you telling me this now?"

Courtney crossed her arms. "In addition to direct military conflict, US intelligence would incite insurrections to weaken governments they wanted to dispose of. They would sow the seeds of discontentment among the population; spread a little money around to organize the trouble makers."

Everett listened. "You're talking about organizing an insurrection. That takes lots of time and lots of resources. We're a little short on both."

"Hear me out," Courtney said. "Lloyd, where were the food distribution centers, and where was the food being kept?"

Lloyd took his ball cap off and scratched his head. "GR had five of the big grocery stores in town up and running. They weren't very well stocked, folks with the Mark were rationed on how much they could purchase and all that, but they were gettin' by."

Tommy added, "The warehouses were over on Fairmont. That's where they kept most of the food. But that's all burnt down. The GR knew the fires were coming. They made sure they took care of their own hide, but they didn't take any precautions to warn anybody else."

Courtney pointed to Tommy. "Bingo! All the survivors are figuring that out about right now. We've got a grass roots insurrection growing in the hearts and minds of Winchester right now. All we have to do is give them a little push."

"How do you suggest we do that?" Everett was beginning to see her plan.

"We write up calls to action on paper and go hand them out all over town. Kevin, Sarah, wasn't someone in your group responsible for the Tallmadge Letter back when the old government was rounding up patriots and Christians?"

Sarah nodded. "Cassie. She worked for the local paper. The government had shut down social media and restricted internet, so she printed up little one-page newspapers. That's part of what triggered the push back."

Everett smiled. "We were seeing copies of the

Talmadge Letter all the way up here."

"I've got a computer and a printer in the house," Tommy said. "I'm out of propane for my generator, but I could hook up an inverter to the truck for electricity."

"And you've got ink?" Courtney was hopeful.

"Let's go see." Tommy motioned for everyone to follow him. "Lloyd, you bring the truck around, hook up the inverter, and pull an extension cord to my bedroom."

"You reckon this here plan will make us some leverage?" Lloyd glanced over to Kevin as he followed Tommy out the door.

Kevin laughed. "I sure hope so, Lloyd. We certainly need it."

Once out of the barn, Everett walked close to Tommy. "The people living in the barn, did they all lose their homes in the fire?"

"Most of them. Some of them were already here; hiding out from the GR. My place has been one of the safe havens for folks who didn't want to take the Mark."

"So the GR never came out here?"

"Oh, they came. I just managed to get them to leave me alone. These GR peacekeepers don't have any loyalty to Luz. They couldn't care less who is signing their paychecks, as long as their belly is full."

"You bribed them to look the other way." Everett glanced over as he walked.

Tommy scowled. "I did. But it was somethin' akin to feedin' an ol' stray cat. Once they learned where the vittles were, you can believe they came back for more."

"It was always the same guys who came around?"

"Same commander. Once he figured out I had a steady stream of resources flowin' through, he began comin' round about twice a month. It was getting tough to make a livin'. I'm not sure if he survived the fire or not. He was an ornery cuss." Tommy walked up onto the front porch. "Y'all will have to excuse the clutter. Lloyd, Devin, and some of my wife's family are all staying with us. It's tight quarters."

Everett and the others removed their ponchos and hung them on the rail of the covered porch to avoid dripping water in the house.

Tommy led the way to the master bedroom and knocked. "Daisy, you decent? We've got company."

"Come on in." A soft southern voice called.

Tommy introduced the team to his wife. Daisy had flowing blonde hair, deep blue eyes and an hour glass figure which was accented by a tight yellow sun dress.

"Tommy don't bring too many ladies to the house. It's a pleasant treat to have some female company." Daisy smiled at Courtney and Sarah as she shook their hands.

Tommy pulled her hair back and kissed her neck. "Don't need to bring no girls around. I done got the prettiest one in Virginia."

Lloyd came in with the cord and plugged in the computer and the printer.

Courtney and Everett sat down at the small desk

and powered on the computer.

"What do we want to say?" Courtney opened a new document.

Everett let Courtney do the typing. "Let's state the obvious. The Global Republic knew the fires were coming. This is evidenced by the precautions they took to protect the buildings where the peacekeepers are staying. They made no effort to warn the citizens of Winchester."

Courtney pecked away on the keyboard. "Okay, that's a good start. How about this. Now they are holed up with provisions while the few survivors in town starve to death."

Kevin stood behind her. "And we need a call to action."

"Okay." Courtney continued typing. "Rally at the Global Republic compound at 5:00 PM. Bring weapons, and let's take back what is rightfully ours!"

Lloyd added, "Abrams Creek runs right by the college. It ain't exactly clean, but it ain't all

bloody no more either. Ain't been no power nor water since the fire. Folks might come just to get a drink."

"Excellent." Courtney included the information about the creek.

"It looks good." Sarah looked over Courtney's shoulder. "Let's address it to the citizens of Winchester."

"How much paper do you have?" Everett turned to look at Tommy.

Tommy opened the bottom drawer of the desk. "Whatever is in the printer, plus that."

Everett put his hand on Courtney's leg. "Maybe we should copy and paste the message two times. If we can get three messages on one piece of paper, we can cut them apart and reach more people."

"Good idea." Courtney completed her task and clicked Print.

Preacher walked into the room and introduced Stewart to the group. Tommy filled them in on the plan.

"What will we be doing while the riot is going on?" Preacher asked.

Everett raised his eyebrows. "Assuming we're successful at inciting a riot, we'll sit back and wait for an opportunity to present itself. If the peacekeepers come out to fire on the crowd, we'll have snipers positioned to take them out. If they try to run, we'll cut them down. If they effectively disperse the crowd and give chase, we'll have ambush locations set up. Unfortunately, when your plan is to create chaos, it's a little hard to predict how everything will play out."

"Where will we go to hand out the papers?" Stewart inquired.

Lloyd held up his hand. "I seen a bunch of folks scroungin' around in the ashes of the Walmart on Pleasant Valley. We could give them a paper."

"Good thinkin', Lloyd." Tommy patted him on the back. "I bet folks are doing the same thing at the other distribution points. Probably over by the warehouse, too."

Everett said, "We should get a move on then. We need to figure out a staging area. Then get these handbills passed out."

"The military calls it an Objective Rally Point or ORP," Kevin said.

"What do you propose for an ORP?" Tommy asked.

Everett pointed to Kevin. "I'll let our tactical coordinator take that one."

"Thanks." Kevin smiled and looked over the model. "These buildings on the north side of the campus, are they all burned out?"

Preacher pointed to several buildings. "All of these are multiple story brick buildings. They have structural issues with the roof, but the lower floors just have heavy smoke damage."

"Then I say we try to make our way there and lay low until the fun starts." Kevin looked up at Tommy.

Tommy nodded. "Lloyd, you go tell Devin to get ready. Preacher, you and Stew head over to the barn and have the men gear up. And get me a list of names of all the hunters. Especially anyone with a good long-range rifle. We'll set them up as snipers."

Kevin said, "If your men can handle passing out the information papers, we'll get on over to the University. I'd like to get a feel for the layout so I can plan where to station our various contingencies."

"That'd be fine with me," Tommy kissed Daisy before walking out the door with the others. "I'll send Preacher and Stew with you. Me, Devin, and Lloyd will have the rest of the boys at the ORP by four o'clock. Anything, in particular, you want us to bring?"

"Food, ammo, and Band-Aids," Kevin replied.

"It was so nice to meet you, Daisy." Courtney waved.

"You too. Y'all will have to come back when I can be a better hostess." She walked with them out of the room.

"We'll do that. See you soon." Sarah smiled.

When they returned, the rain had stopped, but the sky was still cloudy. Preacher pointed to the vehicle in the drive. "That's my old red Chevy with the topper on it. It's a crew cab, but we'll still have to put some folks in the bed of the truck to fit everybody."

Stewart looked at Kevin. "You probably want to ride shotgun. I can ride in the bed of the truck."

"I'll ride with Stewart." Elijah put his hand in the air.

Kevin patted Elijah on the back. "Thanks. Everett, Sarah, and Courtney should all fit in the back seat."

Kevin called out the seating arrangements as the team loaded up into Preacher's truck. "Sarah, you're on the door behind me. Courtney, you're in the middle and Everett is on the driver's side back door. Everyone, have your weapons ready to go in case we hit trouble. Preacher, if we run into a situation, stick the truck at an angle with the passenger's side toward the greatest concentration of hostiles. Sarah and I have the most experience with this sort of thing."

"Yes, sir." Preacher started the vehicle.

Kevin turned around in his seat. "Courtney, can you open that back sliding window? I need to ask Stewart a question before we move out."

"Sure." She slid the glass to the side.

"Stewart," Kevin called.

"Yes?"

"I'm assuming you're Tommy's comms guy. How are you guys set for handhelds?"

"We've got three UHF/VHF handhelds. Maybe eight walkie-talkies. Less than stellar, better than nothing. Everyone is set to channel three on the walkies. We have the three ham handhelds set to 462.6125 which is the same frequency as channel three on the FRS/GMRS walkies."

Everett removed his radio from his vest and scrolled through to find the frequency. "It won't tune to that. It scrolls straight from 462.600 to 462.625."

"Just punch the frequency in manually. And if your radio only displays three digits past the decimal, it will most likely add the 5 on the end if you program it to 462.612."

"Got it." Everett successfully entered the frequency on his radio.

"My team, let's all get our radios on that frequency and do a quick comms check." Kevin removed his radio and made the necessary adjustments.

Courtney and Sarah did likewise, then each of them took turns speaking into their radio.

"Good." Kevin switched his radio off and called toward the back of the truck. "Elijah, you'll always be with Everett and Courtney, so you'll be able to communicate with one of their radios if you need to."

"Yes, yes. That will be fine." The old man waved

through the rear window.

As the truck pulled off of Tommy's property, Kevin turned to Preacher. "If it's possible, let's try to come in from the north. And let me know when we're getting close. I'd like to find a good fallback position in case we have to retreat. It should be somewhere we can safely park the majority of the vehicles."

"We can do that. There's a middle school about a mile and a half north of the university."

"Good. Let's drive by there on the way. What's in between the two?"

"Public park. Swimming pool, soccer field, baseball field, that sort of thing."

Everett looked out the window at the scorched landscape. "And no trees. So lots of open area to cross with no cover."

Preacher replied, "A few maintenance buildings are scattered about; one for the pool and a couple over by the ball fields, but you're right. There's not much cover."

Tommy's farm was roughly eight miles from the university. It took them over a half an hour to reach the middle school, due to the poor condition of the roads.

Kevin grunted as he peered out the window. "It is wide open. That's a lot of ground to cover."

Sarah added, "Especially if someone is injured or if we are transporting a casualty."

Courtney pointed ahead in the direction of the university. "What about that neighborhood?"

"Not much of a neighborhood anymore, but we can take a drive through the streets if you want."

Preacher turned left onto Cork Street. "The neighborhood up on our right cuts straight through to the university. There used to be a lot of brick homes back through there. I doubt they have roofs, but they might be good for cover in a tactical situation."

"Some of the homes could still have people living in them," Everett said.

Kevin nodded. "So let's proceed with caution. If we see any signs of inhabitants, turn around. The last thing we want to do is engage with people who are just trying to defend their homes."

Preacher slowly turned onto Opequon Avenue.

Everett estimated that roughly one in ten of the houses were brick. The other lots were marked only by the concrete footers, stairs, and driveways. A few solitary brick walls stood, the remainder of wood frame houses that had been dressed with a brick façade on the front of the home. "How many streets deep is this neighborhood?"

"Probably about four, but all the streets don't cut through," Preacher continued down the road.

"That's it!" Sarah leaned over the seat and pointed to the right.

Kevin followed the direction of her finger. "Five brick houses in a row."

Everett looked left. "That whole street is brick. Parkview, where does it lead?"

"It comes out right on the campus." Preacher rolled to a stop.

"This is our fallback position. Right behind these houses. Preacher, can you take us on over to the north side of the campus?"

"Yes, sir." Preacher turned the vehicle around and cut through a church parking lot. From there, it was only another 400 yards to the building Kevin had designated as the ORP.

"Where should I park?"

"Pull into that loading dock." Kevin pointed toward the ramp which was obscured from view by the corner of the student center building.

The team exited the vehicle being very gentle as they closed the doors of the truck. Everett walked along the side of the building, peering through the windows around the corner from the loading dock. "It looks empty from here."

Kevin cupped his hands over his eyes to reduce the glare as he took a peek in the window. "Okay. Let's get inside." Using the butt of his folding blade knife which had a glass breaker, Kevin tapped the center of the pane. The glass shattered, and he repeated the process for the other lower panes in the window.

Everett used the stock of his AR to take out the thin metal frame between the panes. He swept the remaining glass out of the bottom frame with his glove then carefully crawled through. "I'll walk around and open those fire doors."

The room he entered was a back office. The desk, computer, and floor were caked in black soot from the fire. The door knob was also black from the fire. Everett opened the door cautiously and scanned the hallway outside before proceeding. As he made his way to the fire doors, he noticed the heavy imprint of his boot on the soot-stained floor. He pushed the bar on the door, and it swung open to the team.

He pointed at his footprints. "If anyone else has been in here since the fire, we'll know."

Courtney walked through the door. "And if the peacekeepers come in after us, we'll be easy to track."

"Unless we pace around the entire building aimlessly," Elijah suggested.

"Actually, that's not a bad idea. If we end up having some time to kill, we can do that. It would be good to know what's in the building anyway." Sarah opened the doors and inspected the offices as they walked through the hallway.

The team reached the front entryway of the student center. A large domed atrium overlooked the street out front.

Everett stared through the smoky windows. "Preacher, Stewart, do either of you guys know what that tower is?"

Stewart looked out the window. "I'm not sure, but that's the direction of the building the peacekeepers are using. Preacher, do you know what it is?"

"No. It's the tallest building on the campus, though."

Kevin gazed at the square brick tower with a pyramid roof top. "I'm sure the GR troops have control of that. They'd be stupid not to."

"Or lazy." Preacher slung his AR-15 over his shoulder as he and Stewart did not have the same single point slings that Everett's team used.

Everett retrieved the small field glasses from his assault pack to get a closer look. "I can't see much.

I'm going to need to look at it from a better angle."

Kevin nodded. "Sarah, you're tactical commander while we're gone. It'll be just me and Everett. We need to keep the lowest profile possible until we can figure out where they have watches set up. Keep your radio on, but don't make any calls unless it's absolutely necessary. They probably have a scanner, and we don't want to let them know we're in the area until we have to.

"You ready to move?"

Everett hung the binoculars around his neck and held his rifle at a low-ready position. "Roger that."

"Be safe Everett!" Courtney's eyes were filled with concern.

"I will."

"I love you," she said.

"You too." He gave her a wink as he followed Kevin.

"Let's move. Stay low, quiet, and close." Kevin led the way back out the fire doors.

As they moved around the corner of the building toward the tower, Everett spotted a four-foot-high metal sign with a map of the campus encased behind a sheet of Plexiglass. "That's just what we need."

Kevin walked over and wiped the soot and ash from the glass. "Hmm. The recon model in Tommy's barn was pretty accurate. This series of buildings must be where the peacekeepers are staying. And this is the building with the tower."

Everett read the label of the tower building out loud. "Health and Life Sciences Building. They must have had a significant amount of nursing and medical programs." Of course, his observation had no bearing on their present predicament. Nothing like that mattered anymore. Yet Everett couldn't help himself from looking back on the past. As he gazed across the ruins of a lost empire, he felt like an archeologist trying to decipher the artifacts of an ancient civilization.

Kevin interrupted his daydream. "There's a building in between, Henkel Hall. If they do have watchmen up in that building, they're exposed going from building to building. We could set up a sniper over here and take them out when they change guards."

"If they change guards. We're just a few hours away from zero hour." Everett grunted.

"If they're in that tower, we have to find a way to eliminate the threat. They can pin down this whole campus with four shooters from up there."

"Or we can take it. Use snipers to keep reinforcements from crossing from the Allen Dining Hall to the Life Sciences Building."

"Yeah. We'll lose some people doing that, but we might have to," Kevin said. "Let's keep moving for now. We need to find a spot where we can get up high and see what type of activity is going on over there."

"What about the theater building? It's across from Life Sciences. It will give us some cover, and let us get close enough to see how many people they have on watch."

"Good, let's do it." Kevin led the way around University Drive to the back of the Bryant Theater Building.

When they reached the side of the building, Kevin peeked in through the window. "Good news. No footprints in the soot."

"And single pane windows."

"That's a blessing and a curse. Easier to get in through, but they make more noise when they break." Kevin turned away from the glass as he struck it with the carbide tip on the butt of his knife. The glass shattered, and the fragments dropped noisily to the ground.

Everett gritted his teeth as he stood motionless for a moment, listening for any indication that the Global Republic peacekeepers had heard the window being smashed.

"Way too loud." Kevin winced. "Let's get inside."

Everett followed Kevin through the window. The two of them worked their way to the east side of the building so they could get a view of the tower.

Everett lifted his binoculars to his eyes. "These windows are really smoky."

"I know, but don't wipe the soot. It'd be as good as hanging a neon sign that says *we're here*!"

Everett took the lanyard from around his neck and passed the field glasses to Kevin. "I don't see any movement or signs that anyone is over there."

"Hmm." Kevin gazed at the building across from them. "Nothing. That's too good be true. The tower looks straight down on their compound. No one would be stupid enough to leave it undefended."

Everett stared through the soot-stained glass. "The weak have one weapon, the error of those who think they are strong."

Kevin nodded. "Bidault?"

"Yeah. A lot of the Agency's core doctrine was developed by the OSS, the CIA's predecessor, when they were working with the French Resistance."

"And that's a good principle to remember." Kevin handed the binoculars back to Everett.

Everett stowed the field glasses in his pack. "Of course, you can't underestimate human complacency."

"Nor her ugly sister, human laziness." Kevin chuckled. "I guess our next step is to go back to the ORP and organize an entry team."

"To take the tower?"

"Yep."

"What if hostiles are in there, and we just didn't see them? Wouldn't it be better to wait for the riots to start? We can position snipers so they can't send reinforcements."

"That's one possible course of action. But my theory is that the riots could be the catalyst which kicks them in the butt and makes them realize that they need that tower. We can still set up snipers. We'll put Elijah, Preacher, and Stewart in the courtyard between the dorms. If anyone tries to leave the GR compound, going toward the tower, they'll have a clear shot. Even if they miss a peacekeeper leaving the compound, they'll have a second chance to take him out when he tries to get from Henkel Hall to the Life Sciences Building."

They returned to the broken window and Everett followed Kevin back out and toward the objective rally point. "Elijah's weapon of choice was a shotgun before you trained him with the AR. I don't know if he's really cut out to be a sniper."

"He's pretty good. I'm not going to put them that far out anyway." Kevin turned to look back toward the tower. "That building is the library. It has windows facing the courtyard. We'll put them in there. They'll have visual and physical cover but they'll be close enough to have an easy shot."

"Sounds like a plan."

The two men spotted no activity on their return trip to the ORP.

CHAPTER 6

When thou goest out to battle against thine enemies, and seest horses, and chariots, and a people more than thou, be not afraid of them: for the Lord thy God is with thee, which brought thee up out of the land of Egypt.

Deuteronomy 20:1

Everett listened as Kevin laid out the overview of the plan to gain control of the tower.

Preacher examined the map which Everett sketched from the sign across the street. Everett labeled each building with a letter rather than the actual name of the building. This tactic provided an additional layer of operational security as only their team would know which building they were referring to if they said building B or building C.

Preacher pointed to one of the boxes on Everett's map. "We've been watching building A, and we haven't seen any activity. The only reason we could think that they wouldn't have tried to hold it is that the dorms where they are holed up, buildings K, L, and M, sit higher on the hill. K and L are only two-story buildings, but being up on that slope still gives them a good vantage point."

Stewart pointed to the map. "Plus, they're on the corner of the campus. The south and east sides have no visual obstructions. It's wide open now that the foliage of the trees has been incinerated. The peacekeepers only have to worry about somebody sneaking up on them from the north or the west. I don't think it is such a bad position. Trying to hold the tower building in addition to the other three would have spread them out pretty thin."

"That's true. If you add another lookout post that requires three men, you'll need nine to fill all three shifts." Kevin rubbed his beard. "Even so, if it were my post, and I had eighty or ninety men under me, I would have assigned watchmen on that tower."

Preacher looked at Courtney and Sarah. "Me and Stewart wouldn't mind being on the entry team and having you girls hold the sniper positions." He turned to Everett. "If it were my wife, I hope a man would volunteer to take her place so she wouldn't have to kick in doors."

Everett smiled. "We appreciate the offer, but the four of us have trained together quite a bit. We've learned how the other members of the team move, and how each of us reacts."

"Then you can count on us to stop anyone from crossing over to your building. I've taken my fair share of deer over the years. And all of them weren't standing still." Stewart patted Everett on the shoulder.

"Okay then. Everyone, do a final weapon check, and let's move out," Kevin said. "We'll escort the sniper team to the library, get inside and assign your positions. The entry team will take the tower. If it's unoccupied, we'll put the snipers in the tower, and the rest of us will return to meet up with Tommy when he arrives with the other men."

Sarah followed Kevin out the doors, with Everett behind her, and Courtney on Everett's six. The sniper team followed from ten yards back.

Kevin moved to the corner of the nearest building. He put his fist in the air as a sign to halt. He dropped to one knee and motioned for Everett to come next to him. He whispered, "Can you hand me those binoculars?"

Everett retrieved the field glasses from his pack and handed them to him. Kevin looked through the binoculars then handed them to Everett, pointing along the creek.

Everett saw a team of six men collecting water in buckets. He scanned the area with the binoculars, but could not see a security team. "Easy pickin's."

"I know, it's tempting. But we can't tip our hand yet." Kevin motioned for everyone to stay low and out of sight until the men were finished retrieving water from the creek.

By the time the men completed their task, the drizzling rain had returned. "Let's give them ten more minutes. I want to make sure they aren't coming back for another load of water before we move."

The time passed slowly standing in the rain. The precipitation wasn't heavy enough to warrant breaking the ponchos back out. Ponchos would encumber their movement in the event that they were to engage in a firefight. Finally, Kevin looked at his watch and gave a nod. The team proceeded quietly along the back side of the buildings.

Preacher waved for the team to stop as they reached the last building before the library. He walked up to Everett's position. "From this corner to the next corner, we're completely exposed to the men on watch at the compound."

Kevin turned and nodded. He retrieved a small mirror from the top pocket of his tactical vest. He leaned his rifle against the wall and lay prone on the ground, extending the mirror just far enough around the corner to get a view of the compound. After several seconds of inspecting the scene, Kevin stood up. He whispered to Everett. "Two guys on the roof, not paying much attention. They look like they just want to get out of the rain. We can time it out and make a run for it when their backs are turned. I can't tell if anyone is looking out the windows. It's too dark inside."

"We don't have a choice, right?"

Kevin answered, "None that I can think of. The entry team will go first. We'll pause to make sure the guards are still turned around then we'll have the sniper team follow."

Everett nodded and relayed the information to everyone else.

Kevin held the mirror out for one more quick glance then led the entry team as they sprinted across the exposed area.

Everett fought the urge to look at the men on the roof as he ran. Sarah and Courtney stayed close to the men as they quickly reached the other side.

Everett took a deep breath and watched as Kevin took a peek from the corner of the library. Kevin motioned for the sniper team to cross. Elijah, Preacher, and Stewart moved briskly and quietly to the corner of the library.

Kevin took one last look to make sure they had not been spotted. "I think we're clear."

Everett exhaled deeply as a sign of his relief. He looked inside the row of windows as they passed, checking for footprints in the soot which covered the floors. "No sign of activity in the library."

"Then let's get this show on the road." Kevin motioned for Sarah and Everett to get on each side of him. "I'm going to try to crack the glass without smashing it. I want you guys to catch the large pieces before they fall to the ground and alert the guards on the roof. Do you both have your gloves on?"

"Check." Sarah held her gloves up.

Everett did likewise, but said nothing.

Kevin firmly pushed the carbide tip on the butt of his knife against the corner of the window. The glass popped and cracks radiated through the pane. "I'll try to dig a piece out with my knife. Each of you keep a hand on either side. If it collapses, I want it to fall inside, not out."

Everett nodded and placed his gloves over the two largest fragments of the window as Kevin attempted to pry a medium-sized sliver of glass with the blade of his knife.

Kevin's piece came out and immediately, the rest of the window fell from its own weight, crashing on the floor inside the library.

Everett grimaced at the loud noise.

Kevin brushed off his gloves and retrieved his mirror to peer around the corner at the men on the roof.

"Did they hear us?" Sarah asked.

Kevin was silent for a moment. Finally, he replied. "I don't think so."

The team climbed in and made their way to the second floor, and then to the southeast corner. Everett walked toward the grimy window. "You guys have a good view of the watchmen on the roof as well as the pathway below from here. If you have to take a shot, you'll have to take out those guys on the roof first. You'll have to hit them through the window. Otherwise, you'll give away your position."

Elijah held his rifle up and looked through the sights. "Yes. It won't be a problem. Just call us on the radio if you need our support."

"Thanks, Elijah." Courtney put her hand on the old prophet's arm then turned to follow the rest of the entry team.

Everett, Kevin, Courtney, and Sarah were down the stairs and back outside in a matter of minutes.

The team had one more short sprint where they could potentially be spotted by the men on the roof. Kevin checked his mirror. "They're not even in view. But still, let's move quickly to be safe."

Kevin led, and the rest of the team followed. They checked for signs of activity before entering. Finding none, they broke out a window and went inside. Within minutes, the team had located the tower.

A large stained glass window allowed light into the tower room which was little more than a hollow brick structure. Everett guessed the inside of a clock tower must look similar. He looked through one of the small pieces of clear glass on the periphery of the stained glass crest of the university. "It's a pretty good view of the compound. If we can get snipers up here, we can pin them down."

Kevin looked out the portals on the other sides of the tower. "This goes right out onto the roof. The ledge provides excellent cover. I say we knock this glass out so our guys will have roof access."

Courtney looked out the window which Kevin was proposing to break out. "What harm would come of waiting until the fireworks start to knock it out?"

Sarah looked over Courtney's shoulder. "Good point. There's no reason to make more noise than we have to right now. If the rioters come, the glass breaking will blend in with the rest of the racket."

Kevin agreed to take Sarah's advice. "Let's get our snipers up here and get back to the ORP."

The next couple of hours passed slowly at the

ORP as the anticipation of the mission grew. Everett looked at his watch, just as he'd done every three to four minutes for the past hour. "Four-thirty."

Sarah stood up from her chair. "I hear a vehicle."

"I hope it's Tommy. He's a half hour late." Everett walked to the office window of the ORP to look out.

"That's him." Courtney pointed at Lloyd's van.

Everett grabbed one of the copies of the map they'd made of the campus and headed toward the fire doors. "I'll send the men in and take the drivers over to the fallback position."

As Everett walked out, he saw Tommy's truck pull in behind Lloyd's. Two other vehicles were following close behind. Most of Tommy's men unloaded from the vehicles and went inside the ORP. Everett jumped into the truck with Tommy. "Have the other vehicles follow you. I'll show you where to park."

As they drove to the fallback position, Everett explained the map with the letters on each building and filled Tommy in on what they had come up with so far. "Did you guys have any success finding rabble-rousers?"

Tommy laughed. "Some men are poets; others are artists, still others musicians and craftsmen. Me? The good Lord gave me the gift of finding rabble-rousers. And for better or worse, they always seem to take my suggestions."

"So you believe in the good Lord now?" Everett smiled.

Tommy held his hand up. "I've always believed.

We may not always see eye to eye, but I believe."

Everett chuckled. "You know, the book of James says that even the devils believe. It says they even tremble in fear of God. The problem is they don't submit to God."

"I can relate to that." Tommy nodded with a big smile. "But you don't have to take on the impossible task of bringing me to Jesus. Preacher has been trying to get me to find religion since before this whole mess got started. Heck, evidently he hadn't even found it himself at the time."

"I was just making an observation." Everett put his hands in the air as if he were backing off. He remembered how much he hated it when John Jones, Ken, or Lisa would try to convince him that following Christ was the rational thing to do. "But you do believe in the Bible, right? All the events that Preacher has told you about, they're coming true, one at a time. You can't deny that."

Tommy sighed. "Yep. They are."

"And you know we've only got a few more years before the whole thing comes to a close. So either way, your sinning days will soon be over."

Tommy swallowed hard. "How about we talk about this some other time? I've got a lot goin' on in my head right now."

"Sure thing." Everett honored Tommy's wish. He remembered how many times he had put off thinking about such things. He'd put it off until he could no longer avoid the subject. And his procrastination had landed him dead smack in the middle of the Apocalypse.

Tommy pulled around to the back of the row of

burned-out brick houses. "Lloyd has a selection of various accoutrements in his van. When things start getting hairy, we'll come back here to gear up for the fight. I'm going to keep two men here with the vehicles to make sure they don't roll away with all our supplies. Not to mention, we'll need 'em to get back home."

"You and Lloyd are going to be mixed in among the rioters?"

Tommy nodded. "Yep. Like I said, I'm a natural born instigator. It'd be a shame to let such a gift go unused on a day like today. Lloyd is coming with me. Devin and five more of my guys will be mixing in the crowd with us. We'll stay until the peacekeepers take action. Once everyone starts to scatter, we'll start tapping anyone from the crowd who looks like they're ready to take it to the next level. I'll bring them back here, organize a direct attack, and hit their compound from the west. I assume your team will be coming in from the north."

"Yeah, that's right. You thought that up on the way here?"

"Figured it out while we were handing out the flyers. People are angry. Might as well help them channel that energy. All the men we dropped off over at the ORP are instructed to work with you. You tell them what needs doin', and they'll get it done. They're all good men."

"Okay then, you've got a good radio, right?"

"Yep." Tommy got out of the truck.

Everett opened the door of the truck and exited the vehicle. "When we're ready to move in on the compound, we'll say something like *minus fifteen*. That would mean T minus fifteen seconds. Whatever number I say is how long until we launch our assault. Let me know how many men you've picked up from the riots. Just give me the number. I'll know what you're talking about, but hopefully, any peacekeepers monitoring a scanner won't have enough information to figure it out."

Tommy shook Everett's hand. "Sounds like a plan."

Everett walked by himself back toward the ORP. As he crossed Pleasant Valley Road, he noticed a gathering of men. He estimated that there were about twelve in the group. Some had ball bats; others carried pry bars. "I bet some of them have pistols, but I doubt they'd take a chance trying to open carry with the Global Republic's standing shoot-on-sight order for anyone in possession of a firearm."

One of the men noticed Everett from a distance. "Hey, you!"

Everett waved at the man and shook his head. "Gotta run." He changed to a brisk sprint to get out of the area before the men got closer to him. He said to himself, "With my weapon and tactical gear, I look more like a GR peacekeeper than a rioter. It's too early in the day for a friendly fire incident." Everett made sure the men weren't pursuing him before he cut around the lake to the ORP.

Everett knocked on the fire doors.

Kevin pushed them open from the inside. "Where's Tommy and the rest of the guys?"

Everett relayed the new plan.

Kevin grimaced. "I guess I was expecting too much if I thought Tommy was actually turning over full tactical command to me."

"He said the guys he dropped off earlier were taking orders straight from you."

Kevin walked back to the office where the map was located. "That's great, but now we've got people running around all over the place doing whatever the heck they want. You can't run an operation like that. That's how people get killed."

Everett shrugged. "It's not the best-case scenario, but I'm convinced Tommy will be able to create a much more effective riot than would happen by itself. When I was at the CIA, anytime the Company went overseas to intentionally destabilize a government, guys like Tommy were always the ones they were looking for. From an intelligence standpoint, he's doing exactly what we want him to be doing. It's messy, but it's a proven strategy."

Kevin looked over the map. "Benny, the guy you called Spindle, he told us about some of that stuff. I'm sure it's effective, it's just when decisions are being made, I can't adjust my course of action if I'm not in the loop."

"I understand. But Tommy is a loose cannon. We knew that coming into this thing. He's not going to conform to our methodology."

Kevin sighed. "I know. But I wish Tommy hadn't put me in charge of anything. When I'm calling the shots, I feel like I'm responsible for every man's life. Loose cannons cause casualties on both sides. It's a variable I'm not used to working with."

Sarah and Courtney walked in. "What's happening?" Courtney asked.

"People are already gathering in the streets. It was a good idea." Everett put his hand on her arm.

"Thanks." She looked at the map. "When do we start to move?"

Kevin looked up at Sarah. "I'm going to take command of most of the fourteen guys Tommy dropped off. We'll be the initial assault team. Sarah, you'll be the tactical coordinator for a five-man team. I'll give you two of Tommy's men plus Everett, Courtney, and yourself. Everett, do you have a problem with that?"

Everett shook his head. "She has more experience."

"Good. You guys are going to take up a position inside the library. The three of you watch that second-floor window where we were earlier. Put the two men from Tommy's team downstairs by the window we came in through. You don't want any rioters or peacekeepers sneaking up on you. I'll cue Tommy with *minus fifteen*. Sarah, count it down, then all of you start taking any shot you have.

"I'll be taking a smaller team inside the fence to sabotage the vehicles once the peacekeepers start taking fire. The parking lot is in your field of fire from the library, so be conscious of what's behind your target when you shoot.

"Once the fireworks start, we can use the radios for minimal coordination. They'll have already figured that they're under a formal attack by that point. So it won't matter as much if they pick up our comms over a scanner. Just don't give away any info over the radios that you don't absolutely have to.

"Any questions?"

"I don't like splitting up our team. We've trained together; we know how to work together. Not having you as coordinator puts everybody at risk." Sarah was obviously in a huff. "Especially you."

Kevin furrowed his brow. "Someone has to lead the primary strike team, Sarah. And we can't have seventeen people on a squad. We have to break it up."

"I don't want to lose you again." Sarah was a warrior, but she was also a wife.

Kevin hugged her. "You won't. I promise."

She put her hand on his cheek. "You can't promise. I know you'll try your best, but you can't promise that."

"I'll assign two men to your team. Then you guys need to get into position." Kevin kissed her forehead and walked out of the room.

Moments later two men who had been dropped off by Tommy walked in.

"I'm Bennett." A young man, late twenties, extended his hand to Everett. He wore camouflage cargo pants and carried an AR-15.

The other man was in his late thirties. He also had an AR-15 slung over his shoulder. "I'm Silas."

Everett figured Kevin had purposely assigned men with compatible weapons and ammo. He shook the two men's hands. "I'm Everett. Nice to meet you. But to be clear, Sarah is running this operation.

She might look like a runway model, but trust me, she saw her share of action in the desert and in the resistance prior to the disappearances."

Sarah blushed as a smile came over her face. "Stop it, Everett. Bennett, Silas, nice to meet you. If you have any ideas, I'm happy to hear them, but if I give an order, it has to be followed immediately and without question. Otherwise, the whole dynamic breaks down and our risk of dying goes up exponentially. If you can't handle that, tell me now. You can go work with Tommy. No hard feelings, at least not on my part. Do you understand?"

Silas nodded." I understand. You won't have any problems out of me. I'm here to win this thing and get these sons of bucks out of my town."

Bennett shook Sarah's hand. "Same here, Ma'am."

"Good. Have either of you served in law enforcement or military?" Sarah asked.

"Tommy never had many friends in law enforcement." Silas smiled. "Maybe a couple, but they had to be careful hanging around the rest of us. And no ma'am, I didn't have the honor of serving."

"Me neither, ma'am," Bennett said. "But we both hunt. Squirrel, rabbit, turkey, deer."

"That helps." Sarah quickly went over basic hand signals with the two men.

"Sounds logical. I'll remember that." Silas tucked his thumb in the sling of his rifle.

"Are you guys any good with the AR-15s?" She inquired.

"Oh yeah. We can shoot," Bennett replied.

Sarah looked the two men over. Both had quad-stack magazine holders on their belts. "You both have five magazines, including the ones in your rifles?"

"Couple extras besides these." Bennett patted the left side pocket of his cargo pants.

Silas said, "I have eight magazines total."

"Okay, conserve ammo. Don't shoot unless you think you can hit someone or if one of your teammates is calling for cover fire. This could be a long fight. Let's move out."

CHAPTER 7

The voice said, Cry. And he said, What shall I cry? All flesh is grass, and all the goodliness thereof is as the flower of the field: The grass withereth, the flower fadeth: because the spirit of the Lord bloweth upon it: surely the people is grass. The grass withereth, the flower fadeth: but the word of our God shall stand for ever.

Isaiah 40:6-8

The rain had paused and Everett was right behind Sarah as they moved toward the library. With Bennett and Silas trailing the rest of the team, the group looked more like militia and less like Global Republic peacekeepers. This was a good thing as they encountered three more groups of people heading toward the compound. One of the groups was only five people, but they had shotguns and were pushing a grocery cart filled with glass bottles which had bits of rag hanging out the top of each one. Everett waved at the man pushing the cart as a sign that they were on the same team and shared a common objective. "Molotov cocktails."

A pickup truck drove down Lowery Drive, passing by the team. Six men were in the bed of the truck whooping and hollering as if they were drunk.

Courtney was directly behind Everett. She turned to Silas. "Those guys look like they might be Lloyd's customers. Do you recognize any of them?"

Silas wrinkled his forehead. "No."

Everett watched as they drove past. "They'll probably be the first to get shot when the GR's patience runs out."

Sarah shook her head. "This is a volatile situation. I don't like it."

The team reached the library and quickly went inside. Sarah looked around. "Bennett, Silas, try to find some cabinets or something to stack up against this window. We want to make it look less accessible to passersby. And at the same time, make sure we can get back out in a hurry if need be. All the exits are locked. Even the fire doors are chained shut. I guess GR fire codes are a little more lax than the old governments. No one gets in here, even if that means shooting. This is our house for now."

"Yes, ma'am." Silas began looking around for furniture to use for a barricade.

Sarah motioned for Everett and Courtney to

follow her to the stairwell. "Let's see if we can get to the third floor. The roof has probably caved in, but we'd have a much better vantage point."

Everett took the lead up the stairs. He pushed against the door. "It's blocked by debris. Should we try another stairwell?"

"Yeah, let's give it a shot." Sarah walked back down to the second floor where they cut through to the opposite side of the building.

Everett carefully traversed the stairs which were littered with scorched roofing material. He pushed the door open. Debris from the collapsed roof was all around, but he managed to get through the door.

Sarah came in behind him. "What a mess."

Everett looked at Courtney as she walked through. "Be careful up here. Lots of hazards are mixed in the rubble."

Sarah pushed against a beam which was blocking the window overlooking the GR compound. "Protestors are gathering around the GR perimeter fence."

Everett and Courtney helped her shove the beam to the side so they could all get close to the window.

Everett wiped an area of residue from the glass so he could see out more clearly. Since the peacekeepers had enough to worry about in the parking lot, it was unlikely that they'd notice the small area of glass that Everett cleaned.

Twenty armed men now stood on the roof of the building. One of the men held a megaphone and spoke with a South African accent. "This is an unlawful assembly. We demand that you disperse immediately."

Everett could hear the response from the crowd. "We want food." Another yelled, "I've got kids to feed."

The guard with the megaphone replied. "The Global Republic is organizing relief efforts. As soon as the convoys arrive, we will begin dispensing aid."

"And when will that be? We're starving now!"

"Why didn't you tell us about the fire?" Another angry person yelled.

Still another protester shouted out, "Why weren't we warned to store food and water?"

"You knew about the blood and the fire!" The voices in the mob sounded angry.

Everett watched one of the drunks from the truck lob a brick over the GR perimeter fence and into a window. The sound of broken glass was followed by the voice of a peacekeeper. "You're under arrest!"

A team of six peacekeepers armed in riot gear emerged from behind the fence to take custody of the man who threw the brick. The rioters jeered and booed as the GR troops restrained the man with zip ties.

A voice that sounded like it could be Tommy screamed out, "You are the criminals! Why are we being arrested?

The collective voice of the crowd grew angrier. A chant began to rise in unison. "Where's our food? Where's our food? Where's our food?"

Everett tried to identify Tommy or Lloyd in the crowd, but everyone had bandanas tied around their faces and hats on their heads.

The man with the bullhorn shouted. "You will disperse immediately! Otherwise, you will be subject to detainment."

"Where's our food? Where's our food?" The mantra grew louder.

Courtney stood next to Everett. "Uh-oh. That looks like teargas."

"Yep." Sarah watched as two peacekeepers began firing teargas into the crowd.

Everett crossed his arms and waited to see how the crowd would react. Those who were near the teargas moved to get out of the vicinity. Soon, a Molotov cocktail landed on the roof. A peacekeeper kicked some of the dirt, which had been spread across the roof to protect it from the plague of fire, over the flame to extinguish it.

"Rubber bullets." Sarah pointed at the shotgun in the hands of a peacekeeper. "The orange stock and forend indicate the weapon is only to be used with less lethal rounds."

Everett watched as the man began firing on the crowd. The people below quickly dispersed, taking cover behind burned-out cars or anything that would shield them from the assault.

Gunfire rang out from below and two peacekeepers fell, one after the other. Courtney pressed against the window looking down at the chaos. "I guess the rioters didn't know those were less lethal rounds."

"Or they didn't care." Sarah raised her weapon.

"It could have been Tommy." Everett held his weapon low.

"Start looking for a target. As soon as we get the

signal from Kevin, we'll start taking out peacekeepers. I've got the guy with the radio. I think he's in charge." Sarah's rifle followed the motion of the man holding the walkie-talkie.

Everett found a target. "I've got the guy on the edge of the roof taking potshots at the crowd." The man Everett had targeted fell backward following the sound of rifle fire from below. "Never mind. I've got the guy lying prone near the ledge."

Courtney said, "I'll take the guy on the corner closest to us."

"Minus fifteen." Kevin's voice came across the radio.

"That's our signal. Fire on zero. Fifteen, fourteen, thirteen . . ."

"Twenty." Tommy's voice followed Kevin's on the radio.

"Tommy picked up an extra twenty shooters." Everett aimed at the center of the man's back as he didn't appear to be wearing heavy body armor.

Sarah continued the countdown. "Three, two, one, fire!"

All three rifles snapped in unison and all three of them hit their targets. Everett's target rolled over and looked right at him as he leveled his rifle in their direction. Everett fired a quick succession of three more shots and the man fell limp.

Gunfire rang out from the tower above them, eliminating three more peacekeepers. Next, the remaining guards on the roof quickly returned to the cover of the building."

Kevin's voice came back over the radio. "I'm taking fire. Sarah, come to me."

"Let's roll." Sarah backed away from the window and led the way back down the stairs.

Everett stayed close. The team exited the library the way they'd come, tapping Bennett and Silas to follow them as they left.

Courtney filled the two men in on the plan. "Kevin was supposed to be getting in the gate to disable the GR vehicles. His team is taking fire, so we're going to back him up."

Sarah led the way to the corner of the next building. "We'll cut across the courtyard here."

"We have no cover." Everett protested. "Shouldn't we cut all the way back around the ORP?"

"It'll take too long. We'll put down cover fire." Sarah stood near the corner. "Cover me."

Everett furrowed his brow. It was obvious that she was making this decision because it was her husband who was in trouble and not because it was the best tactical choice.

Sarah began sprinting across the courtyard and immediately rifle fire rang out from the windows of the GR compound. Everett identified the window the shots had originated from and returned fire.

Sarah made it to the other side, took a position at the corner, and began firing on the building as well.

Everett looked at Courtney. "You go next. Sarah and I are both covering you. Now is the safest time to cross."

She didn't look convinced. "Are you sure?"

He hated to push her into harm's way, especially when it seemed so unnecessary. "I'm sure. Go. Go now!" Everett popped around the building and unleashed a barrage of gunfire as Courtney sprinted to the opposite corner. "Silas, Bennett, you guys both run. I'll cover you."

"Ready when you are," Silas stood behind Everett.

Everett began firing as the two men ran across the courtyard.

He was now the last to go. He peeked at the building. Another shooter was in position in the next window. With only Sarah providing cover fire, Everett's only choice was to run faster than the second shooter could aim. "I'll get his head down before I run." Everett began laying heavy fire into the second window. He kept firing as he began his run to the other side. His magazine emptied out, and he turned his attention to the building where he was running. He bolted to the corner as fast as he could.

"We made it." Sarah leaned up against the wall.

Everett changed magazines. "It was an unnecessary risk, Sarah. And you know it. I'll follow your lead, but don't do that again."

"Let's keep moving." She did not apologize or acknowledge his concern. There was one more dormitory between the team and the perimeter fence of the GR compound. Sarah dashed toward the corner of the last building with Everett, Courtney, Bennett, and Silas close behind.

Elijah's voice came over the radio. "Eight men just came out the back door of building M. They are moving toward building I. It looks like they could be trying to flank you."

"Thanks. If you guys have a shot, take it." Sarah called back. She pointed to Bennett and Silas. "You guys watch that corner so they can't sneak up on us."

Everett looked at the perimeter fence. "That must be the hole Kevin cut to get inside."

Courtney raised her rifle. "There's Kevin, underneath that MaxxPro." She shot one of the peacekeepers who was walking around the side of the armored vehicle, where Kevin was hiding.

Four more peacekeepers came around the side of the vehicle and opened fire on Everett's team.

Everett pushed Courtney back around the corner, then popped out to return a volley of fire.

Gunfire broke out from inside the fence. Everett looked around again to look for a target. Kevin and several of his men were inside the fence, shooting it out with the peacekeepers at close range. "Hold your fire! Kevin and his team are all mixed in with the GR!"

"We've got trouble over here!" Bennett was firing at the opposite corner of the building.

Sarah tapped Everett. "You and Courtney get over there and back up Bennett and Silas. I'll stay here and look for a shot to help Kevin!"

"Roger that." Everett backed off his corner and quickly hustled to the other end of the building.

Elijah's voice came back over the radio. "Down to six, but they're trying to double flank you from both sides of building I. We'll try to hold them off, but a running man is a tough shot from here."

"Courtney, you and Silas hold this corner. Bennett, come with me. We'll cut across to the other side of the building and try to pin them down from the back.

"I'll follow your lead," Bennett replied.

The two of them fired as they hurried to the corner of the next building. Everett went to one knee and peered around the corner to see three men heading in their direction. "You shoot high; I'll shoot low." Everett opened fire on the line of men.

Bennett stood over Everett and leaned around the corner to shoot. The hot brass from Bennett's rifle rained down on Everett's head and back. One of the GR guards fell, and the other two retreated.

"Stay here. Hold them down. I'm going to go work the other corner." Everett patted Bennett on the back as he walked away.

Everett moved his palm from side to side to signal for Courtney to cease fire. He peeked around the corner and laid down a stream of bullets. He waved for Courtney and Silas to come to his position.

"What's up?" Courtney asked.

"I'm going to run up the side of the building and try to push them to the other side so the snipers in the tower can take them. I'll tuck low while I run. You'll have to shoot suppressive fire over my head."

"Everett! That's suicide!" She protested.

"Sitting here and waiting for them to fix us is suicide." He fired several more rounds, changed his magazine, ducked down, and began scurrying toward the back of the building. A peacekeeper stuck his head out and opened fire at Everett. He dropped to the ground and returned fire. Courtney's rifle was clicking off rounds from behind him. The peacekeeper fell limp. Everett continued his assault from a low crawl position, hoping Courtney would be able to eliminate any threat that might appear from around the corner. "Down to four." Everett kept count of the hostiles on the other side of the wall. He was a mere five feet from the corner when the next guard came around. Everett quickly positioned his rifle to return fire, but the man was already shot by either Courtney or Silas. Everett finally reached the end of the wall. He knew it would be his last act among the living if he were to stick his head around that corner. Instead, he changed magazines and dropped the barrel of his rifle to the other side and began firing blindly with only his AR-15 and his wrist exposed to the enemy. He didn't have to hit anything; he needed only to push them to the opposite side of the building so Bennett and the snipers in the tower could get a clear shot.

He pulled the trigger repetitively, holding the stock of the AR-15 with his left hand to keep it steady. Gunfire rang out from all around him. Everett paused to motion for Courtney and Silas to come to his position then continued firing.

Sarah's voice came over the radio. "We're taking heavy casualties. If anyone can get over to the parking lot, we could sure use your help."

"We'll be there when we can, but we've got our own situation we have to deal with first." Courtney arrived at Everett's position.

The radio transmitted Tommy's voice. "I'm coming to you. Hold your horses."

Everett pulled the trigger once more and nothing happened. "Courtney, switch rifles with me. Fast!"

Courtney handed him her rifle and took his as he passed it to her. Silas took aim at the corner of the building in case one of the peacekeepers tried to seize upon the opportunity granted by Everett's magazine being empty.

Everett quickly positioned Courtney's rifle and resumed firing.

Stewart called out over the radio from the tower. "Three guys came out from behind that wall where you guys are working. We took them all but one. He's over behind building H."

"Roger," Silas replied.

Everett changed magazines and looked up at Silas. "Call Bennett and have him join up with us. Courtney, how many magazines do you have?"

"Two."

Everett checked his vest. "I'm down to three. Silas, how are you set?"

Silas shook his head. "Two."

"That's not good. We can't run into another firefight with less than a hundred rounds each." Everett said.

Courtney peered around the corner. "What are these guys running?"

Everett peeked at the corpses of the GR troops on the other side of the wall. "Looks like an AK variant. We might have to take a couple of those rifles if they have lots of ammo."

Bennett met up with them. "You guys okay?"

"Yeah, but we have to get right back in the fight. You and Silas keep watch. Courtney and I will see what we can scavenge off of these guys in the way of weapons." Everett walked to the first corpse and picked up his rifle. "Vektor R4." He pulled the magazine out. "This is 5.56 ammo!"

Courtney pulled a magazine out of the deceased peacekeeper's vest. "These aren't compatible with our ARs. We'll have to strip the ammo out of the mags."

"Let's do it fast. You start pulling rounds out of their mags, Silas, you reload our magazines, I'll collect ammo from the dead and Bennett, you keep watch. If you think you see anything, yell threat. We'll all stop what we're doing and get ready to fight until we confirm it's safe to resume."

Everett quickly hopped from body to body, collecting ammunition from their rifles. Once his task was complete, he assisted Silas with reloading as Courtney was stripping the mags faster than he could load.

"That's it. All our mags are full. I even topped off the one in my rifle." Silas tucked his mags in the pouch on his belt.

"Good. We've still got another eight full mags from the Vektors. Let's strip them out into my assault pack." Everett took his pack off and unzipped the small front pocket.

Once they completed that task, Courtney asked, "Do we go help Sarah or look for this guy in building H?"

Everett exhaled deeply as he considered their next course of action. "I hate to have that guy behind us, but it could be a wild goose chase. Let's see what we can do to help over by the parking lot." Everett pressed the talk button on his radio. "We're coming your way, Sarah."

Seconds later, she replied, "Come around back, we're getting ate up on this side!"

Everett could barely hear her over the constant barrage of gunfire. "Roger that."

Tommy's voice came over the radio. "Everett, if you want to get in position and hang out at the corner, you might have a better opportunity to move in a few minutes."

"No. We need help, and we need it now!" Sarah's voice was frantic.

Tommy came back. "Don't you fret little lady. They're fixin' to have more to worry about than you."

Everett motioned for the team to follow him up the side of the dormitory and back across the courtyard so they could slip around Henkel Hall to be ready for the event Tommy alluded to. Once in position, he looked back toward his team. "I don't know what is getting ready to happen, but I have a feeling that when it goes down, we'll know."

Everett heard a vehicle racing up Wade Miller Drive, toward the back of the GR compound. He stared anxiously toward the corner of the Life Sciences Building, waiting to see the source of the commotion. "Lloyd!" He exclaimed with excitement. Everett pointed toward the old white van barreling toward the perimeter fence.

The van crashed through the fence and immediately drew heavy fire. A group of around twenty men immediately emerged from hiding in ashes of the burned-down hotel across the street.

Everett raised his rifle as peacekeepers came from the front of the building to defend the breach.

He rattled off a volley of bullets. "Tommy's men are attacking through the opening in the fence. Let's give them some cover fire!" Everett and Courtney ducked low and ran to the nearest scorched shell of a car. Everett tried to be more selective about pulling the trigger. He recalled how near they'd come to running out of ammo. He took aim at the corner of Gore Hall, where more GR troops were pouring in. Pop! Pop! Pop! He dropped two of them. As the peacekeepers arrived in the back parking lot, they were focusing on the van and Tommy's men who were rushing the fence. This provided Everett and his team a perfect opportunity to snipe off GR troops with little threat of being shot.

Everett continued to pick off hostiles as the occasion arose. "Call Sarah on the radio. See how she's doing."

Courtney keyed the mic. "Sarah, is it letting up on your side?"

"Yeah, that was a big help. We've got some wounded. I'm going to see what I can do to assist them. You guys keep doing what you're doing."

"Roger that." Courtney raised her rifle and resumed shooting.

One of Tommy's men called over the radio. "GR goons are retreating inside."

Tommy's voice replied, "Then let's get some Molotovs through the windows and start smoking them out. Everett, bring your team up to the van if you can."

Everett motioned for Bennett and Silas to follow him and Courtney. "We're on our way."

Everett weaved
cars for cover so
easy shot from any
parking lot. He step
which had been mov

Tommy stood by
vehicle. "Here's som
first then light a co
through."

Everett took three
Bennett each took two
fabric hanging out the ꜰᴏʀ wicks.

"What's in the bottles?" Everett examined the substance inside.

"Napalm. We mixed gas and Styrofoam. It makes it stickier, so whatever it splashes on is going to burn longer. And for our purposes, it'll smoke like the dickens. We'll have them weasels smoked out of their den in no time." Tommy handed more bricks and bottles to the men behind Everett's team.

"We'll put them to good use." Courtney smiled as if someone had just given her a basket of eggs or a handful of ripe tomatoes.

Everett admired her for her ability to stay upbeat and pleasant in the direst of circumstances. He couldn't resist giving her a quick peck on the cheek, after which, he got right back to the task at hand. He called the sniper team. "Preacher, can you guys watch the windows looking over the back parking lot for the next few minutes? We're going to have to get close."

Stewart replied to the request. "We've got your back. Proceed when ready."

e window he wanted to break
straight for the building. Crash!
ed and rained down on the ground
tt quickly retreated to the van.

first." Bennett held the wicks of his two
while Silas lit them with his lighter. Bennett
ked around the corner of the van then darted
oward the broken window. He lobbed one bottle
through then passed the second to his right hand and
sent it through straight away. The flames flashed
from inside. Bennett hustled back toward the van.

Pop! Pop! Pop! Crack! Crack! Pow! Everett
pulled Courtney back from the edge of the van and
down to the ground. Gunfire erupted from the roof
of the Life Sciences Building where Elijah and the
other snipers were, but it also came from the Global
Republic compound. Shots flew back and forth
from both directions for over a minute. Finally, they
ceased.

Elijah's voice came over the radio. "Threat
eliminated."

Everett looked at Courtney. "Are you okay?"

"Yeah, are you?"

He nodded as he looked around for Bennett. He
didn't see him. Everett peeked past the van door.
"Bennett!" Everett ran to the man who lay in a
growing pool of blood. He bent down to check his
pulse.

More gunfire rang out from the compound. A
bullet struck inches away from Everett's foot.
Everett winced as he screamed out, "I need cover!"
He put one hand under each of Bennett's armpits
and began dragging him back to the safety of the

van.

Courtney and Silas blasted rounds toward the window where the shooter had emerged.

Sweat poured off of Everett's head as he pulled the injured man to the vehicle. He let him down on the ground gently then sat on the bumper for a moment to catch his breath.

"Does he still have a pulse?" Courtney opened Bennett's shirt to locate the entry wound.

"He did. It was weak, but he was alive." Everett panted heavily.

Lloyd passed a mason jar to Courtney. "You can clean him up with this."

Courtney retrieved a bandana from her back pocket and soaked it with the strong smelling liquid from the jar. "Whiskey?"

"Shine," Lloyd replied. "It'll keep him from gettin' infected."

She wiped Bennett's torso, revealing a bullet hole in his abdomen and another in his chest.

Everett watched as the stream of blood grew faint. He took a deep breath and said a silent prayer for his fallen brother in arms.

Courtney put her fingers on Bennett's jugular vein. She looked up at Silas. "He's gone. I'm sorry."

Silas held out his hand toward Everett. "Give me one of them bricks."

Everett handed it to him.

Silas lit two bottles and ran toward the building screaming out in rage and agony. He launched the brick and tossed in the bottles in quick succession. Once again the room exploded into flames.

Everett stood with his rifle leveled, scanning from window to window, ready to eliminate any peacekeeper who might try to shoot at Silas.

Silas returned for another brick and two more bottles. His eyes were filled with grief and vengeance. He returned to the building, breaking yet another window and igniting the room inside into a roaring inferno. As he sprinted back toward the van, a shooter appeared in the third-floor window.

Everett discharged a torrent of gunfire. He watched as the bloody peacekeeper dropped his weapon and slumped forward against the broken pane of the window. Everett looked down, to see Silas lying dead on the pavement. A mixture of blood and brain seeped from the gaping hole in his forehead.

Tommy groaned and shook his head. "Not Silas!"

Lloyd stared at the man's lifeless body. "He was a good man. Finest there ever was."

Everett put his hand on Tommy's shoulder. "We need to get around to the front parking lot. I've got to check on Sarah and Kevin."

The big man turned his attention to Everett. "We'll give you a ride. I've got another half-dozen Molotov cocktails back here. I'd like to get them in the front window. Make sure this place has plenty of smoke."

Tommy turned to the men behind him. "Y'all take cover and watch the back. Kill any of 'em you see tryin' to escape the smoke."

Everett helped Courtney into the back of the van

as Lloyd took the wheel and Tommy got in the front passenger's seat.

Preacher's voice came over the radio. "It looks like the smoke is working. They're coming out onto the roof."

Everett keyed the mic. "Take any shot you get."

Gunfire rang out from the roof of the Life Sciences Building. Return fire could be heard from atop the dorm serving as the GR compound.

Suddenly, bullets peppered the top of the van.

"They're shootin' at us!" Lloyd exclaimed.

"Just keep moving!" Everett covered Courtney with his arms and torso as he saw light streaming in through the bullet holes in the roof of the vehicle.

"I reckon when you smoke a hornet's nest, you expect them to come out stingin'." Tommy held on to the dashboard with one hand as Lloyd swung the van around the curve.

The box containing the bottles filled with Tommy's homemade napalm tipped over as the van hit the curve of the parking lot. Everett and Courtney scrambled to collect them before they broke.

More bullets rained down from above.

Everett hit the door handle and kicked the door open with his foot. He lay on his back and shot back at the peacekeepers sending cover fire in their direction. The van rolled to a stop. Everett grabbed Courtney's arm. "Go! Go! Go!"

The two of them ran for cover behind one of the Global Republic MaxxPros. The heavily armored vehicle provided better protection than the thin sheet metal of the van's walls and roof.

Everett took aim at the roofline, waiting for a clear shot. CRACK, CRACK, CRACK! He sent a peacekeeper tumbling backward.

Courtney kept her rifle trained toward the top of the building as well, taking every shot she could.

"We've got goons coming out the front door!" Kevin's voice came from the other side of the MaxxPro.

Everett was happy to hear Kevin so close by, but the reunion would have to wait. Ten peacekeepers were running out of the building to escape the smoke. Their weapons were up, and they were shooting. Everett continued firing, cutting down two of the runners. Soon, all but two of the remaining escapees were dead at the hands of Courtney and the other shooters who were firing from covered positions all around the parking lot.

Kevin came around to Everett's side of the vehicle. "Two of them are hiding behind that burned- out truck. We've got to take them out before the next wave of goons surface."

Everett nodded. "Where's Sarah?"

"I'm under the truck." Her voice came from beneath the MaxxPro.

Courtney knelt down to look below the vehicle. "Are you okay?"

"I took one in the shin. It's not bad. Kevin patched me up. I can still shoot. If you want to toss me your empty mags, I can reload for you."

Everett removed his pack, squatted down, and slid his magazines to Sarah. "I'm glad you're alright. There's loose ammo in the front pocket."

Kevin pointed across the lot. "I'm going to grab

Tommy and those two guys. We'll push the peacekeepers to the back side of the car. You and Courtney, be waiting for them when they come around. Try not to fire or give away your position until you have a shot."

Everett nodded and led Courtney to the location Kevin had indicated. Everett took aim at the corner of the vehicle. He steadied his breathing as he waited. The prolonged firefight was wearing on his mind and his body.

"There they are!" Courtney fired first.

Everett followed suit. Each of them let out a volley of rounds to ensure the hostiles were dead. Afterward, they rendezvoused with Kevin, Tommy, and the other men.

Courtney removed her pack and took out a canteen of water. She took a long sip and passed it to Everett. "Here. You need to drink."

Everett drank deep and passed the canteen to Tommy. "Where's Lloyd?"

Tommy's gaze fell to the asphalt beneath his feet. His lower lip curled and tightened beneath his thick beard. The lines around his eyes shifted, revealing his deep sorrow. "He's gone."

"I'm so sorry." Everett put his hand on his shoulder.

"One of them heathens up on the roof got him." Tommy took a drink of the canteen and handed it to Kevin.

"He was a good man. He helped us a lot." Kevin took a drink. "We'll get his body and take him home. Don't you worry about that. But for now, we need to wait for the smoke to die down so we can get in there and clear the building."

Kevin looked around at the remaining fighters. "Everybody reload. Drink water if you have it. Address your injuries and be ready to move in."

Kevin dropped to his hands and knees and passed the canteen under the vehicle to Sarah. "How are you holding up?"

"I'm good," she replied.

"Yeah, you're always good. Even when you ain't." Kevin looked up at Courtney. "Can you grab one of the guys and help Sarah back to the ORP?"

"Sure." Courtney squatted down and looked under the MaxxPro. "Come on, let's get you out of here."

Everett put his hand on Courtney's back. "You can stay with Sarah if you want."

Sarah winced in pain as she inched out from beneath the truck. "I don't need a babysitter. Courtney is one of the best-trained people on this operation. And I doubt she wants to sit this one out."

Everett knew Sarah was right. "There's more 5.56 ammo in the back of Preacher's truck. Bring as much as you can when you come back."

Tommy pointed to two of his men. "Russ, you and Jimmy get our wounded out of the area. If they can walk, send 'em back to the trucks. If they can't, help 'em over to the road then drive back and pick 'em up in a truck."

"You got it, Tommy." Russ waved as he and Jimmy walked away.

Everett called to the men on the roof of the Life Sciences Building. "Elijah, you guys stay vigilant. It ain't over yet." He wanted to let them know not to let their guard down without tipping the team's hand and letting the peacekeepers know they intended to make entry. "Is everybody okay up there?"

"Stewart was hit," Preacher said.

"Is it bad?" Everett inquired.

Preacher's voice came back over the radio. "Headshot. He's in glory with our Lord right now."

"At least he's in heaven." Tommy shook his head. "Right after the disappearances, him and Preacher both got right. Lloyd might have too if I hadn't razzed Preacher and Stew so hard about all of it. Lloyd's probably in hell right now. And it's probably my fault."

Everett looked over at him. "You can't blame yourself. Every man makes his own decision about whether he'll accept the free gift of salvation. Lloyd had his opportunities. He made his decision."

Tommy shook his head. "Maybe if he had just one more chance. Maybe if he'd known today would be his last."

"Very few people know for certain when their time will come." Everett sipped his water. "Although, when you're coming into this sort of a situation, you have to know it might be the last thing you'll ever do. We're not out of the woods yet." He put his arm around the big man's neck. "And as of this moment, you still have one more chance to repent."

Tears streamed down Tommy's cheeks and were lost in his long beard. "I don't feel much like I deserve it. Especially after knowing ol' Lloyd is gone."

"None of us deserves it." Everett patted him on the back. "But Christ died to atone for everybody's sin. Even yours."

Tommy began to sob. "Oh, Jesus, I'm sorry. What a fool I've been. I've wasted my whole life trying to be a big shot. I've been a horrible friend to Lloyd and a bad example to all the men who looked up to me." Tommy wiped his eyes and looked up toward the sky. "I don't know how much of my life is left, but whatever there is, Lord, you can have it."

Everett hugged him. "Welcome to the family."

"You made a good decision. Congratulations!" Kevin put his arm around Tommy.

Everett looked back over his shoulder. "The rioters are creeping back out of the shadows."

Kevin turned around toward the row of brick dormitories. "Yep."

Everett surveyed the entire surrounding area. Men were emerging from the corners of the building and coming over the hill behind the parking lot. He watched as three of them crossed over the downed fence and began picking up weapons of the fallen peacekeepers. "We're not going to be in control of this situation for very long if this keeps happening."

Kevin nodded. "Let's get the bodies of our men loaded up into the van. Make sure you get all the weapons we came with."

Tommy looked around at his men. "Guys, you heard the man. Let's go. And I want a few of those peacekeeper guns for souvenirs. Let's get some of that gear too. I don't mind the rioters having some of it, but we've earned our share of the loot."

Kevin nodded in agreement. "Okay, but let's be quick about it. These are desperate, hungry people. We want to be out of the area before they make entry into the compound and start scavenging for food."

"They've got no training. If the rioters enter that compound, any GR troops holed up in there will eat them alive." Everett watched as Tommy's men began stripping the deceased peacekeepers of their weapons, vests, helmets, and boots.

"I know, but if we go in with an untrained horde, we'll be the ones who die." Kevin followed Tommy toward the van. "I hate to say it, but most of these rioters have the Mark. There's nothing we can do for them."

Everett nodded as he walked alongside Kevin. He knew they were lost souls. Yet he still felt compassion for them. He pressed the talk key on his radio. "Courtney, hang out at the ORP. We're scratching the last part of this operation. It looks like the situation is going to take care of itself."

"Roger that." Her voice came back over the radio.

Everett hit the mic again. "Preacher, if you and Elijah can manage to get Stewart down to your entry point, we'll be by to pick you up shortly."

"We'll manage," Elijah replied.

Everett, Kevin, and Tommy collected the bodies of Bennett and Silas, loading them into the back of the van with the other corpses.

"Hey, where are you guys going with all those guns?" One of the growing number of men coming across the broken-down perimeter fence called out to Tommy's men.

Tommy leveled his weapon toward the man. "We're leaving plenty for y'all. But we put our butts on the line for this mission. We're all on the same team here, so don't create a problem where there ain't one. Trust me; you don't want that any more than I do."

Everett helped Kevin get Lloyd's body moved to the back of the van then walked over to stand by Tommy with his rifle at a low ready position.

The man who Tommy had addressed grumbled and began talking to some men in the mob who were collecting weapons.

Kevin observed what was happening. "We need to move fast. Tommy, have your guys start exiting the parking lot area."

Tommy stuck his fingers in his mouth and let out a screeching whistle. "Leave everything else. Get on back to the trucks and watch your backs."

Everett sat in the driver's seat. He started the ignition and put the van into reverse. "Hang on."

Tommy sat in the rear with the sliding side door open, ready to fire in case the mob turned on them before they could get out of sight. Kevin rode shotgun and held his weapon out the window as a show of force. Five of Tommy's men walked beside the van as Everett backed out of the lot.

Everett drove slowly down Wade Miller Drive so the men walking beside them could use the van for cover if a firefight were to break out. He saw elements of the mob entering the back doors of the GR compound as they pulled away. He drove to the side of the Life Sciences Building where Preacher and Elijah stood next to Stewart's body.

Everett got out to help load Stewart into the back. "We can walk back to the ORP if you guys want to roll on over to the fallback position and meet up with the rest of your men."

Tommy helped to position Stewart's corpse next to the others. "Okay. We'll see you back at the farm."

Tommy took the wheel of the van and Everett slid the side door shut. Everett waved, as he, Kevin, Preacher, and the prophet walked back to the Objective Rally Point.

Everett's body felt extremely heavy. He was completely exhausted. The adrenaline that had sustained him over the past several hours was gone. He fought to put one foot in front of the other as they journeyed back. He couldn't think about the trip back to the farm, the long road to the landslide area, and finally, a grueling hike back across the rough terrain, made by the mass of earth and debris which slid down the face of the mountain during the Great Quake.

When they arrived at the ORP, Everett could hear gunfire erupting from the Global Republic compound on the other side of the campus. "I hope they finish off the peacekeepers."

Kevin helped Sarah into the bed of the truck and then crawled in to stay beside her. "They will. Over a hundred people are in that mob. I suspect more will show up to fight for the spoils. At most, we're talking about ten or fifteen peacekeepers holed up in the dorm. The GR goons don't stand a chance."

"I hope you're right." Everett closed the tailgate. "Sarah, how are you feeling?"

"Good, thanks." Her face didn't display the same confidence in her situation that her words implied.

Courtney turned to the old prophet. "Elijah, can you pray for Sarah's leg?"

"Yes, of course." Elijah put his hands over the tailgate, placing one on her wounded shin and the other on her prosthetic leg. "Everyone, gather around me."

Everett, Courtney, and Preacher all put a hand on Elijah's back. Kevin held Sarah's hand and bowed his head.

The old man bowed his head. "Dearest Father, great and mighty Jehovah. We ask that you show your mercy to this precious child. Heal her. Restore her strength."

Elijah continued to pray, but in another language. Everett assumed it was Hebrew. Afterward, they loaded up. Preacher in the driver's seat, Elijah riding shotgun, and Everett and Courtney in the back seat.

Everett tried to stay awake. "Talk to me. How was Sarah doing? Emotionally, I mean."

Courtney held her eyes open wide as if she were fighting off sleep also. "I think she's worried that she'll lose her foot. She had a team of doctors, custom-fitted prosthetic, and months of physical therapy when she lost her leg. The fact that none of that is available seems to be worrying her."

"That's understandable." Everett watched the buildings closely for possible threats as they traveled through the burned-out town. "How are you?"

"What do you mean?"

"How are you holding up? We were in a stressful environment today. It's not normal. I wish you didn't have to be exposed to all of that."

She shrugged. "Nobody likes war. But we have to do what we have to do. It's survival. I feel about the same as everybody else I guess. I'm tired more than anything."

He took her hand. "Me too."

Everett breathed a sigh of relief as Preacher reached the Winchester city limit. Barring any unforeseen disaster, they were home free.

Minutes later, Everett was fast asleep.

CHAPTER 8

Now Peter and John went up together into the temple at the hour of prayer, being the ninth hour. And a certain man lame from his mother's womb was carried, whom they laid daily at the gate of the temple which is called Beautiful, to ask alms of them that entered into the temple; Who seeing Peter and John about to go into the temple asked an alms. And Peter, fastening his eyes upon him with John, said, Look on us. And he gave heed unto them, expecting to receive something of them. Then Peter said, Silver and gold have I none; but such as I have give I thee: In the name of Jesus Christ of Nazareth rise up and walk. And he took him by the right hand, and lifted him up: and immediately his feet and ankle bones received strength. And he leaping up stood, and walked, and entered with them into the temple, walking, and leaping, and praising God.

Acts 3:1-8

Everett awoke to Elijah's voice.

"Wake up. We're here." Elijah reached over the seat and gently nudged Everett.

Everett yawned and looked out the window. They had arrived at Tommy's place. He glanced over to see Courtney sleeping with her head against the window. He stroked her leg. "Time to get up, sleepy head."

She took a deep breath and stretched her arms. "I can't wait to get back to my sleeping bag."

Everett opened the back door and got out of the truck.

Tommy pulled the van behind the house and cut the engine. He exited the vehicle and walked over to the truck. "Preacher, I've got a list of the men who died. I need to walk over to the barn and inform the families. I need you to drive these good folks back to their mountain. I'm sure they'd like to get home before dark."

"I'm low on gas."

"Can you get them there and drive home?"

Preacher nodded. "Yeah, but that's about it."

Tommy patted him on the shoulder. "I'll give

you five gallons to give you a buffer. We'll go back to Winchester tomorrow and get the fuel out of those GR vehicles. I didn't see anyone with gas cans or cars in that mob. The gas should still be there."

Tommy extended his hand to Everett. "Y'all did good work. I'm mighty thankful for your help. I owe you one. A big one. If you ever need anything, don't hesitate. Preacher will be monitoring Stew's radio. You know how to reach us."

"It serves our interest as well to not have a Global Republic outpost nearby. Thank you for organizing the raid. I'm sorry it cost so many lives." Everett got back in the truck.

"Freedom is never free. We'll see y'all soon." Tommy closed Everett's door and waved.

Everett drifted back to sleep as he waited for Preacher to get his gas so they could be on their way home.

His eyes opened when the truck came to a stop. Everett looked up to see the pile of earth and stone blocking the road. "This is our stop. Thanks for the ride."

"It's the least I could do. You all be safe. I'll be praying for you." The man smiled.

Everett, Courtney, and Elijah exited the cab of the truck and helped Kevin get Sarah out the back.

"I can fireman carry you if you want." Kevin watched her artificial limb as it came to the ground, and she put all of her weight on it.

She balanced herself on her prosthetic, holding to the bed of the truck. "You can't carry me all the way to the other side of the landslide. Besides, it's very rugged terrain. The least little slip and you'll go straight down with all that extra weight."

"I can do it. I'll let Everett, Elijah, and Courtney carry our gear."

She pursed her lips. "No thanks. If two of you can walk on either side of me, I can swing my fake leg from point to point. It will be slow going, but much safer than a fireman carry on such an uneven walking surface."

Kevin nodded. "Everett, can you get the left side?"

He handed his rifle to Courtney. "Sure."

Each of them worked with her, slowly climbing onto the mound of dirt, rock and tree limbs. The three of them developed a synchronized rhythm where Everett and Kevin would take a step forward then pause, allowing Sarah to swing her artificial leg forward. They repeated this process over and over.

Elijah and Courtney followed close behind, carrying the rifles and assault packs for the group.

It was an arduous journey, taking more than twice as long as it took that morning, but they finally arrived on the other side of the landslide. The team loaded up into Elijah's old truck and drove back to the creek.

Everett got out and looked at the clear water. "I'm going to get some clean clothes, wash up, eat something, and go to bed."

Sarah looked at the stream. "If you guys don't mind. I'm going to clean up while I'm here. Courtney, could I ask you to bring me a change of clothes down from the cave?"

"Sure. No problem at all. I'll bring you some soap too." Courtney headed up the trail.

Kevin helped Sarah toward the creek. "I'm going to stay with Sarah and help her get washed up. I'll get her to the cave and come back later."

"I can come back down after Sarah is dressed and help you get her to the cave. See you in a bit." Everett waved as he followed Elijah and Courtney up the trail.

By the time Everett was cleaned up, the sun was down. He had to traverse the trail back up to the cave by flashlight. His stomach growled. He was famished from the long day and the gruesome battle. No one had the strength to cook. Everett ate two MREs and a box of cookies before turning in. Unlike many of Tommy's men, Everett was alive. He was safe, and he was tired.

As he slept Wednesday night, Everett dreamed of the vicious attack on the Global Republic compound. Fear and anxiety caused him to toss and turn in his sleeping bag on the hard floor of the cave. He could hear screaming. It was that of a woman. His mind imagined the horrible things that must be happening to her. He looked around the vivid dreamscape of the raid. "Where's Courtney? Is that her screaming? Oh, God, please don't let it be Courtney!"

The shrill-pitched cry grew louder, piercing through his sleep. His eyes opened wide to the utter darkness of the cave. The screaming continued. Everett swept his hand across the ground next to him where he'd left his flashlight. "Why didn't I leave my gun next to me?" He found his flashlight and clicked it on, shining it toward his rifle leaning against the cave wall, ten feet away. "I have to get my gun before the threat gets to Courtney or me." He stumbled out of the sleeping bag as he darted toward the weapon. He switched on the light which was mounted on the rifle's fore grip and scanned the cave.

Sarah was sitting up in her sleeping bag, kicking with both legs and screaming at the top of her lungs. By now, Kevin was out of his sleeping bag, flashlight on and holding Sarah.

Courtney awoke and crawled over to her. "Shhhh. It was just a dream. I was having them too."

"No! No! No!" Sarah sounded frantic. "It's not a dream!"

"What's not a dream, baby?" Kevin kept his arms around hers in a futile effort to keep her still.

Elijah stooped beside her with his flashlight on as well.

Sarah cried out. "My legs! My legs!"

Everett watched as Kevin and Courtney shined their lights on Sarah's legs which she had kicked out of the sleeping bag. She continued to kick. Everett stared closer. He'd never seen her sleep with her prosthetic on before. And he'd never had trouble distinguishing the real leg from the artificial one. Everett furrowed his brow and looked closer. "I must not be totally awake yet." He murmured to himself.

Everett raised the rifle and pointed the light

toward the cave wall. There stood Sarah's prosthetic, right where she'd kept it every night since they'd moved to the cave. "Hmm."

Sarah calmed down to some degree. "I'd always felt tingles or an itch in my missing leg." She whimpered for a moment to catch her breath. "Even though I knew it wasn't there, I'd scratch the bed, or the couch, or my prosthetic, or whatever was in the space where my leg belonged."

She gasped for breath. "I was asleep and felt an itch. I reached down to scratch, and there it was!"

Everett turned his attention back to the beams of Kevin and Courtney's flashlights. Sarah had two legs. She had two feet, with five toes each that she was wiggling. She ran her hands up and down both legs, touching her knees, her calves, her ankles, the balls of her feet, and finally her toes.

Kevin ran his hand across the leg that wasn't there the night before when they went to sleep. "I don't believe it! How can this be?"

Elijah chuckled with his arms crossed.

Courtney shined her light up at the old prophet.

Elijah looked at Kevin. "And that is why you don't see many miracles. Because you don't believe. Even after all he has done for you. Bringing you back to the land of the living. How quickly you forget the blessed works of the Almighty."

Sarah's tears turned from shock to an expression of joy. She looked up at Elijah. "Thank you."

"No, no, no." He shook his finger. "I haven't done anything. Thank your Heavenly Father and his holy Son, Yeshua. Give glory to him in whom we live and move and have our being!"

Sarah wiped her tears and looked toward heaven. "Thank you, Jesus. Thank you, God!"

Kevin held her close and stroked his fingers across her legs. "The bullet hole is gone also." He bowed his head. "Thank you, God. Forgive my unbelief."

Elijah rested his hand gently on Sarah's shoulder. "The Scriptures say that in the last days God will show signs in the heavens above and wonders in the earth below. Surely, you will have trying times, and you will be pushed to the very ends of yourselves. But hold on to these precious memories, when the God of heaven has revealed himself to you. Savor these expressions of his mercy and grace. Recall them to your mind when your faith is tried."

Elijah stared directly into Kevin's eyes. "And do not discount them as having another explanation. I know what the enemy has been whispering in your ear. He tells you that you were not truly dead, but merely unconscious. He says that your experience in the underworld was a figment of your imagination. And he causes you to conveniently forget your bullet-riddled torso. Where did your wounds go? How did you heal so quickly?"

Kevin's mouth hung open. "I . . . I don't actually think that. I know it was God. But you're right. Those thoughts, they cross my mind from time to time. Exactly the way you explained it. How did you know?"

Elijah nodded. "The enemy's strategy has always been to discredit or explain away the miracles of God. Pharaoh's priests mimicked the miracles performed by Moses. They cast down their staffs and they too turned into serpents. They struck the water, and it too turned to blood. The evolutionists convinced the entire world that over billions and billions of years, the universe came to be, on its own, and out of nothing. And trust me, you will see Angelo Luz perform great miracles, signs and wonders, in keeping with his father's method of deception."

Courtney smiled. "Thank you for praying for her, Elijah."

"It was you who suggested that I pray for her leg." He chuckled.

"I meant for you to pray for the bullet hole in her shin." Courtney looked down at Sarah's new leg with an expression of amazement.

"Well, fortunately for Sarah, you weren't more specific." Elijah returned to his sleeping bag and reclined onto his back.

Courtney hugged Sarah. "Do you want to try to walk?"

Sarah dried her eyes. A tremendous grin stretched from one side of her face to the other. "Yeah."

Kevin stood on one side of Sarah and Courtney on the other. Each of them helped her up to stand on her own two feet, for the first time in years.

Sarah pulled her hands away, standing on her own strength. "I'm fine. I can walk perfectly. My leg is just as good as it was before I lost it! Maybe better." Sarah walked around the cave.

"When God moves, his work is complete." Elijah crawled inside his sleeping bag. "He formed the sun, the moon, the planets, the stars, most of which are much larger than our sun, all from nothing. Restoring your leg is quite a small thing in comparison." Elijah rolled over as if he were going back to sleep.

"It's not small to me." Sarah put a pair of long pants over the shorts in which she'd been sleeping. She grabbed her jacket. "You guys can go back to sleep. I'm going for a walk."

Kevin kissed her and held her close. "Do you mind if I tag along?"

"Not at all." She smiled and ran her hand through his beard.

"You guys be safe." Everett got back into his sleeping bag, next to Courtney. Despite the excitement, he was back to sleep in a matter of minutes.

Everett awoke Thursday, unsure of the time. He looked at the beam coming from Courtney's flashlight. "What time is it?"

"Afternoon, sleepy head. Everyone else has been up for hours." She knelt beside him and gave him a kiss.

"Have you been outside?"

"Yeah. It's gorgeous. Other than looking like a moonscape that is. The sky is bright and blue. A mild breeze is blowing. The temperature is probably around seventy. Much warmer than the cave. Get dressed and come on out."

"Okay. I'll do that." Everett's body felt sore from the previous day's activity. He stretched out some of the stiffness and got dressed. He put on his sunglasses as he exited the cave. Even so, he had to squint at the abrupt change from absolute darkness to daylight.

Sarah had managed to build a fire. "Good morning." She fed some twigs into the flames.

"Courtney said it's afternoon." He shielded his eyes with his hands.

"Whatever. We haven't been back to sleep yet. So, for us it's getting ready to be bedtime." She laughed.

"It's nice and dark in the cave. Your eyes will never know the difference." Everett poured water from a jug into the metal percolator and placed it on the grate over the flames. "How did you manage to get a fire going?"

"Kevin and I scrounged up some lightly-burned charcoal from the base of some trees. We pulled dead branches around the creek which weren't burned and used them for tinder to get the charcoal going."

"The dead branches weren't wet?"

Sarah pointed at a plastic bucket full of wood shavings. "We whittled them down to where they were dry. These are drying out. We'll be able to use them in a day or two."

"What did you guys eat for breakfast?" Everett inquired.

"Eggs, oatmeal, toast and jelly." Kevin repositioned each of the solar panels to line up with the sun.

"Toast? Who made bread?" Everett asked.

"Elijah. We saved some for you." Courtney passed a small bundle wrapped in a clean towel.

"Thanks. Where is Elijah?" Everett pulled back the corners of the towel, revealing a small loaf of bread.

"He walked to his barn to feed the goats and chickens." Courtney placed the pan on the grate and cracked two eggs for Everett.

"By himself?"

"He took Samson and Delilah back to the barn. Danger went with him. I offered to walk with him, but he said he wanted to pray while he walked." Courtney stirred the eggs with the spatula.

Everett asked, "Did he have a gun?"

"He took his old shotgun," she replied.

Everett poured some of the warm water from the percolator into his bowl of instant oatmeal. "That's something I guess." He topped the water off and filled the inner basket of the percolator with coffee.

Kevin looked at Courtney. "My batteries are almost recharged. You should give me yours to charge next."

"Thanks. We should take advantage of the sunny days when we get them." Courtney unscrewed the cap on her flashlight and handed the batteries to Kevin.

"Yeah, winter will be here before you know it." Everett set his oatmeal to the side and removed the batteries from his flashlight. He handed them to Kevin.

Sarah rolled her eyes in disgust. "Oh. Don't talk to me about winter. It was bad enough being cooped up in the cabin all winter."

Courtney held her hand up in the air. "Stop it! I can't even think about that right now. At least we had windows and a fireplace last winter." She tilted the pan and moved the eggs out onto a plate with the spatula. "Enjoy!"

Everett took the eggs, soft-scrambled the way he liked them. "Thank you." He took a bite with his bread. Small comforts like fresh eggs and homemade bread were the only things he had left to remind him that the world was ever anything more than a menacing nightmare.

He finished eating and poured himself a cup of coffee in the metal canteen cup. Everett took a sip and looked down the path that had been created by their footprints in the ash. "What is Elijah carrying?"

Kevin peered down the hill. "I don't know."

Elijah held two clear plastic bags with what appeared to be meat inside. "Stoke up the fire," he said as he arrived at the makeshift campsite just outside the cave entrance.

"What do you have there?" Everett tried to identify the meat.

"Goat. What else?" Elijah passed one of the bags to Everett.

Everett inspected the meat which had been cleaned and skinned. "I'm sorry you had to kill one of your goats."

"That is why we have them." The old prophet handed the other bag to Sarah. "I separated out the heart, brain, kidneys, and liver. I know you girls aren't very fond of the organs, but I assure you, Danger and Sox will be much less picky about what part of the goat they are eating."

"Oh." Sarah's nose crinkled, the corners of her

mouth turned down, and she passed the bag of goat organs to Kevin. "Can you do something with this?" She looked away as she held her arm out to him.

Kevin looked slyly at Elijah as he took the bag. "Sure thing." He set the bag down and entered the cave. "I'll grab some pots and be right back."

Danger sniffed the bag as soon as Kevin turned his back.

Elijah bent down to open the bag and cut a few pieces off with his knife. He let Danger eat them from his hand.

Sox returned from exploring over the hill. As his name suggested, the cat had four white feet that looked much like socks or booties which went up to the joints of his legs. The sides and bottoms of his feet were no longer the pristine white color they had been. Like everything else in this world, they were stained black by ash and soot. The cat sniffed around Elijah's hand, rubbing up against the prophet's leg.

Elijah cut a smaller piece from the bag of organs. "You must teach these humans to be grateful for what the Lord has provided."

Courtney's eyes looked worried. "It wasn't Samson or Delilah, was it?"

"No child." Elijah emptied the organs into a pot. "It was one of the unnamed goats. You don't name livestock that you plan to eat. I shouldn't have named Samson nor Delilah. Their day may come, but they will be the last to go. And if I'm not here when that day comes, promise me that they will go together. They won't be happy without each other."

Courtney nodded. "Okay. Aren't you trying to

grow food for them?"

Elijah nodded. "I'm going to take wheat over to the plot this afternoon. It's late September. The first frost could be as early as next week. Or, God could be gracious and give us another month. Regardless, the corn will not have time to mature. The wheat may perform better. It should stay green until winter, providing food for the animals. Then it should reemerge in the spring and develop heads a couple of months later.

"Of course, this is assuming that the judgments don't wipe out everything."

"Including us." Kevin set the large Dutch oven on the grate and opened the bag of goat meat.

Elijah chuckled as he walked into the cave. "To be absent from the body is to be present with the Lord."

Sarah put her hand on Courtney's shoulder. "I'm okay with going home. This world isn't very enjoyable anymore. But, I hope we can all go together."

"Aww. That's so sweet!" Courtney held Sarah's hand.

Kevin rolled his eyes. "Yeah, just like Jones Town."

"Shut up, Kevin." Sarah stood. "Wash that meat off your hands and come inside the cave. I need you to help me stay warm. I've got to get some sleep."

"If you insist." Kevin winked at Everett. "Do you mind keeping an eye on the cook pots?"

Everett smiled. "Not at all. You guys get some rest."

"Thanks. Your batteries should be charged in

about half an hour. The charger is right inside the cave entrance, so you'll be able to see to retrieve your batteries. Bring the panels back in when it gets dark." Kevin washed his hands with a small amount of water from the jug and followed Sarah into the cave.

"Good night." Courtney waved.

"I could use a little help with getting the wheat in the ground." Elijah looked at Courtney as he emerged from the cave with a one-gallon plastic zipper bag of wheat.

"Sure. Do you mind, Everett?"

"Go ahead. Take a radio, a rifle, and at least four magazines. I doubt many people are going to be out and about today, but if they are, they'll be the most desperate sort you've ever seen."

"Okay. We'll bring Cupcake for back up." She collected her things and blew Everett a kiss as she followed Elijah down the hill. Courtney patted her leg. "Come on, Cupcake!"

Everett waved and reached down to scratch the cat which had taken a seat near his feet. "It's just me and you, Sox."

Everett retrieved his Bible which he had placed near the door of the cave. He turned to Revelation chapter eight to review the next phase of tribulation. "And the third angel sounded, and there fell a great star from heaven, burning as it were a lamp, and it fell upon the third part of the rivers, and upon the fountains of waters; and the name of the star is called Wormwood: and the third part of the waters became wormwood; and many men died of the waters, because they were made bitter. And the fourth angel sounded, and the third part of the sun was smitten, and the third part of the moon, and the third part of the stars; so as the third part of them was darkened, and the day shone not for a third part of it, and the night likewise. And I beheld, and heard an angel flying through the midst of heaven, saying with a loud voice, Woe, woe, woe, to the inhabiters of the earth by reason of the other voices of the trumpet of the three angels, which are yet to sound!"

"Do you hear that Sox? Woe, woe, woe to the inhabiters of the earth. He's talking about you and me. We're the inhabiters. Have you ever had anybody give you three woes in a row?" Everett stared at the cat as if he actually expected an answer.

Sox looked away from Everett and began licking his back leg.

Everett smiled and watched the small animal groom himself, without a care in the world. "You're lucky that you can't understand me. You'd be freaking out right now."

Everett read the passage over several more times. Afterward, he looked at his Jewish calendar which he'd lined up with the Gregorian calendar to know where the feast days fell. "Sukkot starts at sundown tomorrow night. I hope the third angel can give us a little more time before he sends Wormwood."

Everett checked the goat meat stewing in the large pot then replaced the heavy cast iron cover. Even though the landscape appeared bleak and miserable, he took in the fresh air and time outside in the sun, knowing that he would soon be cooped up in the cave. "Wormwood or not, winter is right around the corner."

"What do you say, Sox? Do you want to walk down to the creek with me and wash some dishes?"

Sox found a nook between the rocks at the entrance of the cave. The cat worked himself snuggly inside and closed his eyes for a nap.

"That's what I figured." Everett peered sideways at the feline. He gathered the breakfast dishes in an empty bucket. Everett pulled the Dutch oven to the side of the grate so the goat meat wouldn't burn or overcook during his time away. He positioned the second pot containing the goat organs at the other end of the grate.

He picked up the bucket and started down the hill. Once he arrived at the creek, he collected water and washed the dishes in a bucket with a very small amount of soap. He poured the water out, twenty yards away from the creek then refilled the bucket to rinse them. As much of a hassle as washing dishes seemed at present, it would become immeasurably more difficult once winter arrived.

Everett walked back up the hill, pulled the two pots back over the hot coals, found a comfortable position, and continued reading his Bible. Besides the information concerning the end, he desperately needed the faith and strength to endure. And there was no other source to acquire such attributes besides God's Holy Word.

Two hours later, Courtney and Elijah returned from their excursion.

"How did it go?" Everett closed his Bible.

"Good. We got the seeds in the ground."

Courtney found a seat next to Everett.

Danger sniffed the pot of meat.

"Nope. That one's ours." Courtney lifted the top from the pot of organs. She winced as she drew a small bit out with a fork and set it on a rock to cool for the dog. "You get the yucky stuff."

Everett looked over at Elijah. "How far back have you been in the cave?"

"Not much past the storage corridor."

"Could you go further if you wanted? Is it accessible?"

"Yes. It gets tight. You'd have to crawl, but it may open back up. I couldn't say for sure."

Everett considered Elijah's answer. "Crawl, like hands and knees or scoot on your belly? Is there room on either side if you wanted to turn around."

Elijah nodded. "Hands and knees. It's a low tunnel. Something like a large drainage pipe. Why do you ask?"

Everett shrugged. "Just curious. I'm thinking of doing a little spelunking tonight. We've still got plenty of sun. The solar batteries are topped off, so it won't be too much of a drain to recharge the flashlight batteries. We're using flashlights in the cave when we're just sitting around anyway."

Courtney furrowed her brow. "Be careful, Everett. It sounds dangerous. You don't want to take any unnecessary risks. We can't exactly call 911 if you get trapped or injured."

"I'll be safe. But I want to find out where the corridor leads."

The hours passed uneventfully. Sarah and Kevin

emerged from the cave in time for dinner, which consisted of stewed goat and rice. No one was very talkative during the meal. A combination of the fine food and all of them being tired made for a quiet atmosphere.

Everett finished his plate. "You guys look well rested."

Kevin collected the dishes in the bucket. "We are, thanks."

"I hope we're able to sleep tonight." Sarah assisted Kevin with the dishes.

"I don't expect that you'll be growing any new legs tonight." Elijah laughed.

"It was a pleasant surprise, even if it did freak me out a little." Sarah followed Kevin down the hill to wash the dinner plates and utensils.

Everett checked his flashlight. "Elijah, Courtney, if you two will excuse me, I'm going caving."

"Why don't I tail you as far as possible? If you get into trouble, you can call out to me," Courtney offered.

"Sure. But I don't intend on going very far if it looks dicey." Everett made his way through the cave entrance.

Courtney followed him. "Okay, but for my peace of mind, I'm going to tag along."

"Suit yourself." Everett began ascending the ladder.

Courtney followed him up to the storage area, past the long corridor where they'd stashed their supplies, and to the place where the corridor became lower and narrower. "This is pretty tight. I think I'm going to hang out here. Give me a yell if you need help."

Everett crawled on his hands and knees. The top of the tunnel lowered to less than three feet high. He took a deep breath and continued forward for another ten yards. He began to feel claustrophobic in the restrictive space, yet he carried on. The ceiling dropped more, to a height of less than two feet. He called loudly back to Courtney. "This is my limit, any lower and I'm done. I'll have to back out if the tunnel doesn't open up soon."

"Don't push yourself," she pleaded from several yards back down the tunnel.

Finally, the tunnel opened up. Everett inched his way out of the slim passageway and out onto a wide flat surface. He stood up and shined his light all around. A massively high domed ceiling stood twenty feet above him. The back wall of the room dropped below the level where he stood. He walked forward, shining his light toward the ground. Ten feet beyond the tunnel, the floor dropped off. He peered over the ledge and looked down, but darkness swallowed the beam of his flashlight. He found a pebble and tossed it over the side. Everett listened as it bounced from wall to wall and fell into the abyss. Finally, he heard the faintest splash. "Water!"

Everett crawled back into the small opening of the tunnel and began his return trip. He called to Courtney. "I'm coming back."

"What did you find?"

"Water." He replied.

Everett sat outside of the cave Friday evening as

the sun set behind the mountains. He watched the vivid colors, bright oranges, hot pinks, and hues of purple fill the sky. He took Courtney's hand and held it tight. "I hope this isn't our last sunset."

Courtney sighed and looked over at Elijah. "What do you think? Will the next wave start tonight?"

Elijah whittled on a stick with his pocket knife to pass the time. "Who knows?" He picked up a pile of the shavings and tossed them into the fire pit. The hot coals immediately reignited.

Sarah put her hand on Kevin's leg. "Remind us what Sukkot is again."

"It is also known as the Feast of Booths or the Feast of Tabernacles." The old man did not look up from his stick and his knife. "Sukkot comes from the word *sukkah* which means hut. Jews build little huts or booths outside and have dinner in them on Sukkot. They do this to commemorate the time they spent in the desert living in temporary shelters while they were on their way to the Promised Land. When they arrived, of course, they constructed permanent residences."

Elijah looked up at the evening sky, streaked with color. "For you, children of the New Covenant, you might think about the time you're spending in your temporary dwellings."

"Yeah, I'll be happy to get out of this cave and back into a house someday." Kevin nodded.

Elijah chuckled. "No, no. In Second Corinthians, Paul compares our earthly bodies to tents or temporary shelters. He says when they are destroyed, we will be given new bodies, which he compares to buildings, built by God. These dwellings will be eternal."

"Hmm." Kevin looked at Elijah. "That sounds good too."

Elijah looked back down at the stick he was whittling. "Some scholars believe that Messiah was born on Sukkot. It falls during the time when Romans would typically collect taxes which is where Joseph and Mary were going when Yeshua was born. In an agrarian culture, governments want to get their cut of the goods as soon as the harvests are in.

"Those who hold tight to this reasoning say that it was on the Feast of Tabernacles that God tabernacled with men."

"A tabernacle is basically a tent." Courtney squinted as if she were considering the concept. "So, saying God tabernacled with men is essentially saying God went camping with men. I don't get it."

Elijah smiled at her the way a father might look at his child. "Why not? He took on a temporary body, to live among us, to teach us how to walk in his light, to shed his blood in atonement for our sins, to be resurrected, and finally, to ascend back to his permanent home. Given the way he was treated while he was here, it wasn't much of a camping trip from his perspective. But the time he spent in his earthly tent, it is the difference between eternity in heaven and eternity in hell for you and me."

Sarah crossed her arms. "One of the men in our survival group, Noah, said something to the effect of thinking the Second Coming of Christ might be during the Feast of Tabernacles. I rarely paid any attention to the Bible studies, at all. But I remember him using that word, tabernacled. Something about God will tabernacle with man. I thought it was odd to hear it used as a verb I guess. But, for whatever reason, it stuck with me."

"It could be true. Was Noah among those who disappeared?"

Sarah swallowed hard. "Yeah. He was a good man. He had such a beautiful family. Sox belonged to his little girl, Lacy. She was just too cute. I've seen combat and been through some pretty tough stuff in my life, but watching them all disappear was more than I could handle. I never thought anything could break me like that, but I had a total meltdown when that happened."

Kevin looked curious. "Wait. Elijah, how can you say it could be true? The Second Coming already happened."

"No, no. The Rapture already happened. The return of Jesus to collect his saints. In the Second Coming, he will be crowned King of Kings and Lord of Lords. He will rule on this earth for one thousand years."

"The Bible says that?" Sarah asked.

"Revelation twenty, verse four," Everett replied.

She shook her head. "I've read Revelation several times. I don't know how I missed it."

"I've read it too, but it sounds new to me." Kevin put his arm around Sarah. "I guess it's like your head is so rattled by all the other stuff in the preceding chapters that it's hard to grasp what's going on by then. Besides, when I'm reading Revelation, it's usually to try to figure out how we're going to survive the next wave of destruction. I try not to get more than three or four judgments ahead of where we're at. I just can't handle thinking about all of it at once."

Elijah rocked to and fro as he whittled. "That is understandable. It is not an easy time to be alive. But, those who survive to the end without taking the Mark and those who are beheaded for the gospel and are resurrected, will reign with Messiah for one thousand years."

"Then what happens?" Sarah asked.

"Then, Satan will be released for a short time, to deceive the nations one last time. Afterward, he will be cast into the lake of fire for eternity and God will make a new heaven and a new earth. That will be the final chapter."

"That's all literal?" Kevin inquired. "Couldn't some of that be symbolic? A lot of stuff in Revelation is symbolic, right?"

"Some of it is symbolic, no doubt about it. The woman who is protected by God for three and a half years is a symbol for the nation of Israel. But the new heaven and the new earth cannot be symbols for anything. They are exactly what God has said they are." Elijah folded his knife and stuck it in his pants pocket.

Everett directed his thoughts toward the Millennium, the new heaven and the new earth. It seemed so far away from the doom-laden realm he currently inhabited. "The sun is gone. It's getting chilly out here."

Courtney zipped up her jacket. "It's warmer than it is in the cave."

"I could sleep outside." Sarah pushed another lump of lightly seared wood into the fire.

Kevin protested. "Not me. The temperature is going to drop. The cave will be warmer. Plus it shields us from the wind and any rain that might come."

Everett added, "Or hail, or blood. Don't forget; atmospheric conditions ain't what they used to be." As the last light faded behind the mountains, Everett grew more anxious about the arrival of Wormwood. "But, for now, I guess it is warmer out here than in the cave. Do you guys mind if we listen to the radio for a while?"

"Sure. Let's hear what the most high and prepotent propaganda machine is spewing out." Courtney's voice was filled with disdain for the self-proclaimed global order.

Everett ducked into the cave, retrieved the radio, and returned to his seat near the fire. He switched on the dial. He immediately heard Athaliah Jennings' voice. Sarcastically, he said, "Uh- oh. They brought out the GR Propaganda Secretary. This must be an important lie."

Everyone grew still and quiet to listen to the staticky broadcast.

"His Most High and Prepotent Majesty has issued an urgent warning to those living in the western hemisphere. The Great Quake has affected the orbit of the earth around the sun and scientists now believe the planet is on a collision course with the asteroid 2019 WD10. Astronomers have been aware of the large comet for many years but were certain that the object posed no threat to earth. However, the projections have changed, due to the shift in earth's orbit.

"The size of the asteroid is estimated to be fifty-five miles in diameter. A collision with such a large meteor would likely be an extinction level event. But there is hope. The Watchers, who are maintaining constant contact with His Majesty and the Pope, have assisted GRASA in developing a plan. With the help and understanding of the cosmos from the Watchers, the Global Republic Aeronautics and Space Administration has been able to repurpose one of the rockets scheduled to deliver replacement communication and observation satellites. This vessel will deliver a nuclear payload to the center of WD10, which will break it up, preventing the earth from being hit by such a tremendously large object.

"The calculations and measurements were only made possible by the Watchers. We must be grateful that they have revealed themselves to us at such a time as this. We must also remember to thank them in our prayers for giving us His Majesty. Since he is a son of the Watchers, born of a human woman, he has proved to be the perfect intercessor, if you will, between these gods and mankind.

"It breaks my heart to think there are still people who have not yet placed their trust in His High and Most Prepotent Majesty, Angelo Luz. Without him, we would all perish. But, in his mercy, he has worked to save even the unbeliever from this most catastrophic event.

"But please, allow me to continue relaying this

most important segment of this evening's broadcast. While the meteor will be destroyed, it is likely that earth will still collide with the debris field. Smaller asteroids, perhaps as large as a half of a mile wide may still come crashing down.

"His Majesty has requested that all global citizens make provisions to shelter in place for a prolonged period of time. The Global Republic will be limited in what they can do to help for the first week or two after we've experienced the effects of the debris field.

"We urge you not to panic. You have over two months to prepare. Our best estimates tell us that the asteroid will be in view of the earth on the first of December. As our planet comes around the sun, and we have a clear shot with the rocket, we will fire the nuclear payload to eliminate the threat. The device will strike the comet on December 4th. Earth should collide with the outer layer of the debris field approximately three days later, on December 7th."

Everett grabbed his Bible and took out the Jewish calendar he kept folded in the back. "Hanukkah. The threat was announced on Sukkot, and we'll be struck by the remnants of Wormwood on Hanukkah."

Courtney shook her head. "At least they're telling us this time."

"Yeah, so we can pray to the Watchers and thank them. Can you believe that garbage?" Sarah sounded incensed.

Elijah took a deep breath as he looked up at the sky. "The children of darkness have been praying to them for ages. Satan, Nimrod, Semiramis, Tammuz, under all their various names have been worshiped as gods, almost since the beginning. These Watchers are the same demons with a new look. I suppose you could call it rebranding. Nevertheless, they are up to their same old tricks."

Kevin rolled his eyes. "I liked the part where Jennings fawned over Luz's mercy." He mocked the Press Secretary's voice. "He's sparing even the unbeliever." Kevin shook his head in disgust. "Yeah, right. So he can execute us on primetime television."

Everett snorted. "Debris field of a fifty-mile-wide asteroid. Luz is going to have to take a rain check on his new reality show."

Courtney corrected him. "Fifty-five-mile-wide asteroid."

"Even worse." Everett pursed his lips.

"So. Two months to get ready for it." Sarah put her elbows on her knees and rested her chin in her hand.

"A little more." Everett consulted his hand-drawn Gregorian calendar that he kept with the Jewish version. "We've got roughly ten weeks. It's good to know that it's coming. We can make the most of the time."

Courtney picked up Sox who was rubbing her leg. "We can take action. Not much, but we can do something. But I feel so horrible for all the people who are already living on a knife-edge and starving to death. They're pretty much doomed."

Everett tossed a piece of wood in the fire. "I wish we could help. For our brothers and sisters, we can pray. For those who have taken the Mark, nothing can save them now."

Sarah scratched Danger. "Why do we always get the brunt of the judgments? The hail, blood, and fire only fell on the western hemisphere. Now we're getting the worst of Wormwood too."

Elijah's face was lit by the glow of the fire. "Luz's seat of authority is in DC, New Atlantis, or whatever they want to call it. While the entire earth is under the Almighty's judgment, DC is the current bullseye. But remember, the Seal Judgments were evenly distributed. And those living in nations that were impoverished prior to the First Seal had no means to prepare. They were as Courtney said, living on a knife-edge."

Kevin looked at Everett. "Wormwood is supposed to poison the fresh water supplies, is that right?"

"Yeah. A third of the fresh water on earth. If it somehow contaminates all the lakes, streams, rivers, and ponds all the way from northern Canada to southern Chile, that would be roughly one-third." Everett hated to think of the amount of death headed their way.

Courtney stroked the cat's back. "The water you found, do you think it will be safe?"

Everett looked at Elijah. "God has a mission for Elijah that hasn't been fulfilled yet. He's bulletproof. God has to provide water for him. I'm assuming the water I found at the back of the cave will be drinkable. It's deep. I think it's coming from an underground spring."

Elijah laughed. "Read the whole story. I

wouldn't quite consider myself bulletproof."

"Well." Everett smiled at him. "For now anyways."

CHAPTER 9

And the carcases of this people shall be meat for the fowls of the heaven, and for the beasts of the earth; and none shall fray them away. Then will I cause to cease from the cities of Judah, and from the streets of Jerusalem, the voice of mirth, and the voice of gladness, the voice of the bridegroom, and the voice of the bride: for the land shall be desolate.

Jeremiah 7:33-34

Over the next few weeks, the coming destruction weighed heavy on the minds of everyone in the group. And with each passing day, the mountain air grew colder.

Everett and Courtney finished cleaning up the dishes from breakfast.

Sarah emerged from the cave. "Do you guys want to go with me for a little jog?"

"Kevin usually goes with you," Courtney replied.

"He's going to try to call Tommy over the radio." Sarah leaned against the rock and stretched her leg.

Everett was curious. "What does he want to talk to Tommy about?"

Sarah switched to stretch the other leg. "He wants to see if they've heard anything new. Ask how they're coming along with their preps for the Wormwood impact. That sort of thing. Basically just keeping his ear to the tracks."

"That's smart. Where are you running to?" Everett inquired.

"To Elijah's. I offered to feed the animals so he can get a break."

Everett turned to Courtney. "I'm game. What do you think?"

"Sure. I'll change shoes and grab the rifles."

The three of them geared up and began jogging toward Elijah's property.

Danger followed close for the long run down the busted-up pavement.

Everett breathed heavily. He had trouble keeping up. Sarah took up running immediately after her leg was restored.

Everett called out. "Hold on!" He tightened the sling of his HK G36C so the rifle wouldn't bounce so much on his back as he fought to stay close to

Sarah. Courtney had run with Sarah on a few occasions, so she managed to maintain a shorter distance between herself and Sarah than Everett did. Still, her heavy breathing revealed that she was maxed out.

As they neared the farm, Everett lost sight of Sarah. Courtney remained in his view. He pushed himself for the last stretch of the run. "This is good training," he said to himself between gasps for air. Finally, he arrived.

Sarah sat on a rock sipping from her canteen. She took another drink and passed it to Courtney. "What took you guys so long?"

Courtney drank from the canteen and handed it to Everett. "Okay, Sarah. You put us to shame. Is that what you want to hear?"

Everett breathed deeply. "Some more than others." He sipped the water and replaced the cap.

"I like to take advantage of the weather. If we get heavy snow like last year, we'll be spending a lot of time inside. And snow or not, the days are getting shorter."

Everett walked to the barn and looked over the goats. The remaining animals appeared much thinner than the last time he'd seen them. He opened the gate to let them out. All of them rushed toward the small field of wheat.

Courtney smacked Samson on the head. "Don't even think about it! You know better by now."

"Go! Get! Get out of here!" Sarah shooed away the other goats, chasing them toward the woods so they could graze on the new growth sprouting up from the forest floor.

Everett walked near the goats, keeping them all in close proximity to one another.

Sarah and Courtney let the chickens out to forage for bugs, worms, and tender shoots on the other side of the barn.

Everett counted the goats. "Thirteen. Samson and Delilah get to spend the winter with us, so that's eleven remaining. We've been eating one goat a week. That will leave four more for slaughter before the Wormwood impact. I guess we could make jerky with the other six. Maybe cook a couple off right before impact. As cold as it is in the cave, fully cooked meat will probably keep for at least a week without spoiling," he mumbled to himself.

He watched over the herd, corralling them back each time one goat ventured too far away from the rest. Everett observed the forest floor in amazement at how rapidly the small tufts of grass, saplings, and wild bushes had emerged from the ashes. "Life finds a way. Even though we're living in the harshest conditions in history, life still goes on." He looked up toward heaven. "What an awesome God who designed all of this."

An hour later, Courtney called out. "Are the goats about full?"

Everett watched as his small herd seemed to be getting pickier about their eating. "I think so," he yelled.

"Bring them in," Sarah called back

Everett tried pushing the group back toward the barn, but the goats had their own idea. "I don't think they're ready."

Courtney walked over to Everett's location.

"You have to be smarter than the animals you're working with."

"You realize that sounds a little insulting, right?"

She winked and gave him a quick kiss on the cheek. "Watch." She pulled her backpack around to the front and stuck her hand inside. She brought out a fistful of deer corn. Courtney sprinkled the kernels around her feet. Immediately, the goats began to follow her.

Everett pursed his lips. "Bribing and outsmarting are two different things."

When they arrived back at the barn, Sarah had used the same method to convince the chickens to return to their enclosure. "You guys ready to head back?"

Everett nodded. "Yeah. But don't wait up for me. I might take my time getting back."

"Don't worry. I won't." Sarah winked.

"Me too. I want to make sure my husband doesn't get lost." Courtney put her arm around Everett's arm and pulled him close.

"See you guys back at the cave." Sarah zipped up her pack. She hung her rifle across her back and broke into a quick sprint, with Danger staying close on her heels.

A single gunshot rang out in the distance.

"What was that?" Courtney stopped in her tracks.

Everett put his hand up signaling for Courtney to be quiet for a moment. He could still hear the trailing blast echoing off of the hills below. He shook his head. "It could have been from a mile away. With no foliage in the trees, the sound travels much farther." He stood silent for another moment, scouring the blackened landscape for movement or signs of life.

Courtney tugged his arm. "Let's go home."

"Okay." Everett turned reluctantly and continued toward the cave.

When they arrived, Elijah and Kevin were preparing dinner.

"Smells good. What are you guys cooking?" Courtney took her rifle from over her shoulder.

"Goat and rice stew." Kevin used a pair of tongs to poke the piece of bone floating in the pot, forcing it beneath the water.

Elijah patted out a piece of dough, round like a pizza, but much thicker. "And grilled flatbread."

"That sounds great." Everett had worked up a good appetite.

"Do I have time to go clean up in the stream before dinner?" Courtney asked.

"Yeah," Kevin replied. "But tell Sarah that you're going. She was waiting for you guys to get back. She didn't want Everett to walk up at an inopportune time."

Courtney chuckled. "I'll take her with me."

Everett remembered the gunshot. "Make sure you keep your rifle where you can get to it quickly. And take the whistle."

Everett looked in the pot. "What else is in your stew besides goat bone and rice?"

"Those are the main ingredients. I put some onion powder, garlic powder and a half of a can of those dehydrated mixed vegetables." Kevin continued to prod the pot with the tongs.

"Sounds pretty good. I never knew you were such a chef." Everett looked on as Kevin stirred with the utensil.

"This is camping food. I can cook camping food. Just don't let me in a proper kitchen."

"There is very little threat of that. Very little, indeed." Elijah appeared discouraged by the limited resources available for preparing the meal. Nevertheless, he brushed olive oil on the dough and placed the flat loaf on the grill. "How were the animals?" Elijah sprinkled his hands with flour, pulled another ball of dough from the bowl, and began patting it out.

"Samson said he misses you."

Elijah fought back a grin as if he were afraid to admit how much he loved the old goat. "Don't tease me. Balaam's donkey spoke in the Book of Genesis. I've often wondered what old Samson might be thinking."

"They all got their bellies full, foraging in the woods."

Elijah nodded. "The new growth is getting easier for them to find. Did they obey when you told them to return to the barn?"

"Courtney figured out a little trick for that." Everett smiled as he placed a piece of wood in the coals below the grate where Kevin's soup was simmering.

The time passed slowly and Everett grew antsy waiting for Courtney and Sarah to return. His mind began to suggest what might be keeping them. He imagined the worse. He envisioned the desperate sort of persons who were still alive despite the earth and sky conspiring to wipe mankind from the face of the planet. He pictured the sordid creeps to whom the gun belonged, slithering up on the girls from behind and then taking their rifles. "I'm going to go tell the girls that dinner is ready."

Kevin furrowed his brow. "They might not be decent."

"I'll only go three-quarters of the way down the hill. I'll yell until they hear me." Everett slung his rifle over his back.

"If you're hungry, I'm sure they won't mind if you go ahead and eat. I'll eat with you."

Everett forced a smile of gratitude so not to alert Kevin of his growing fear. "No. I'm fine. I'd just rather act in an abundance of caution, times being what they are."

"Okay. But don't get too close. Sarah will freak on you."

Everett nodded. "I'll keep my distance." He hustled down the trail, listening as he sprinted.

"Courtney!" His voice echoed through the hollow. "Courtney!" He yelled again.

"What?"

Her voice had the effect of a choir of angels on his soul. They had been gone a little longer than usual for a bath, but the sinister prank that his mind had played in those few minutes had taken him to the edge of sanity. "Dinner is ready!"

"Okay. We're coming now!" She yelled from below.

He cupped his hands over his mouth to direct the sound. "Are you dressed?"

"We're decent!" Sarah's voice came back.

Everett walked down the trail to find Courtney and Sarah picking up their rifles with towels wrapped around their heads. "You girls were gone for quite a while."

"We were talking. Girl stuff, you know," Sarah said.

"Sure." He smiled. "I just wanted to make sure you two were safe."

"Thanks." Courtney took his hand and walked beside him until the trail became too narrow.

That evening, the group ate Kevin's soup and the bread which Elijah had prepared. Afterward, they played several hands of cards, listened to the radio, and sat by the campfire, enjoying the remaining time they had to be outside before the impact with Wormwood and the subsequent winter.

The next morning after breakfast, Everett tapped Courtney on the shoulder. He whispered, "Are you up for running with Sarah to the barn and back?"

"Is it a covert operation?" She looked from side to side in mock suspicion.

"No. But I'm determined not to be the person in the worst shape of this whole camp. I thought I'd let you in on it if you're game."

Courtney tapped her lips with her finger. "Yeah. She did sort of gloat about it yesterday, didn't she. I don't see anything wrong with a little friendly competition, but my shins are killing me right now."

"You'll work it out. But easy on the competition talk. We don't want her to see us coming."

Sarah popped out of the cave. "Hey!"

Everett was startled. "What's up?"

She asked, "I don't know. What are you guys talking about?"

Courtney put her arms around Everett. "Sweet nothings."

"Oh." Sarah rolled her eyes. "Then never mind. Are you guys running with me today?"

"We hadn't really thought about it, but yeah. I guess we could come." Everett feigned an attitude of nonchalance.

Sarah stretched her legs. "I'll go slow, but you guys have to at least try to keep up."

"Okay. We'll do our best." Courtney tightened her jaw.

Everett knew from looking at her that she was all in from this point forward.

Sarah slung her pack over her shoulder then picked up her rifle. "Ready?"

Everett reached his arm through his rifle sling, pulling it as tight as he could get it so it would bounce less. "Ready when you are."

Courtney adjusted the barrel of her Mini 14 so it wouldn't interfere with her stride. "Let's do it!"

Sarah clapped her hands. "Cupcake! Come on, boy!"

Danger let out a brief whine and looked up at Elijah. The dog lay at the prophet's feet, wagging his tail.

Everett tried to suppress his laughter. "I think you wore him out yesterday."

Elijah waved. "Tell Samson and Delilah that I'll be around later this afternoon."

"We'll do." Courtney waved as she dashed off.

Sarah was already gone. Everett took a deep breath, knowing the agony he was about to experience from his shin splints. He'd done all he could to stretch them out that morning, but his shins hurt. He focused on Sarah who was already twenty yards in front of him, forcing his mind to ignore the pain. He caught up with Courtney. He glanced at her face which was wincing in pain with each step.

"I'll run it out huh?" She scowled.

"Eventually." Everett winked and kept up his pace.

Sarah turned around and jogged in place. From thirty yards ahead of them, she waved. "Come on! Push yourselves! You gotta dig deep!"

"She knows we're in pain. She's enjoying this." Courtney grunted low.

Everett spoke softly. "He who laughs last, laughs loudest."

As Everett and Courtney came within ten yards of Sarah, she turned around and resumed her steady clip toward the barn.

Everett regulated his breathing. His legs hurt, but his heart and lungs were working just fine. Prior to the collapse, he would hit the gym every morning, dedicating several hours a week to cardiovascular training. Courtney had been a runner before the world fell apart. It wouldn't take her long to bounce back either. Determined to keep up, Everett refused to let the pain stop him.

Sarah quickly regained her thirty-yard lead. She slowed down, still facing forward. She held one fist in the air, the signal the team used for *halt*.

Everett slowed his stride as they gradually

caught up with Sarah. He scanned the surrounding area for signs of trouble.

"What is it?" Courtney whispered.

Everett shook his head. "I don't know. But something alerted her."

Sarah appeared unhurried as she removed her rifle from her back. She motioned for Everett and Courtney to continue to her position.

Everett took his HK from over his shoulder as he caught his breath and kept walking. Courtney did likewise.

As they approached, Everett heard motorbikes in the distance. He looked at Sarah. "Motorcycles?"

She nodded.

"Do you think it's Tommy?" Courtney inquired.

"Probably." Everett resumed walking down the crumbling pavement of the road.

"Why would they be coming from the east side of the mountain?" Sarah asked.

Everett shrugged his shoulders. "Fewer obstacles. They don't have to ride across the landslide."

"But they have to come through Woodstock. It's a populated area. At least it used to be." Courtney furrowed her brow.

Sarah moved her head from side to side slowly. "Kevin just talked to Tommy yesterday. He didn't say anything about coming up here. He knows how jumpy we are."

Courtney added, "And he knows the risks of surprising jumpy people who usually have their fingers wrapped around a trigger."

"They could be in trouble. Maybe they didn't

have time to call." Everett listened as the motors came closer. "Either way, we'll proceed with caution."

Sarah removed her backpack and knelt down. She unzipped the pack and took out two magazines. She slung the pack back over her shoulder and tucked the magazines in her waist. "How many mags do you guys have?"

Everett gritted his teeth. "One."

"One extra?" Sarah looked at him curiously.

"No. One magazine." Everett sighed in disgust at his own ignorance. "I was determined to keep up with you today, so I wanted to keep my load light."

Sarah rolled her eyes. "Arghhh. What about you, Courtney?"

Courtney lowered her head as if she'd just been caught with her hand in the cookie jar. "One magazine. No extras."

"And we've all got different weapons, so neither of you can use my mags." Sarah shelled out five rounds from each of her extra mags. "At least we're all running 5.56." She handed five rounds to Everett and five to Courtney. "These are in case you run out, but don't run out. Make every shot count. I guess if we need cover fire, I'll have to be the one laying it down."

"We can lay down short three round bursts if you need cover." Everett was very disappointed in himself.

"Not Courtney. She's only got a twenty-round mag."

Courtney looked down at the ground. "Sorry."

"No time for apologies. Let's just hope it's

Tommy and his boys." Sarah held her rifle low and began moving quickly down the road.

Everett stayed close behind Sarah. *Why did I let myself think it was okay to have a little fun? This is the Apocalypse. Literally. We're always one mistake away from death. My carelessness may cost me my life. Or worse. It could be Courtney who dies.* Everett shook the thoughts away from his head. Guilt and regret clouded his judgment. "Not now!" he said aloud.

"What?" Courtney was close behind him.

"Nothing." He glanced backward. "Sorry, I put us in this position. I love you."

"I love you, too. And it's my fault as much as it is yours. Let's just get through this."

He nodded. He appreciated the fact that she didn't blame him, but as her husband, he knew that the responsibility fell solely on his shoulders.

He listened as he walked. The noise of the motorbikes grew louder then suddenly stopped.

Sarah paused and turned around. "Do you think Tommy and his boys would be taking a break at the barn? Because that's about where it sounds like they stopped."

Everett shook his head. "Not Tommy. Some of his boys could be ripping us off, but I saw his face. His conversion was sincere and it was total."

"You don't think a hungry belly would inspire him to backslide a little?" Sarah seemed less convinced than Everett.

"No. But Devin, on the other hand. Who knows? That boy is capable of anything." Everett thought for a moment. "Tommy, Preacher, and Devin are the only ones who know where we're at. I'm sure Preacher wouldn't be up here either."

Courtney sneered, "It doesn't really matter who it is. We need those animals to get through what's coming."

"Agreed." Sarah quickened her pace. "We'll stay to the right of the road and use the ditch for cover. I'll take the position nearest to the house. Courtney, you travel down to the bend in the road and Everett you go on around another ten yards. You'll take the first shot. As they are trying to locate your position, I'll line up my next three shots. Once they figure out how close I am, they'll be coming at me with everything they've got, so it will be up to you guys to pick them off."

"It's a good plan. I apologize for putting us in this position." Everett followed Sarah toward the right side of the road.

"You didn't know we had a surprise waiting for us today. I'm just glad we were here to intervene."

Everett knew she was being generous with her grace. "Thanks."

The three of them reached a location where they could see all the motorcycles. Six dirt bikes and two quadrunners were parked outside of the barn. Three of the dirt bikes had riders with helmets and long guns standing watch.

Sarah reclined against the left side of the ditch. "It looks like one shotgun, a deer rifle, and an AR-15. That shotgun will be bad news for me at this range. Try to take him first if you have a shot. When they start looking for you, I'll take the AR next. The deer rifle is detrimental, but it's lever action. He's got to rack a round every time he fires. Get going and stay low! If you're spotted, we lose the element of surprise, and we don't have enough ammo for a prolonged, entrenched firefight."

Everett nodded and began low-crawling along the ditch to his position. Courtney wriggled along behind him. They reached the bend in the road. Everett turned and put his hand on Courtney's arm. He closed his eyes and whispered a prayer. "God. Watch over us. Especially my beautiful wife."

She blew him a kiss with a smile. "Thanks. Now get going."

Everett slithered through the mud, with his stomach in the dirt, using his feet and elbows to propel himself forward. He reached his position and slowly looked over the road. The rider with the shotgun was turned around with his attention on the two goats, which were bleating at having their legs tied together with a rope, securing them to the back of the ATVs. The man with the AK, however, was looking right in his direction.

"If I take out the shotgun first, the guy with the AK will see my muzzle flash." He hated to venture from Sarah's instruction, but he had to adjust the plan. "I can take them both before Sarah gets off a shot. I have to." He raised his rifle into position at a snail's pace so the man with the AK wouldn't detect his movement. Once the barrel was over the edge of the asphalt, Everett turned the rifle right side up so he could take aim through the reflex sight.

A head shot was out of the question. The weapon wasn't configured for a long-range shot, but at this range, he'd have no problem hitting the gunman in the center of mass. Everett placed the red dot in the center of the illuminated circle on what he imagined to be near the bottom of the man's sternum. He took a breath and released it, squeezing the trigger with the pad of his finger.

Pop! The man dropped his weapon and grabbed his chest. Everett had no time for such an elaborate process of aim taking before his next shot. He quickly placed the glowing red pinpoint on the rider with the shotgun who was pointing his weapon in Everett's direction. He fired three times. POW! POW! POW! The shotgun fell to the ground just as a projectile struck the pavement, inches from Everett's face. Debris from the road flew into Everett's right eye. He turned to the side, wiped the additional chunks of dirt and asphalt from his brow and eyelid then blinked his eye repeatedly to clear the obstruction.

He could hear the exchange of gunfire and knew he must get back in the battle as rapidly as possible. To lighten his load, Everett had also neglected to bring water, leaving him to rely completely on his tear ducts to uncloud his vision. Blinking several more times and blotting the corner of his eye with the back of his hand, he was finally able to see well enough to shoot.

He popped up from cover and began firing at the remaining two men who were attempting to get on a bike while shooting at Sarah and Courtney. The two survivors worked as a team. Both had AR-15s. One would fire while the other got on the bike. The engine of the bike roared, and the two men tore out across the yard toward the road. Everett let out a volley of fire at the riders who were heading straight for him. The man on the back of the bike fired at Everett while his partner drove.

Several rounds peppered the pavement near Everett's head, forcing him to take cover. He waited for the bike to get closer then sprang from cover once again. He fired several times. The man in the rear of the dirt bike turned around to fire at Everett once more, sending a stream of lead projectiles in the direction of the ditch. Once more, he had to take cover in the recess of the ditch. Everett listened for the gunfire to cease then came up from the respective safety of the ravine. The riders were fleeing, but he knew he had to take the shot. The guy on the bike had practiced shooting and riding at the same time. Whether they were self-taught or had received training from the military, the riders knew what they were doing. They also knew where the food was and they would likely be back. Everett pulled the trigger. The rifle fired and the bolt locked back. Everett's magazine was empty. He'd hit the man in the rear, but the rider remained on the back of the bike.

Everett hit the magazine release, catching the mag as it dropped. He dug the five rounds, which Sarah had given him, out of his pocket. Adrenaline pumped through his chest, causing his hands to shake as he tried to push the shells into the top of the magazine. One of the brass rounds slipped from his fingers. He expeditiously retrieved the single bullet he dropped and clicked it into place along with the other four. He racked a round into the chamber, stood up, and took aim. The bikes were out of sight. He listened as the engines roared in the distance growing less and less audible.

"Everett!" Sarah's voice rang out from behind him.

He turned, first to see that Courtney seemed to be okay, then he looked at Sarah. She circled her finger in the air, signaling for Everett and Courtney to rally around her. Everett bent low as he hustled back up the ditch to her location.

She changed her magazine. "How many rounds do you have?"

"Five," Everett responded.

Courtney looked at her rifle. "I'm out."

Sarah took the magazine back out of her AR-15. "This is the mag I took ten rounds out of. It's all I've got." She shelled five rounds out of the magazine, handed them to Courtney, and popped the mag back in the well. "That leaves me fifteen rounds. I'll take point. One of the guys who went down had an AR. We'll approach the barn, kick their rifles away, and Courtney, you pat them down. We don't want someone playing possum so they can pull a handgun on us the second we turn around. We'll see if we can get more ammo from the guy with the AR. You guys can take turns reloading your mags then we've got to clear the barn, inside and around back. Those quads could have had more than one rider each. The dirt bikes may have also, for that matter.

"Ready?" Sarah took point and raised her rifle.

Everett held his rifle low. "Ready when you are."

Sarah tucked low and advanced toward the barn with Everett and Courtney right behind her. They reached the first downed combatant. Sarah kicked his shotgun away and scanned the area for threats. Courtney patted down his back side. Everett kicked the man over onto his back, keeping his sight trained on the body. Courtney frisked the man from the front side. His helmet rolled off, and Everett looked into his hollow eyes. He was sure this particular hostile would not be giving them any more trouble.

"Clear." Courtney stood up.

Next Sarah moved to the man with the AR-15, kicking his rifle away. Everett and Courtney repeated the task of checking for a secondary weapon.

"Two extra magazines in the side pocket of his cargo pants." Courtney held them up.

"Good." Sarah took one. "Changing." She switched her mag for the fresh one, tucking her other magazine in her waist. "Set."

Everett stood watch with Sarah as Courtney loaded another fifteen rounds into the magazine of her Mini 14.

"Set." Courtney handed the half-empty mag to Everett.

He removed the shells from it and tossed it on the ground. "I'm going to check the rifle to see if I can get more bullets."

"We've got you covered. Go ahead." Sarah pivoted from the entrance of the barn to the left side.

Everett pulled the magazine from the AR and extracted the shells. The rider who'd carried the AR-15 never got off a shot. Everett topped off his mag and slammed it back into the magazine well. "Set."

The team continued to clear each remaining hostile. Once the task was completed, they unloaded the various weapons tossed about on the ground. The shells and magazines were collected in Sarah's pack.

Next, the three of them stacked up at the entrance to the barn. Sarah nodded to let Everett and Courtney know she was ready. She entered quickly, turning left. Everett came in right behind her and covered the area to the right. Courtney walked through the door last and scanned the area. The goats and chickens had all left, fleeing the chaos of the gunfight.

Everett walked back to the stalls on the right side of the barn. His heart stopped as he peered around the corner. A blast from a silver revolver rang out, leaving him temporarily blind and deaf. He pulled the trigger of his HK repeatedly. When he looked down, two women lay, slumped up against the wall of the barn. He stood motionless over them. Immediately, the regret began to creep in. "Oh, no. What have I done?"

Sarah moved passed Everett, quickly clearing the remaining stalls.

Courtney stood behind him. "Don't start that, Everett."

"Girls. I just killed two women."

"You just survived someone shooting at you from close range. And the only reason you're still here is because you pulled the trigger. Sarah and I are girls. When we pick up guns and go play with the boys, we accept the fact that we're not going to get any special treatment."

Everett looked at the two lifeless corpses. "But they were just hiding. I don't even think the second one had a gun."

"Then her idiot friend is to blame for her death. The second she pulled that trigger, she sealed both of their fates. You had no choice." Courtney put her hand on his back. "Come on. We still have to clear the back."

Everett felt sick to his stomach. He felt light-headed as if he needed to sit down. "I'm feeling dizzy. You better take second position behind Sarah."

"Snap out of it, Everett. Your meltdown is going to have to wait a few more minutes." Sarah held her rifle up as she exited the barn.

Courtney trailed behind her.

Everett focused on his wife. *I've got to keep Courtney safe.* He repeated the phrase over and over. He followed the girls around the corner. What if he saw another woman with a gun? Would he hesitate? *I've got to keep Courtney safe.* Repeating his mantra, he was determined to do anything necessary to fulfill its purpose.

Sarah scanned the hill behind the barn. "I think we're clear."

Everett exhaled. The weight of what he'd just done hit him. His stomach churned, and he threw up.

Courtney patted him on the back. "Everett. It's okay. You did what you had to do."

"Thanks." He knew she was right, but his mind

wasn't about to let the issue go.

Sarah gave him a reassuring squeeze on the shoulder. "We need to check all of the hostiles for a pulse and figure out what we're going to do with the bodies."

Courtney put her arm around Everett. "Come on. You'll be okay."

Wishing he had brought water to rinse his mouth, Everett straightened up.

As they came around the corner of the barn, Sarah raised her weapon "Don't even think about it!"

Everett came around the corner to see one of the hostiles crawling toward the pile of emptied weapons. The bloody figure still wore a motorcycle helmet and was bleeding from the torso and the thigh. Everett approached with his rifle pointed at the hostile. "Lie down, pull off your helmet, and place your hands on your head."

The helmet came off revealing the rough face of a young man, about Everett's age. Everett was relieved that it wasn't a female. It was the person who'd had the AR-15, standing guard, the first hostile Everett had shot.

"I'm dying. I need a doctor." The man's voice was weak.

Courtney's training as a subcontractor for the NSA covered profiling. Though she'd never been directly involved in an interrogation, her analysis had been passed on to other agencies for the purpose of information gathering. It was understood that she'd be the one who would handle the questioning. "You're a long way from a hospital, but I'll see what I can do to help you." She turned to Sarah. "Can I get some water for the gentleman?"

Obviously, the man was no gentleman. Everett doubted that such a thing existed on this God-forsaken planet. He'd just shot a woman himself. If Everett ever had been a gentleman, those qualities had been erased by the hardscrabble struggle to survive. Yet, he understood that Courtney was going with the old you-get-more-flies-with-honey approach.

Sarah handed the canteen to Courtney. "Everett, watch her. I'm going to check the others for a pulse."

Everett nodded and watched as Courtney took a drink of the water for herself. "Oh. That's good. You must be thirsty. Would you like some water?"

The man rolled over slightly, looking at the canteen. "Yes, please."

"Okay. I'll give you some, but first, you have to give me something. How many people are in your survival group, and where did you guys come from?"

The man lost his hopeful expression. "I can't tell you that."

"Listen, I don't have any intention of going after them. If you have friends or family at your compound, they'll never hear anything from us. We just want to know if we should expect more trouble."

The man shook his head. "There won't be no trouble. All that's left of our bunch is old people and kids."

Courtney held the water out to the man. He

reached out to take it. She snatched it away. "There are no little kids. The youngest people left behind by the disappearances were fifteen. That was two and a half years ago. They'd all be close to eighteen by now. Are you telling me you have a bunch of eighteen-year-olds at your compound? The GR considers that military age."

Everett stepped on the man's hand gently to flatten it out. He looked closely through the dirt and grime. "He has the Mark."

Courtney glanced over at his hand and nodded. She stared at the man as she waited for an answer.

"Some. And some of the girls had babies after."

Courtney shook her head. "I think you're lying to me. The oldest possible child is a year and a half old. I'd call that a baby, not a kid. I hope you realize that you're making it very hard for me to be able to help you. And that's a shame. I've got water. Maybe we could get you patched up. Even in your condition, you could probably navigate a quadrunner back to your people who could probably take care of you until you heal up."

Sarah called out from inside. "I've got a pulse on the girl in the barn."

"Okay. This guy doesn't want to talk. Why don't you come out here and keep him company? We'll go chat with the girl," Courtney replied. She turned to the man. "I hope I don't find out you're lying to me. I'm going to be really angry. I mean really angry!"

"Wait. Don't leave. I'll tell you." He held his hand up.

"Be quick about it." Courtney took another drink

and exaggerated her satisfaction from the water. "Oh, that's good water."

"We've got four people standing guard back at our place."

"Where is it? How many males and how many females?"

"Let me have a drink," he pleaded.

"Nope. This quit being about me helping you when you lied. Now it's about me not getting angry and hurting you even more." She pointed to the corpses strewn about. "I shot a lot of your friends here. Don't think I won't hurt you. Anyway, we're not getting anywhere. I'm done dealing with you."

"Okay, two males, two females. We're all at a farm on the west side of Woodstock."

"I said we're done." Courtney led the way into the barn.

Sarah cracked a faint smile as she passed Courtney. "You're good," she whispered.

Everett followed Courtney back toward the stall where he'd shot the two women. Knowing guilt and regret were lying in wait for him, Everett steeled himself for the grisly sight.

The older woman lay face down in a pool of her own blood. She was the one who'd fired at Everett. The other woman, much younger, twenty or twenty-one, Everett guessed, was propped up against the side of the barn stall.

Courtney squatted next to her. "Hey."

The girl's breathing sounded shallow, but her eyes appeared fully alert. She looked at Courtney, but said nothing.

"Have some water." Courtney unscrewed the top

of the canteen and held it to the girl's lips.

She sipped the water. The girl was in bad shape. Her blood-soaked hand covered the side of her stomach. The lower half of her shirt was red and wet.

"Was that your mom?" Courtney asked.

The girl shook her head slightly. "No. That was Bobby's mom. My mom disappeared."

"Who's Bobby?"

"My boyfriend." Her voice was faint.

"Did Bobby come here with you?"

She licked her lips. "Yeah."

"Where are you guys from?"

"Woodstock." The girl looked at the canteen.

"And you're all staying together?" Courtney gave her another sip.

Water dripped down the girl's mouth. "Yes."

Courtney wiped the girl's chin with her shirt sleeve. "I'm Courtney. What's your name?"

"Crystal."

"How many other people from your group stayed behind?"

"Are you going to hurt them?"

"No. We just need to know if they're going to come back to hurt us. We would have never shot you, not in a million years, but Bobby's mom shot at my husband. He had no choice."

"He didn't have to shoot me." Crystal glanced up at Everett.

He looked away.

Courtney said, "You know; the Bible says the companion of fools will be destroyed. When you chose to associate with people of poor character, you have to accept the consequences. I'm sorry this had to happen to you, but you made a choice to come up here with this group. It's not fair to blame my husband.

"I notice that you don't have the Mark. Are you a Christian?"

"I guess not," Crystal replied. "I'm still here, ain't I?"

"We're still here. We're Christians."

"Yeah, right. Some Christians. Killing everybody. You're going to hell, just like Jacob Rolston and just like me. Rolston had that big mega church, and he's still here. My mom used to drag me to church every Sunday. I went down front. I said the prayer. It didn't do me a bit of good."

"Crystal, we're defending our lives. We won't survive if we let people steal our food. And judging from the way your group was armed, they weren't going to give our goats back if we'd asked nicely.

"But forget about that for a moment. You know it's not a magic prayer, right? We don't say abracadabra, Jesus, don't let me go to hell, and expect an enchanted fire insurance policy. Being saved means accepting the blood of Christ, but it also means repenting of your sins."

"My mom told me all of that. Why don't you just let me die?"

"Crystal, it's not too late. You can sincerely ask God to forgive you. Tell him that you repent of your sins and mean it this time. Jesus wants to forgive you so bad."

"I won't be around long enough to live a life of repentance."

"Then it should be easy," Courtney said matter-of-factly.

"Maybe he can forgive me, but I can't forgive him."

"What does that even mean?"

"I was eight months pregnant when the disappearances happened. I woke up that morning, and my baby was gone. Gone. My belly had shrunk down to normal size. My baby just disappeared. You have no idea what that's like, so you can't even begin to understand how I feel."

Courtney's eyes were wide. "You're right. I can't. But you can't blame God. Part of repentance is accepting responsibility for your actions. If you'd been right with God, Jesus would have taken you too. We missed the rapture. We figured it all out the day of the disappearances, but we had no one to blame but ourselves. So, we repented, and God forgave us."

Crystal shook her head. "I'll tell you what you want to know. But promise you'll leave me alone to die in peace."

Courtney swallowed hard as if she was fighting not to get emotional. "Okay. I promise. How many people from your group stayed behind?"

"Four. Greg, his girlfriend, and another couple they're friends with. It's Greg's farm where we stay. He runs the place, like some kind of a boss. When the Global Republic quit supplying us with what we needed, Greg offered people food and security in exchange for working on his farm, running raiding missions, or whatever. He probably won't come up here himself, but he might bring in others to take our place. We had to keep going further and further from the farm to find food. My guess is that he'll eventually send somebody back up here. Especially if anyone got away to tell him what happened. It's not the first time he's lost a raiding team. He'll definitely want his guns, bikes, and quads back. The roads are so shot out; that's the only way anyone can get around.

"He says it's share and share alike, but he has his own private stash of food and supplies. He sure doesn't share in the risk when we go out on raids."

Courtney nodded and looked up at Everett. "Sounds like a real nice guy."

"So can you just leave me alone now?"

Courtney gave the girl another drink of water. "Sure. But think about what I said. You still have a chance to get right with God."

"I'll think about it." Crystal's eyes closed, maybe for the last time.

Everett walked outside, with Courtney trailing behind. He glanced at the man near Sarah's feet. "How's he doing?"

She shook her head. "I don't think he needs a guard anymore. What about the girl?"

"She's on her way out." Everett looked at the ATVs. "We need to find those goats before they get too far away. Do you two know how to operate a quadrunner?"

Sarah nodded. "I do."

Courtney inspected the handlebars. "Sort of like a jet ski?"

"More like a motorcycle." Everett walked her through the basic operations of the controls.

"Okay. Let me try." Courtney got on the ATV, squeezed the clutch, and started the engine.

"Give it some gas and ease off the clutch," Everett instructed.

Courtney complied. "Okay." The quadrunner jerked forward and stalled.

"A little slower letting off the clutch. Wait till you've gone a few feet before you take your hand all the way off." Everett watched with his arms crossed as she tried again.

Courtney took off without a hitch, driving the quad out to the road and coming back. "How was that?"

Everett nodded. "Much better. Now try switching gears, but wait until you have some speed built up."

Courtney zoomed up the tattered pavement over the hill and returned to Everett. He selected a dirt bike and started the engine. "I think the goats headed over the hill. Hopefully, they stayed together." He led the way across the forest floor which was green with new growth, picking a path between the burned-out stumps of the trees which had been consumed by the fire. He looked across the hollow as he crested the first hill but saw nothing. Everett continued to ride over the next hill, and there they were, grazing on the tender shoots scattered about the ground. Everett cut his engine and waited for Courtney and Sarah to arrive on the two quadrunners. The girls pulled up and cut their engines as well.

Everett pointed toward the ravine to the right. "We'll circle around them and drive them back the way we came. Courtney, you take the middle. Sarah, you ride on her right, and I'll take the left. Keep it in first gear, nice and slow. If we push 'em too hard, they might scatter, which will make our job even harder. Besides, we don't want to stress them out. They've had enough to deal with today."

"I didn't see the chickens." Courtney started her ATV.

"Probably went the other way." Sarah nodded over her shoulder, toward the barn.

The three of them drove in single file, around the small herd of goats. Once they were in position, they spread out and began moving the goats back to the barn.

By the time they came over the last hill, the goats had become less wary of the vehicles and required a gentle nudge with a foot from time to time.

"We've still got to clear these bodies." Sarah looked tired.

"And find the chickens." Courtney sounded as if she had very little energy as well.

Everett hated the thought of moving the corpses. He was exhausted also, but he knew the job had to be done. "You two go look for the chickens. I doubt they're very far. I'll take care of the corpses."

"Where are you going to put them?" Courtney asked.

Everett stared blankly down the hill. "I'll haul them to the downed tree blocking the road. It will be a sign to others, warning them, come no further."

Sarah nodded. "That sounds good. We can't bury all these people. It would take us two days to scavenge enough material to burn them."

"Is the fallen tree far enough? Won't we smell them?" Courtney crinkled her nose.

"Not at the cave." Everett began hoisting one of the dead hostiles onto the rear of the quadrunner.

"What about from here? We're going to have to guard the barn around the clock." Courtney helped him lift the body.

Everett secured the corpse with a bungee cord which was attached to the back rack. "I don't know. We'll have to talk that over as a group. We may have to accelerate our plan and slaughter all the goats now. Trying to hold a barn is risky. This Greg guy could send a team up here at night and take us out easily."

"We've got night vision. We could set up an overwatch position. Up there, near that rock." Courtney pointed across the road. "You'd be able to see them coming up the road. We could take them out before they ever get into position to attack the barn."

"Assuming they come that way." Everett mounted the quad.

"They'd be coming from Woodstock. How else would they come?" She inquired.

"You've got a point. Still, we have to discuss it with Kevin and Elijah before we make a decision. Worry about finding the chickens for now." Everett rode the ATV down the tattered pavement toward the giant tree which blocked the mountain road. When he arrived, he backed up to the downed tree and pushed the corpse over the trunk, making no particular fuss about the way the body fell.

He wasted no time getting back on the quad and going to collect the next corpse. He murmured to himself, "I'll check to see if the girl is dead yet. We've got to get the goats back in the barn before they wander off." Everett looked at Crystal. She could be passed out or she could be dead. He didn't know. He decided to first drag the body of the older woman to the ATV. She felt light compared to the man he'd just left draped over the fallen tree trunk. He hoisted her onto the back. The rack still had space for Crystal's body, and Everett couldn't afford to be wasting trips. He knelt beside her. "Crystal. Are you awake?"

She didn't respond.

He pulled her away from the wall, put his arms beneath her armpits and lifted her up. He carried her to the quadrunner and placed her gently beside the woman. He pulled the bungee cord tightly across their bodies to keep them from shifting or falling off on the bumpy ride and started back down the hill. Once more, he backed up to the tree and unhooked the cord from the rack. Everett grabbed Crystal around the waist and laid her across the tree. Next, he repeated the process for the older woman. He mounted the quad and prepared to return to the barn.

"Uhhhh. Help." A faint sound came from behind him, sending chills up his spine.

He turned to see Crystal pushing herself off the tree and sliding down onto the asphalt. "Oh no. God, please give me strength." He stepped off the ATV and walked over to the girl. "Crystal?"

She rolled over onto her back and lifted a hand.

"It hurts so bad. Please help me. Please."

Everett shook his head. "I don't have any medicine. I'm sorry. I can't help." Guilt rushed through his veins to his core, turning his stomach sour.

"I'm cold." She lowered her arm and wrapped it around her shoulder.

Everett watched the pitiful display of a young woman dying in agony. Dying, because he'd shot her.

Crystal's breath was labored, revealing her pain.

Everett walked back toward the quadrunner. "Lord, give me wisdom." He slowly loosened the sling which held his rifle tightly on his back. He removed the weapon and slowly turned around. He looked on silently as Crystal's chest raised and lowered, fighting to breathe.

His lip quivered as he raised the rifle to his shoulder. He swallowed hard and took up the slack in the trigger. He blinked repeatedly to clear the tears welling up in his eyes so he could see clearly. He lined up the sight with the side of Crystal's head and squeezed the trigger.

The shot echoed off the surrounding hills and continued to ring out for what seemed like an eternity to Everett. The sound lingered in the air like a beacon of shame, letting the world know that he'd killed yet another woman. He lowered his eyes in despair and humiliation, wondering if he'd just lost the last ounce of his humanity. For the next few moments, he stood motionless, wallowing in his self-hatred and anger.

Minutes later, Courtney and Sarah raced down

the hill on the other quadrunner.

"Everett!" Courtney's voice called out.

He forced himself to turn around.

"Are you okay?" Sarah jumped off the bike with her weapon drawn. "We heard gunfire."

"Crystal was still alive. She was suffering." Everett motioned toward the corpse with the barrel of his gun. His voice was dry and lifeless. He returned to his quad.

Courtney looked into his hurting eyes. "Are you going to be okay?"

"Yeah. Did you find the chickens?"

"We found them," she replied. "We were working them back toward the barn when we heard the gunshot. We've got to get back and finish up. Why don't you head on back over to the cave and get cleaned up? Sarah and I can move the rest of the bodies once the chickens are back in the coop."

"I'll be fine." He started the engine and raced back up the hill, leaving the girls behind.

Two hours later, the three of them arrived back at the cave.

"What took you guys so long?" Kevin looked Sarah over. "I was gearing up to come looking for you."

"Long story." Sarah plopped down near the entrance to the cave. "Could you bring us some MREs and water? We've had a pretty rough day."

Kevin eyeballed the bundle of weapons Everett held. "Okay, but I need to hear what happened."

"Can we tell you while we eat? We're famished." Courtney sat on the ground.

"Sure." Kevin disappeared into the cave. Minutes later, he returned with three MREs.

Elijah followed him with two canteens of water. "Good heavens, are you alright?"

Everett, Courtney, and Sarah told the story of their experience as they ate.

"We can't keep the vehicles here," Kevin said.

"We left them down by the creek. Mainly, because we didn't want to spook you coming up the trail." Everett sipped his water.

Kevin shook his head. "We can't even keep them by the creek. We can't do anything that would lead them back to the cave. They could smoke us out or trap us inside until they think we're dead. The cave is great for natural disasters, but tactically, it's a death trap. Only one way in and one way out."

Courtney nodded. "So what do you think? Keep the vehicles back at the barn?"

Kevin rubbed his beard. "I don't know."

"The ATVs can get us around where the truck won't go." Sarah continued eating. "They might come in handy."

Kevin nodded. "And they might bring us a heap of trouble. We've got enough of that as it is. If this guy thinks we have them, he's not going to stop looking until he finds them."

Sarah took a drink. "We can't let him get them back. He'll be a persistent source of danger if he has his transportation."

Kevin said, "Then we torch them. Drive them down to where you stacked the bodies and torch them."

"Maybe it doesn't have to be all or nothing.

What if we keep one quadrunner and one dirt bike? He probably isn't going to risk losing another raiding team and more guns over two vehicles." Everett opened the last pouch in his MRE.

"Hmm." Kevin glanced toward the sky and scratched his chin.

"Two dirt bikes. Let's keep one quad and two dirt bikes. Who votes for that plan?" Sarah held her hand up and gestured for Courtney to cast her ballot by raising her hand also.

Courtney continued chewing and put her hand up.

"Come on, Everett. It was your idea. At least vote for your own idea," Sarah chided.

Everett placed his hand in the air.

"I didn't know we were voting on it." Kevin furrowed his brow. "Okay. Two bikes and one ATV. We'll strip the spare parts, drain the gas, and use the tires to ignite the fire. We'll keep the quad at the barn and stash the bikes up on the landslide. We'll figure out a way to camouflage them."

"Were any of the goats taken or injured?" Elijah asked.

Courtney winked at the old prophet. "Samson and Delilah are fine, Elijah."

"That brings us to our next order of business. Are we going to set up a guard at the barn?" Sarah tossed her trash into the small fire burning in the pit.

Kevin looked at Elijah. "I guess we'll have to. The cave smelled like a zoo when we kept six animals in there for a couple of days. I can't imagine keeping the whole herd in there for the next seven weeks."

"We could keep the animals tied up outside of the cave," Elijah said.

Kevin shook his head. "Same problem. That lets people know we're here and sets us up to get smoked out or trapped inside."

Everett said, "It makes sense to have a guard at the barn. If they're coming back, it would be better to take them on there than have them find their way to the cave."

Kevin pointed at Everett. "I agree."

"We'll be spreading ourselves thin. Who is going to stay at the barn, and who is going to keep watch over the cave?" Sarah inquired.

Everett still wore a long face. The killing of the two women weighed heavily on him. "We'll take shifts. Three at the barn, plus Danger. One person works overwatch; one stays on duty inside the barn, and the third person sleeps. The positions rotate."

Sarah patted the dog and ruffled his ears. "Except for you, Cupcake. You're on duty twenty-four seven."

"The two people who are at the cave keep a close watch, but they'd be on light duty until their shift at the barn came back around." Everett finished laying out the division of labor.

"I'm fine with that." Kevin looked at the others.

Everyone seemed to be in agreement about Everett's proposed course of action.

Everett spent the rest of the day cleaning his rifle and inspecting the captured weapons with Kevin. When dusk finally came, exhaustion sucked Everett into a deep sleep, despite the images of the two women he'd killed being played over and over in his mind.

CHAPTER 10

Let us come before his presence with thanksgiving, and make a joyful noise unto him with psalms. For the Lord is a great God, and a great King above all gods.

Psalm 95:2-3

Thursday morning, Everett powered off the PVS14 night vision scope mounted on the top of his AR-15 as the first hint of dawn broke across the sky. He hit the switch at the base of the rail mount which flipped the PVS14 to the side, giving him an unobstructed view of the EOTech reflex sight. He changed the setting on the reflex sight to full power. This rifle was designated to the person on after-dark overwatch duty since it was set up with the team's best night optics.

The glorified foxhole, which Kevin referred to as the LPOP, shielded Everett's body from the wind, but the cold November air made its way through the wool blanket and to the core of Everett's bones. He shivered as he looked at his watch. "One more hour."

Everett peered down the hill then across the road at the barn. A steady stream of smoke came out of the stove pipe extending from the wall of the barn. He imagined how warm it must be inside. Elijah had kept a small stove in the barn to help break the winter chill for his goats. However, since the large potbelly stove was the only thing from Elijah's house to survive the fire, Everett, Kevin, Courtney, and Sarah had replaced the small stove with the large potbelly. Even with the drafty walls of the barn, it kept the area inside much warmer than the cave.

One month had passed since the skirmish at the barn. Everett saw no more signs of trouble coming up from Woodstock. The freezing nighttime temperatures put an end to the rancid scent of the decomposing bodies strewn about the pavement, only a few hundred yards down the mountain. The stench, which served as a putrid reminder of Everett's unthinkable act, finally faded away. But not the guilt. While they came less often, he still experienced regular nightmares, visions of Crystal and the other woman's frightened faces.

"Eight hours in the foxhole. It's an appropriate sentence for my crimes. I can't say I'll miss it, though. Courtney and I have light duty for the next two days. It'll be nice to be back in the cave for a change." He sighed. "Only two more weeks until we hit the meteor's debris field. I'll probably miss this stinking foxhole." Talking to himself had become more and more common since the commencement of the guard shifts. Everett spent quite a bit of time praying, but chattering to himself helped him to stay awake.

The hour passed slowly and Everett emerged from the observation post dugout. His legs were stiff from being still in the cold air. He could get out and walk around if he wanted, but that meant leaving the hole, the wool blanket, and the small amount of body heat that amassed inside the foxhole. Everett knocked on the door before entering. The slight courtesy kept the person inside from being startled and thereby reduced the chances of a friendly-fire incident.

"Happy Thanksgiving!" Courtney met him at the door with a steaming cup of hot chocolate.

"Happy Thanksgiving to you." He gave her a hug and took the mug. "Hot chocolate. You're kidding!"

"Kevin and Sarah have a stash of it for special occasions."

He sipped the warm beverage. "I've never needed it like I do right now. Is Kevin awake?"

"I'm up." Kevin descended the ladder from the barn loft. "How is it out there?"

"Cold. A few flurries." Everett took another sip. "And boring."

Kevin zipped up his jacket, put his gloves on, and pulled his face mask over his head. "Just the way we like it." He tucked his walkie-talkie in his pocket, grabbed his AK-47, and headed out the door.

Courtney took Everett by the hand. "Come on up to the loft. We can snuggle for a few hours before Elijah and Sarah get here with the big lunch."

Everett smiled. "What do you mean by snuggle?"

Courtney turned around as she began climbing the ladder. "I mean, snuggle; as in keep each other warm. It smells like goat poop in here, Everett. Don't be gross."

"Oh." Everett's voice betrayed his disappointment.

She pulled off her boots, lay down and zipped up her sleeping bag. "But we'll be back in the cave tonight." She winked. "Alone."

Everett's smile slowly returned. "Okay." He removed his shoes and wriggled down inside the other sleeping bag. "Do you know what Elijah is making for Thanksgiving?"

"Chicken, of course. Canned green beans, instant mashed potatoes, canned cranberry sauce, and mushroom gravy."

"Mushroom gravy?"

"Yeah. It's just canned mushroom soup so you can put it on your chicken, your potatoes, green beans, or whatever."

"Wow. He's pulling out all the stops. It'll be just like Thanksgiving before the world blew up."

"Oh! I almost forgot. Pumpkin pie. He's grinding wheat to make his own crust, and he's using canned pumpkin."

"That will be fantastic. I guess it will be the first time we've all been together for more than a minute or two since we started the alternating guard shifts out here at the barn."

Courtney pulled the top of the sleeping bag up to the bottom of her chin. "Yeah. We're in close quarters inside the cave, so it's been nice having a little breathing room. Besides, it'll all be over within two weeks. Once the last animals are butchered, there will be no need to guard the barn. Did you guys decide what to do about the quadrunner after we move back to the cave?"

"We think it would be best to leave it here. We're going to take a few critical components off the engine, so it won't run." Everett closed his eyes.

"I'll monitor the radio for a while if you want to take a little nap."

"I'm fine. I just need to rest my eyes for a few seconds. The cold air makes them feel dry." Less than a minute later, he was fast asleep.

Everett awoke to the sound of Danger barking outside. He sprang from inside the sleeping bag, grabbing his HK rifle. "Courtney!"

She answered from down in the barn. "Relax. It's just Elijah and Sarah coming down the hill on the quad."

Everett laid his gun on the sleeping bag, put his boots on, and grabbed his jacket. He slung his rifle across his back and descended the ladder. "How long was I out?"

"About four hours." Courtney placed more wood in the stove and closed the door. "Help me set up the table."

Everett looked at the wood boards and concrete

blocks that were normally used as a table inside the barn. "We're eating outside?"

"Yeah, the weather feels like it could get up to fifty today. Anyway, it's not fair for Elijah to go through all that trouble of putting together a nice Thanksgiving meal only to have us eat it amongst the fragrant bouquet of goat manure." Courtney placed the boards against the wall near the door.

Everett assisted her with the boards then grabbed two blocks and began hauling them outside. "Happy Thanksgiving." Everett nodded his greeting to Elijah and Sarah.

"And to you, my friend." Elijah pointed toward the LPOP. "Sarah, won't you run and fetch Kevin. We must get everything set up so we may eat while the food is still hot."

"Sure thing. Happy Thanksgiving, Everett." She waved as she walked away.

Soon, the entire team was working together to get the table set up. Sarah had brought an orange sheet which worked perfectly as a festive tablecloth. Courtney set the table while the men found buckets to use as chairs. With Sarah's assistance, Elijah removed the various dishes from the box secured to the back of the ATV.

"Come. Everyone, take a seat. And grab the hand of the person next to you." Elijah bowed his head. He offered a quick prayer, thanking the Lord for the provision and protection of the team. He asked God for mercy, comfort, and his blessing on all their Christian brothers and sisters who were suffering through this day with much less than what the group had.

"Amen." Everett took a piece of chicken and passed the plate. "Wow. This smells just like a Thanksgiving turkey."

"Sage and rosemary. It's what I've always used on my turkeys." Elijah spooned out a scoop of mashed potatoes. "We do the best we can with what we have to work with."

"You're too humble, Elijah. This is a magnificent meal, by any standard." Sarah chuckled.

The team continued eating and enjoying each other's company. They took their time and, in the grand tradition of Thanksgiving, everyone had seconds. The conversation lingered over the pumpkin pie and three pots of coffee. The sun beamed brightly, chasing away the chill. During the meal, all the members of the group laughed and smiled, and forgot the terrible times in which they existed. Though it was fleeting, they enjoyed the moment.

After the meal, Courtney and Everett helped Elijah place the dishes in the box on the back of the quadrunner.

"Everett and I will take the dirty dishes back. We'll wash them and put them up." Courtney took a stack of plates from Elijah's hand.

"Bless you child. Be sure to take some leftovers as well. We have plenty." Elijah smiled.

"We've got food at the cave. You guys keep the leftovers." Everett placed an empty bowl carefully in the box.

Elijah portioned out some green beans, potatoes, a slice of pie, and a piece of chicken in a dish, handing it to Courtney with a wink. "We'll share.

That's what Thanksgiving is all about."

"Thanks, Elijah." She placed the dish on top of the dirty dishes which were going back to the cave.

Everett assisted Kevin with setting the table back up inside the barn. "No trouble so far. Only two weeks to go."

Kevin stacked the concrete blocks on the dirt floor of the barn. "Yeah, but we'll be vigilant until the last day. You saw how unexpected it was when you guys happened upon it last month. You never know when trouble is right around the corner."

Everett saw the wisdom in Kevin's comment. "Yep. The second you let your guard down. That's when it hits you."

Once the table was put away, Everett and Courtney said their farewells and got on the quadrunner.

"Y'all be safe." Kevin waved as he picked up his rifle and returned to the observation post across the road from the barn.

Everett and Courtney waved as they rode away. The two of them stopped at the creek to wash the dishes before returning to the cave. Everett groaned as he bent over to draw water into the bucket they kept near the creek for just such a purpose. "I'm so full I could pop."

Courtney chuckled. "I know. If we could curl up on the couch and watch *It's a Wonderful Life*, all would be right with the world."

Everett snorted. "I'd like to see George Bailey try to get by in the Apocalypse. What was the amount of money he was trying to kill himself over?"

Courtney rolled her eyes. "I don't know, like eight grand I think."

Everett shivered at the touch of the cold creek water. "Even so, I wouldn't commit suicide by plunging into icy waters. There's a smarter way to get your life insurance money than that."

Courtney rinsed a plate and stacked it on top of the other clean ones. "You're missing the point. The moral of the story is that George Bailey was instituting a permanent solution to a temporary problem."

"No, I get it. I'm just saying the movie wouldn't play well today. Anybody who can't handle being down eight thousand dollars would be eaten alive in a world where the sky rains blood and fire, where earthquakes, famine, and plague are the rule rather than the exception, and where the western hemisphere is bracing for impact with a giant comet."

Courtney pretended to smack an invisible gavel on a make-believe block. "Wrong, wrong, wrong. If it were on tonight, the whole planet would tune in to watch Jimmy Stewart strolling down the quaint little streets of Bedford Falls. Forget about George Bailey being such a sissy. They'd want to remember a time when even insurmountable problems like missing eight thousand dollars had a solution."

Everett washed the last dish and handed it to Courtney to rinse. "Maybe we'll see if it's playing on the radio tonight. You never know."

She rinsed the dish and placed it with the others. "I thought you wanted to snuggle, but we can listen to the radio, if that's what you'd rather do."

"Oh, it's either or, is it?"

She winked and threw her arms around his neck. She kissed him. "No. It's not either or. I'm just teasing."

"You know you drive me crazy, right?" He held her close and gave her a long passionate kiss.

They hauled the dishes up to the cave, leaving the quad at the bottom of the trail, near the creek. Once inside, Everett exchanged all of his batteries for fresh ones and placed the cells they'd used over the past two days into the charger.

"Do you want some tea?" Courtney placed several small pieces of charred wood in the small rocket stove which Elijah had built from creek stone inside the cave. The team learned the hard way that the cave did not have sufficient airflow for a large fire in the cathedral area. However, the small amount of smoke produced by the rocket stove easily vented out the storage corridor.

"Sure." Everett turned on the radio and took a seat on his sleeping bag.

Courtney filled the kettle with water and joined Everett. Sox emerged from inside Courtney's sleeping bag, stretched, and took a seat in Courtney's lap. She stroked his back. "He's hungry. Bring him a piece of that chicken."

"Chicken? Why don't we give him some potatoes and gravy?"

"It's Thanksgiving, Everett. Give him a tiny piece of chicken. You can mix it in with the potatoes."

Everett looked Sox in the eyes. "You realize this is a people holiday. You should feel bad for imposing yourself."

"Stop it, Everett! Don't say that to him. There were cats on the Mayflower, so they probably participated in the first Thanksgiving."

Everett stood up to bring Sox his celebratory meal. "I've never heard that. I don't know what history book you were reading."

"All ships used to travel with cats. They kept the boat free of mice and rats. They had an official title, the Ship's Cat."

"You're making this up." Everett tore tiny shreds of chicken and mixed them into the potatoes which he then spooned into the cat's food bowl.

Courtney laughed. "I'm not making it up. I can't believe you've never heard of it."

Everett placed the bowl several feet away. "Here's your food. Now, can I have my wife back?"

Sox leaped out of Courtney's lap and sauntered over to the bowl. The loud smacking sounds he made as he ate were his stamp of approval that the meal was indeed pleasing.

"I'm glad you like it." Everett returned to his seat putting his arm around Courtney. He scrolled through the stations on AM and FM.

"There's only one station. The GR propaganda radio." Courtney pursed her lips as she watched Everett search in vain for something else.

"I know. I'm just checking to see if anyone might have a pirate station up." Once he was satisfied that there were no other alternatives, he tuned to the GR station.

The female reporter's voice had a distinct British

accent. "The Falcon Twenty rocket which will launch a week from Saturday has been cleared by GRASA. The final inspections were made yesterday afternoon, and the GRASA spokesperson assured the Global Republic Broadcasting Network that all systems are go for the mission to disintegrate the comet 2019 WD10. The Space Agency has designated the comet, Wormwood, which is derived from a Greek word meaning *bitter*. While we have devised a plan to overcome the complete destruction of our planet threatened by this celestial object, the fallout will bring a very *bitter* period indeed, especially for the Western Hemisphere.

"His Majesty has pledged a massive relief effort to commence on Monday, December 11th. The initial three-day period following the collision with the debris field will be spent assessing damage to GR infrastructure, particularly in the capital city of New Atlantis. Emergency management protocols are already in place, and plans exist to bring the government back online within seventy-two hours of impact.

"Minister to the Americas Richard Clay and GREMA Director Vivian Brown issued a statement today, reiterating the Global Republic's call for everyone in the Western Hemisphere to store up food and water, and to seek shelter below ground if possible. While relief efforts will begin immediately after the government comes back online, it could be as much as a month before teams are able to reach remote areas and locations which are hardest hit by the debris field."

Courtney laughed. "It took four days to get water to the Superdome after Katrina. The GR is still recovering from the mega quake two and a half years ago. They haven't even started to deal with the blood and fire. What makes them think they'll be able to respond to this in a month?"

Everett answered, "They're just keeping up appearances. If you tell everyone that it's going to be six months to a year before they can even think about reestablishing communications, supply chains, medical and police services, people might start forming their own government."

Courtney rolled her eyes. "Well, we can't have that, now can we?"

The reporter continued. "His High and Most Prepotent Majesty Angelo Luz has decided to attend the rededication ceremony of the new Jewish Temple in Jerusalem. The eight-day ceremony will begin at sundown on December 7th and end with an extravaganza on the evening of December 15th. Supreme Pontiff of the Universal Church, His Holiness, Pope Peter of Rome as well as the Global Republic Minister of Religion Jacob Ralston will also be in attendance. His Majesty and Pope Peter both place high hopes on the celebration and the rededication of the temple. It is their ambition that this will once and for all bring unity between Jews and the Global Republic Ministry of Religion.

"It has been widely reported that many Jews, particularly those in the former Israeli territories, are using counterfeit implants which have circumvented the Mark system. Others have avoided the Mark by operating in black-market barter exchanges. These exchanges are often run by criminal organizations which sell tainted goods and expose participants to extreme levels of violence."

Everett crossed his arms and shook his head. "Unlike the GR, which wouldn't hurt a flea."

"Keeping up appearances. Remember, it's all propaganda." Courtney scratched Sox under his chin.

The GRBN reporter expounded upon the news item. "Speculation about why His Majesty has been so tolerant and patient with the Jewish People in the area centers around the fact that his mother was of Jewish descent.

"It is expected that after much research by the Temple Institute that His Majesty will be named as the Messiah of the Jewish prophecies. While most other cultures, like Hinduism, Buddhism, Islam, and Zoroastrianism have officially recognized His Majesty as the coming savior, Jewish leaders have been slow in confirming that he is indeed the one of whom the Hebrew texts have spoken."

Courtney turned off the radio. "Sorry, I can only stomach so much of this garbage at a time." She took the cat out of her lap and let him go explore the cave. "Besides, wasn't there something else you had in mind?"

Everett leaned in for a kiss. "Yeah. I've got a few ideas."

CHAPTER 11

And the third angel sounded, and there fell a great star from heaven, burning as it were a lamp, and it fell upon the third part of the rivers, and upon the fountains of waters; And the name of the star is called Wormwood: and the third part of the waters became wormwood; and many men died of the waters, because they were made bitter.

Revelation 8:10-11

On the evening of December 4th, Everett and the rest of the group listened to the play-by-play coverage of GRASA Mission Control being broadcast over the Global Republic Broadcast Network radio station.

The GRBN reporter, Harrison Yates, provided commentary on the mission in real time. "Listeners in Ontario, Quebec, and the eastern portion of the former United States will have an unobstructed view of the detonation of the nuclear device. Even if you have minimal cloud coverage in your area, the blast will still be visible. Those of you with clear skies will witness an extraordinary event unlike anyone has ever seen.

"The specialized Thor's Hammer satellite has docked with Wormwood and is currently boring a hole which will be used by the satellite's anchoring device. This will ensure that the nuclear blast retains the maximum effect on the comet upon detonation. Mission Control has stated that they will trigger the device in twenty minutes.

"All of us here at GRBN wait with bated breath for confirmation that the mission is a success. I needn't remind any of you that the fate of the planet hangs in the balance."

Everett gazed up at the heavens. "I guess we should be able to see it then."

Elijah tossed a piece of wood into the camp fire. "It's been a while since I saw fireworks."

Courtney sat shivering beside Everett, her arm wrapped around his. "This is crazy. I'm so anxious. I know how the Bible says everything will end. And obviously, it's been right about all of it so far, but still, a lot could go wrong."

Everett gave her hand a squeeze. "It's normal to be a little apprehensive. Everyone else on the planet is right now."

Kevin stood away from the fire, staring out into the darkness. Sarah got up from the rock she'd been sitting on and walked over to him. "What's bothering you?"

Kevin looked around the camp, at the cave entrance, then back out into the void of night. "I hope we've covered all our bases. That's all."

Sarah rubbed his back. "The batteries are all charged. We'll slaughter the last goat tomorrow."

"Hahmm." Elijah cleared his throat.

Sarah turned around with a smile. "Sorry. Not Samson and Delilah, of course. The last goat slated to be killed, I mean."

Courtney added, "We've collected enough new growth from the forest to make a month's worth of fodder for the goats and the chickens."

"I've stacked enough charred wood to last us for about four weeks in the rocket stove if we use it sparingly," Everett said.

"We've stored lots of water." Elijah whittled away at a small branch.

"We'll take the ATV back to the barn Wednesday morning, pull the spark plugs, distributor, and the fuel line. We'll drain the gas and bring it back with us. We've done our best, Kevin." Everett looked up at his friend. "It's time to trust God with the rest."

Kevin turned around and offered a smile to Everett. "You're right. I guess obsessing over everything gives me something to do besides worry."

"Worrying is negative faith." Elijah continued to whittle.

"Thanks, but we're not all prophets with perfect trust in the Almighty." Kevin walked over to the campfire and found a seat.

"Who has perfect trust?" Elijah snickered. "I simply made a statement. I've never claimed to have perfect faith. I will say that I believe the Scriptures perfectly. If God says something is to be, I believe it. But after all I've seen and done, that is more about logic and experience.

"Perfect faith is about being ready to accept God's will for your life, no matter what. Even when you have no idea what the outcome may be, how awful the suffering, or how deep the grief. If you can accept that, as Job did, as John, James, Peter, and Paul; when you are willing to drink from his cup without protest or fear, then you have perfect faith."

Everett took Elijah's comments to heart. He believed in God. He had no doubt that everything would turn out just as the Scriptures predicted, but was he ready to endure immeasurable suffering? Could he persevere through the trials of Job? He quivered as he considered it. "I hope I never have to find out," he mumbled to himself.

The voice of Harrison Yates came over the radio. "We have less than two minutes remaining before GRASA Mission Control triggers the device which will break up Wormwood into much smaller meteors. Many of those smaller rocks will be burned up by earth's atmosphere, long before they make contact with the surface of the planet. Inevitably, we will have some very large asteroids that will cause extensive damage, but unlike hitting Wormwood as a single object, our species will survive. We will go on. We will rebuild."

Everyone in the group, including Elijah, stood up and silently looked out at the stars. Danger barked and wagged his tail as if he wanted to be let in on the joke. Sarah patted her leg, signaling for the dog to come stay beside her. Courtney held Everett's hand with her left and with her right, she reached out and took hold of Elijah's hand.

Yates began the countdown. "One minute more until the detonation."

Everett sighed deeply. He became conscious that he was squeezing Courtney's hand too tightly. He regulated his breathing and loosened his grip.

Harrison Yates reached the final countdown. "Eight, seven, six, five, four, three, two, one . . ."

Everett held his breath as he kept his eyes wide open, gazing toward the sky. A bright, brilliant flash erupted into a ball of light, only a fraction of the size of the moon, but much brighter. He turned away for a moment, not sure if it was safe to continue looking. He glanced back at the distant fireball. The outer edges began to fade, but the blast remained visible for several more seconds. "Wow."

"Folks, we are awaiting confirmation that the mission was a success. Everyone with a view of the sky in the eastern region of North America just witnessed a tremendous blast and we are diligently standing by to hear back from GRASA Mission Control to confirm that the comet has been demolished." Harrison Yates stopped talking, something that rarely happened.

Courtney looked at Everett. "Do you think it worked?"

Everett shrugged, still looking out into space.

Yates resumed his commentary. "Citizens of the Global Republic, the comet Wormwood has been destroyed. As we have said from the beginning, you will still need to seek shelter, underground if possible, and prepare to stay in place. The Global Republic advises those living in the Western Hemisphere to go underground Thursday morning and remain there until Friday night. You should have provisions to survive on your own for one month.

"The debris field that the earth will collide with on Thursday evening contains huge meteors. Undoubtedly, these objects will cause significant damage and loss of life.

"In the coming hours, we will be receiving images taken by Argus, a secondary surveillance satellite launched at the same time as Thor's Hammer, which will give us some approximate answers about the size of the various fragments left behind by the destruction of Wormwood. It will be very difficult to pinpoint where the larger chunks will land, but at least we'll know what the planet is in for, as a whole. "

Elijah stood up and brushed off his backside. "The show is over. I'm going to sleep. I shall see you all in the morning."

"Good night." Courtney waved.

"Me, too." Sarah yawned and turned to Kevin. "Are you ready to go to bed?"

"Sure. Everett, are you guys going to stay up with the fire or should I put it out?" Kevin pulled Sarah's hand while he waited for Everett's reply.

"I'm going to sit up and watch it burn out. Soon, it will be too cold to be out here at night, even with the fire. I'm going to take advantage of it while I can."

Kevin waved. "Sure thing. See you in the morning."

"I'm going to grab a blanket if we're going to be sitting out here longer." Courtney tussled Everett's hair as she walked toward the cave. "I'll be right back."

Everett looked up with a wink. "I'll be here."

The two of them sat under the stars for what might be one of the last nights. Already well below freezing, the night-time temperatures would continue to fall over the coming months. Once the fire burned out, they retreated to the relative warmth of the cave. At a constant fifty-four degrees, the cavern offered year-round temperature control. While not the optimum climate by anyone's standard, it eliminated exposure risks like frostbite and heat stroke.

The following two days provided an adequate amount of last-minute tasks to keep the team busy. By late Thursday morning, the list of assigned responsibilities had been completed, and the only thing left to do was wait.

Everett finished his plate. "I couldn't eat another bite."

"The goat was fantastic, Elijah. I'm full as a tick." Courtney took Everett's plate and stacked it on top of hers.

"Thank you. I'm glad you enjoyed it. We'll have leftovers for the next few days." Elijah continued to cut off the remaining meat from the goat on the spit, suspended above the coals of the fire.

Kevin held his stomach as he stood up. "I'm going to put in a quick call to Tommy before we bring the antenna inside."

"Tell him I said to be safe, and I'll talk to him when the smoke clears." Everett began disconnecting the solar panels so he could bring them into the cave.

"I'll take the dishes down to the creek." Sarah collected the remaining plates.

Courtney slung her rifle over her back. "I'll come along and give you a hand."

Everett looked up at the sky. "Don't be long. With the sun shining, we may not be able to tell when the meteor shower begins. We have to be ready to take shelter at a moment's notice."

Courtney shielded her eyes from the sun and looked up. "We'll be on the lookout."

Everett continued his task of reeling up the cables and stowing them inside the cave. As a precautionary measure, he moved all the individual components of the solar array back into the cathedral, well away from the cave entrance.

Once that task was completed, he found Kevin and gave him a hand dismantling the ham antenna. "What did Tommy have to say?"

Kevin spooled the wire from the antenna around a stick. "He said to tell you hello."

"Hello?"

"Howdy, I think was the exact word he used."

"Is his group ready?"

"They've done all they can. How did you put it? Do your best and trust God with the rest, right?"

Everett smiled. "That's all any of us can do."

"Tommy said they are hunkering down. If he gets a direct impact of a large meteor on top of the house or the barn, there's nothing they can do, but he has those dirt mounds all the way around, which will help to shield against any smaller asteroids with an angle to their trajectory."

"Yeah, surviving a direct impact is a tall order. The girls still aren't back yet, huh?"

Kevin looked down the trail. "Not yet."

Everett looked up in time to see a bright glowing object shining like a spotlight in the eastern sky. He held his hand up to block the sun so he could get a better look at the fireball. "Here it comes!"

Kevin looked up, blocking the sun with his forearm in order to see what Everett was pointing toward. He turned around and surveyed the rest of the sky. He pointed toward the west. "There goes another one. Just above the mountain."

Everett turned to see a comet descending with a

long glowing tail and a trail of smoke. He stuck his fingers under his tongue and whistled as loudly as he could. "Courtney! Sarah! Get back here! It's starting!"

Kevin collected the remaining pieces of the antenna stand, scooping them up in a hurry.

Everett patted him on the back. "If you can handle this, I'm going to run down to the creek and grab the girls. I'm not sure they heard me."

"Sure. Go ahead." Kevin carried the equipment inside the cave.

Everett dashed down the trail. "Courtney! Sarah!" He heard no reply. A loud boom rang out from across the hollow. Everett pushed to run faster. He reached the creek to find the girls finishing up with the dishes. "Hurry! It's started. We have to get to the cave." Everett pointed at the sky.

Courtney looked up. An expression of concern covered her face. "Oh no!"

Sarah followed her gaze and pointed at the sky. "There's another one. And another one. Four, five . . ."

"We have to go right now!" Everett picked up the plastic crate containing the dishes and grabbed Courtney's hand.

BOOM! A meteorite the size of a garbage can struck the trail between Everett and the cave. The shock wave knocked them from their feet, causing Everett to drop the crate of dishes.

"That could have been us!" Courtney pushed herself up off the ground onto her hands and knees.

"It still might be. We have to go! Come on! Get up!" Everett helped Courtney back to her feet.

Sarah scrambled to collect the dishes which were strewn about the ground.

"Forget about the dishes, Sarah. We have plenty of others in the cave. We have to get to safety!" Everett grabbed Sarah's hand, pulling her up.

Another loud boom was heard in the distance, motivating the three of them to hustle up the hill.

Everett reached the crater left by the impact of the meteor on the trail. "Go around it. We have no idea what the chemical makeup of Wormwood was. If it poisons the water, we know it ain't healthy."

Courtney and Sarah followed Everett as he picked a path that took them up a steep incline, avoiding the crater.

"Ah! Ouch!" Courtney lost her footing and slipped down the embankment.

Everett climbed back down to help her. "Are you okay?"

"I rolled my ankle."

Sarah turned around to help her. "Can you walk?"

She moved her foot in a circular motion. "It seems okay."

Fifty yards away, another meteor about the size of a beach ball struck the forest floor. The ground rumbled. Everett grimaced. "Our odds are getting worse by the second." He and Sarah assisted Courtney in getting back up.

"How's that?" Sarah paused to wait for Courtney.

Courtney put her weight on her foot. "I'm good. I can walk."

Everett climbed back up the small cliff then

lowered his hand to Courtney. "Grab hold. I'll pull you up. Sarah, give her a little nudge from behind."

"Roger." Sarah grabbed Courtney's belt and hoisted her up as Everett pulled.

Once Courtney was safely up the incline, Everett gave Sarah a hand.

The three of them were soon on top of the ridge, and Everett led the way back to the trail. "Can you run?"

Courtney winced in pain. "I can walk."

Everett felt anxious but didn't want to show his high level of concern to the girls. "That's okay. Sarah, why don't you go ahead and run back to the cave. Kevin might need some help getting the rest of the ham equipment away from the entrance."

Sarah paused. "Are you sure? If Courtney can't walk, you'll need my help to carry her."

"I'll be fine. Go ahead." Courtney waved her on.

"Alright then. I'll see you there." Sarah began sprinting toward the cavern.

"You should go too. Run back. I'll be there in a few minutes." Courtney pulled her hand away from Everett's.

"And let you beat me to heaven? Not in a million years." Everett winked and gave her a smile to lighten the mood.

She grinned and walked beside him. "I love you, Everett Carroll."

"And I love you, Courtney Carroll." Everett wrapped his arm around her allowing her to put part of her weight on him so they could move a little faster. His eyes darted back and forth from the sky and the trail, watching for obstacles so they wouldn't trip. At a glance, he could still see three large fireballs. One of them was competing with the sun, in relative size and brightness, from Everett's perspective. "We need to get to the cave before that big boy hits."

Courtney looked up at the giant glowing ball that seemed to float down to earth like a colossal flare. "Okay."

Everett pushed her to keep going as quickly as possible. "We're almost there."

Twenty feet away, a smaller meteor hit. It was only the size of a football when it struck, but the ground trembled beneath their feet.

"There's the cave! We're almost home." Everett held her tightly as she seemed to be getting weaker.

Another distant reverberation shook the earth, evidence of yet one more massive asteroid striking the planet.

Sarah came to the door of the cave. "Do you need some help?"

Courtney's limp grew worse.

Everett looked up at the mammoth fireball coming closer and closer to the ground. "Yes. Please!"

Sarah jogged over to Courtney and put her arm around her. "I've got you."

Everett held his wife from the opposite side of Sarah as he watched the comet smoke and flare brighter. "We need to run!"

"Okay." Sarah hurried, in step with Everett.

They reached the mouth of the cave and helped Courtney inside. Sarah followed her in, and Everett entered last.

"Get back! Everybody! All the way back to the cathedral!" Everett helped Courtney limp to the innermost area of the cavern.

BOOOOM! The earth shook, taking them all to the ground. Everett grabbed Courtney and fell backward, breaking her fall.

"Are you okay?" She gazed into his eyes.

He'd fallen directly on his back, knocking the air out of his lungs. He gasped for breath and nodded. Once he regained his breath, he said, "I'm fine. How about you?"

She smiled. "I'm okay, thanks to you."

Danger barked and yelped in fear. Samson and Delilah bleated as they fought to regain their balance. Sox darted to the safety of Courtney's sleeping bag, burrowing deep inside. Even the rooster and the two hens cackled a sound of sure distress at the violent shaking of the earth.

Elijah took a seat on his sleeping bag. He bowed his head. "Lord, I pray that you will watch over us, your children. Spare us from this plague as you spared your children from the plagues of Egypt. Amen." The old prophet looked up. "Is everyone alright?"

Everett brushed off the seat of his pants and surveyed the room with his flashlight. "All present and accounted for."

"And now we wait." Kevin sat next to Sarah and put his arm around her.

Every few minutes, the walls of the cave would rattle as the larger meteorites hit outside. The group sat silently and listened for the next hour as the bombardment continued.

Everett climbed up the ladder and located the first aid supplies. He located an Ace bandage and brought it back down. He removed Courtney's shoe and sock. He lightly touched the swollen area. "Does that hurt?"

"No. It looks worse than it feels."

Everett wrapped the bandage firmly around her foot and ankle. "Is that too tight?"

"It seems to be okay."

"If it feels like the Ace bandage is cutting off the circulation, let me know. I'll rewrap it." Everett picked up the small radio and tugged the antenna to make sure the end which ran outside of the cave was still secured to the bit of root by the cave entrance. He turned on the radio, but only static could be heard. "I guess the GRBN are in their bunkers also."

"We need something to get our minds off of the impending doom." Sarah scooted closer to Kevin.

Courtney moved her foot in a circular motion then looked up at Elijah. "Why don't you tell us about Hanukkah?"

Elijah glanced from person to person. "Does everyone want to hear about it?"

"Yes, please!" Sarah replied.

"Believe it or not, the story has great relevance to the time in which we are now living.

"I'm sure most of you are students of history and need no back story, but just to recap, Alexander the Great's empire fragmented after his death. Seleucus, one of his generals, took control of Babylonia and expanded his territory throughout the Near East to become what is known as the Seleucid Empire. The seventh ruler of this Seleucid Empire was Antiochus Epiphanes. He had a rather colorful rise to power, but that's another story altogether.

"While Antiochus was in Egypt, the Jews revolted, overthrowing the puppet leader which Antiochus appointed as High Priest over the Jews. When Antiochus received news of the rebellion, he returned to Jerusalem and put down the uprising with a violent iron fist. He put an end to the sacrifices in the temple and slaughtered a pig upon the altar of God, the supreme abomination.

"The Jews launched a guerilla warfare campaign against the Seleucid Empire and eventually won the victory.

"Of course, the temple had to be rededicated. To do so, the priests needed the holy oil to burn in the lamp for eight days. Unfortunately, they had only enough oil for one day. The priests burned the lamp, and that one day's worth of oil miraculously lasted the entire eight-day period."

"Oh. And how does that pertain to us?" Sarah inquired.

Elijah raised his eyebrows. "Daniel prophesied of the antichrist who would put an end to the daily sacrifice and commit an abomination in the temple."

"Maybe Daniel was talking about Antiochus," Kevin said.

"He may have been. Antiochus Epiphanes could have been the near fulfillment of this prophecy, but we know that it will be fulfilled again, in the person of the antichrist, Angelo Luz."

"A near and far fulfillment of the same prophecy?" Sarah sounded confused.

"Yes, child. Messiah tells us in Matthew twenty-four to watch for the fulfillment of this prophecy in the last days. Antiochus Epiphanes died some 160 years prior to the Messiah's birth. So, it could not have been him of whom Christ spoke."

"Daniel speaks of Alexander the Great and the division of the Macedonian Empire, right?" Everett pulled Courtney's sock back over her foot so it wouldn't get cold.

"Yes. The goat in Daniel chapter eight tells of a great conqueror. As the horn, representing authority, is broken off the goat, four other horns grow up to take its place. These are the four leaders who took control of the divided Macedonian Empire, one of them being Seleucus.

"When speaking of the desecrated temple, Daniel says in chapter eleven, 'but the people that do know their God shall be strong, and do exploits.' That may well have a near and far fulfillment. It is quite possible that it spoke of the Maccabees, who overthrew the Seleucid Empire, and it may have been a prophecy of you. Perhaps it foretold of your battle against the GR outpost in Winchester and the courageous acts against Luz by your brothers and sisters around the world."

Everett smiled as he considered that his life could be a fulfillment of Bible prophecy. "Sort of gives you a sense of purpose, doesn't it?"

Courtney grinned. "Yes, it does."

BOOOOOM! Tremors shot across the floor; the walls shook, and everyone jumped from shock.

Everett's heart raced. "That was close. It sounded like it could have been near the entrance. I better check it out."

Kevin clicked on his flashlight. "I'll come with you."

The two men made their way to the front of the cavern. Everett shined his light toward the opening. "It's caved in."

"We're trapped." Kevin moved his light from side to side, examining the rubble blocking the exit.

Everett nodded. "Yep, but let's not use that language with the girls. It won't help. I'm sure we'll be able to dig out."

More rumblings could be heard from outside. "But we better wait until the earth has cleared the debris field before we give it a try." Everett turned to go back.

When he returned to the cathedral, Courtney asked, "What happened?"

"A meteorite struck near the entrance. Some mud and rock came inside the cave." Everett took his seat next to Courtney.

"But we can still get out, right?" Sarah's voice sounded concerned.

Everett feigned a lack of genuine concern. "Yeah, it's just rubble. We'll get it cleared in no time. But we don't want to be near the entrance while the sky is still falling in."

Elijah stood up and walked over to the rocket stove. "Why don't I make my famous apple latkes? You can't celebrate Hanukkah without latkes."

"That would be fantastic, Elijah." Everett welcomed the distraction from the ongoing apocalyptic bombardment.

"Can I help?" Sarah asked.

"Yes, please. Will you bring me a box of instant mashed potatoes and a jar of apple sauce from the pantry?" Elijah pointed toward the elevated storage area above the cathedral. "And let Kevin hold the ladder for you. I don't want the next shaker to cause you to fall."

Elijah lit the stove, mixed up his batter, and managed to dispel the atmosphere of fear and worry with his warm latkes. Sox, Danger, and the goats even managed to get a taste. The heavy spirit of concern lingered in the background, but the group made a conscious effort to stay positive for the duration of the violent meteor shower.

CHAPTER 12

And the fourth angel sounded, and the third part of the sun was smitten, and the third part of the moon, and the third part of the stars; so as the third part of them was darkened, and the day shone not for a third part of it, and the night likewise.

Revelation 8:12

Everett awoke from a fitful night's sleep. He flicked his flashlight on to see the time on his watch. "Six thirty." He rolled over and lay still, listening for rumbles that might signal that the meteorites were still falling. All was quiet. The last impact to wake him up had been at 3:00 in the morning. Everett could hear nothing, except the steady rhythmic breathing of Courtney, whose sleeping bag was huddled up close to his. Everett closed his eyes and prayed silently inside the warm comfort of the covers he was in no hurry to leave.

He finished praying and flicked his light on once again to check the time. "Five past seven." He quietly slipped out of his bag and put on his jacket. As carefully as possible, he lit the rocket stove and started a pot of coffee. Everett read a few Psalms by flashlight while he waited for the coffee to brew. He sipped his coffee then made his way up to the cave entrance.

"This is a mess." A large slab of stone from the roof of the entrance jutted down at a steep slant, with the bottom toward the cathedral and the top angled out in the direction of the entrance. Everett leaned on the slab. It didn't move. He pushed and kicked at the block. "It won't budge."

Mud and rubble lay at the base of the grand stone. An eighteen-inch gap between the top of the slab and the cave ceiling was also filled with smaller pieces of broken stone and earth. The wire antenna to the AM/FM radio ran out from beneath the bottom of the slab. Everett tugged gently on the wire. "Seems secure. But who knows if it's cut on the other side."

"We're stuck, huh?" Kevin's voice accompanied a secondary flashlight beam examining the giant slab of rock.

Everett turned around. "We might be able to dig out through that gap." He shined his light to the space separating the slab and the ceiling.

Kevin's light bounced from wall to wall and

floor to ceiling. "My guess is that we're roughly five feet away from the previous entrance. We'll have a lot of digging to do."

"Do you have other plans?"

"No." Kevin snickered. "But we need to dig out five feet without hitting any other obstructions that are too big to move."

Everett directed the beam of his flashlight on the slab. "The top is probably two feet closer to the outside than the bottom. We might only have about three feet to dig."

"If we don't have additional rock and debris on top of the entrance. Something caused it to cave in. We could have a huge meteorite sitting above the exit. Or, it could have hit higher up on the hill, causing mud and rock to slide down from above." Kevin combed his beard with his fingers. "Or the worst case scenario, we've got a layer of mud and rock, sitting on top of a giant meteorite, sitting on top of this immovable slab of stone."

Everett grimaced. "Did anyone ever tell you that you can be quite a downer sometimes?"

"Just keepin' it real, bro. Just keepin' it real."

"Well, don't keep it too real with the girls. Let's assume that we can dig out until we're proven wrong."

"On the bright side, I haven't heard any more impacts."

Everett patted Kevin on the back. "See there; you can find something positive to say after all."

"Don't get used to it." Kevin smiled. "What do you say we grab some shovels and start trying to dig out?"

Everett led the way back toward the cathedral. "I'll second that motion."

Courtney, Sarah, and Elijah were all awake when the two men returned to the cathedral.

"How does it look?" Courtney asked.

Everett preempted a response from Kevin. "I think we can dig out."

"I can help," Sarah offered.

Elijah stood up. "Yes, I too will assist you. Tell me what I must do."

"Thanks," Everett said. "Elijah, if you and Sarah can round up some buckets, we can use them to move the mud and rock out of the way as we dig. Kevin and I will get the tools from the upper storage area."

Courtney flexed her bum ankle. "I can help also if you need me."

Everett held up his hand. "No. You rest your foot. If you can manage to keep the animals out of our way, that will be a big help."

"Roger that." Courtney held Sox in her lap as she sat on her sleeping bag.

Everett and Kevin found the shovels and rendezvoused with Elijah and Sarah near the blocked entrance. Everett positioned the buckets below the gap and began striking the mud and rock with the point of his shovel.

Kevin assisted him. "Looks like you've got one big rock, right in the middle of everything."

Everett worked around the large boulder that seemed to be blocking the gap. "Yeah, I see that. We'll get as much material cleared from around it as possible and see if we can move it."

The two men half-filled the buckets below their work area.

Elijah replaced those buckets with empty ones. "We'll dump these out before they get too heavy."

Sarah assisted him in taking the rock and dirt to the far corner of the cave.

Kevin whispered to Everett while Elijah and Sarah were gone with the buckets. "That stone ain't moving."

Everett gritted his teeth. "I know. But I'm not giving up yet. We've got a hammer and a chisel up in the storage area."

Kevin shook his head. "That will take forever."

"Which is exactly how long we'll be here if we don't clear that rock." The frustration of the situation hit Everett hard.

"I'll get the hammer and chisel." Kevin walked away.

Sarah returned and placed her bucket next to Elijah's. "What's the prognosis?"

"It's going to take some work, but we'll get out." Everett nodded to make his statement more convincing to everyone, including himself.

Kevin returned in a few minutes, handing the tools to Everett. "Here you go."

Everett positioned the tip of the chisel on the boulder, nearest to the top of the slab. He swung the hammer. TINK! Tiny fragments of the stone sprayed everywhere. "You didn't happen to see any safety glasses when you were digging around in the tools, did you?"

Kevin shook his head. "No. Do you want some sunglasses?"

"It's hard enough to see as it is." Everett furrowed his brow.

Sarah put her hands on her hips. "If you get rock in your eye, it might be even harder to see."

"Try these." Elijah took his readers out of his jacket pocket.

Everett placed the glasses on his eyes. "Wow. Everything looks bigger and closer." He carefully swung the hammer at the butt of the chisel. Tink! Tink! Tink!

Once he felt more comfortable with the glasses, he resumed hitting the chisel with all his might. TINK! TINK! TINK!

Twenty minutes into the experiment, he'd made a dent in the rock not much larger than a golf ball. He rubbed his right shoulder.

"Let me give it a few swings." Kevin stepped closer to Everett.

Elijah raised his index finger. "Wise King Solomon said, 'If the iron be blunt, and he do not whet the edge, then must he put to more strength: but wisdom is profitable to direct.' Might I suggest that we sharpen the chisel?"

"Sure." Everett handed the chisel to Elijah and the hammer to Kevin.

Elijah left to sharpen the chisel. Everett and the others waited for him to return. Courtney hobbled into the cave entrance area. "Sounds like you guys are working hard."

Everett nodded. "We've got to split up that big rock."

Courtney flipped one of the empty buckets and took a seat. "That's how they used to quarry stone.

They'd turn the chisel slightly with each strike until it drilled out a hole then place a wedge between two slips of metal called feathers."

Everett listened closely. "Go on."

"That's all I know about it." She shrugged.

Desperate for information, Everett asked, "How many holes? How deep? How far apart? Anything else you can remember will help."

She looked up at the rock. "You'd have to have a wedge and two feathers for each hole. We don't have any, so it doesn't matter."

Everett strained to think what he could use for a wedge. "What about an ax head?"

Courtney glanced up at him. "Maybe."

Everett looked at Kevin. "What could we use for the feathers? Some kind of shim."

Sarah interjected. "We could use the punches in our gun maintenance kit."

"We'll probably ruin the punches." Kevin looked up at Everett. "Of course, we won't need them much if we don't get out of here."

"Exactly," Everett replied.

Elijah returned with the chisel and a round sharpening stone. "Try this. I'll sharpen it every half hour or so. It's easier to keep the edge than to put a new one on it."

Courtney looked at his whet rock. "It looks like a hockey puck."

"That's what it's called, the Puck. It's a rougher grit than the stone I use for my knife. The Puck is specifically made for tools; axes, machetes, chisels, that sort of thing." Elijah passed the sharpening tool to Courtney to inspect.

"Here we go." Kevin put Elijah's reading glasses on and began swinging the hammer against the chisel, turning it slightly with each blow, as Courtney had suggested.

"I'll get the ax and see what I can find to use for shims." Sarah left the work area.

Everett watched Kevin from behind. "It does seem to be moving faster since Elijah sharpened it."

TINK! TINK! TINK! Kevin continued for fifteen minutes then paused to inspect the progress.

Everett took the tools from him. "Take a break. I'll work on it for a while."

Courtney pointed to the opening. "You should begin making another hole. You'll have to make a long slit, big enough for the ax head."

Everett nodded. He took the glasses from Kevin and positioned the chisel next to the existing hole. TINK! TINK! TINK!

Sarah returned with the ax. "I can take a few swings. You guys are going to be sore if we don't split the work up between everyone."

Everett handed her the tools and the glasses. "Okay, thanks. Start a new one right about here." He pointed to a spot beside the existing holes.

As Sarah began pounding away at the rock, Everett inspected the ax. "I doubt we can salvage the handle. I guess we'll just cut it off and make a new one. What do you guys think?"

Elijah nodded. "If we can pry the metal wedges out of the top of the ax handle, perhaps we can save it. Wood being the scarce commodity that it is, fashioning a new handle will be a challenge."

Everett looked closely at the thin steel wedges

inserted in the top of the handle. "I suppose we could pick them out with a screwdriver and some needle nose pliers. It's going to be a big project."

Courtney held out her hand. "Then let me take charge of that one. I'm feeling pretty useless as it is."

Everett passed the ax to her. "Thanks. I'll get you some tools." He made his way up the ladder into the storage area. Everett shined his flashlight into the toolbox and selected various sized screwdrivers and a pair of needle nose pliers. He scratched through the box picking out a set of Allen wrenches. "Maybe we can use these for shims. We'll need more than a couple of punches to shim an ax head."

Twenty minutes later, Everett returned to the work area and handed the tools to Courtney. "Take a break, Kevin. I'll give it a few whacks."

Elijah intercepted the chisel. "Let me put a quick edge on it. Let's make the most of your strength."

The hours passed, and the team continued their effort at splitting the boulder. Elijah stood up. "I vote that we break for lunch. We've got plenty of leftover goat and perhaps a few latkes."

Everett nodded. "That sounds fantastic. Let me know when it's ready. I'm going to keep working for a while longer."

"Yeah, I'll stay with Everett," Kevin said.

Elijah stood up. "Fine. Sarah, will you help me with the meal?"

"Sure. You guys don't' wear yourselves out." She waved as she walked away.

Everett asked Courtney, "How are you doing with the handle?"

She didn't look up from her project. "I've got a hold of the first wedge. It seems like it's getting loose. I'll get it, eventually."

"I'm sure you will. But, can I borrow it for a second? I need to see where we need to work on the hole." Everett held out his hand.

She looked up and passed him the ax. "Here you go."

Kevin held the handle so Everett could place the ax head against the slit they'd carved. "Looks like it needs to be wider."

"And deeper." Everett passed the ax back to Courtney.

The two men continued beating the chisel against the rock for the next forty minutes.

Sarah walked into the work area. "The food is ready. You guys come eat. You'll have more energy after lunch."

Everett nodded and placed the tools atop one of the buckets as he followed Sarah. He felt tired, and they still had a lot of work to do. "Courtney, can you walk by yourself or do you need a hand?"

"I can hobble. I'm fine."

Everett insisted and helped her back to the cathedral.

Elijah brought plates around to everyone and asked God to bless the food.

"This is delicious, Elijah." Everett devoured his meal. He'd built up quite an appetite working on the boulder all morning.

"Fantastic, as usual." Sarah took another bite.

Courtney finished chewing. "Can we listen to the radio? It might help us to feel a little less claustrophobic."

"I'm not sure if the antenna was cut by the slab when it fell, but I'll try." Everett placed his plate on the ground and pointed at Danger who was already eyeballing the remainder of his meal. "Don't even think about it." Everett found the radio and switched it on. "It sounds like we have a signal. It's staticky, but it's something."

The reporter was difficult to make out through the static. "The Global Republic is urging all survivors not to drink surface water. The comet contained a very high percentage of arsenic and radium. Arsenic was one of the primary elements making up Wormwood. When the planet collided with the debris field, the meteorites, which fell to earth, rained the poisonous matter across the lakes, ponds, and streams all across North and South America. The Atlantic Ocean has also been heavily polluted by the fallout of the comet.

"We are unable to provide an estimate of how long the effects of the contamination will last, but GREMA Director Vivian Brown issued a statement early this morning urging all Global Republic citizens to locate underground streams and deep wells for drinking and bathing. Her statement said that arsenic can be absorbed through the skin as well as through the digestive system. Due to the extremely high levels of arsenic contained in surface water, drinking or bathing may result in vomiting, diarrhea, confusion, and even death.

"If you think you have arsenic poisoning already, the best course of action is to locate a clean water source and drink lots of fluids. Dehydration from arsenic poisoning is likely to be one of the main causes for loss of life in this disaster.

"Besides the loss of human life, this event is going to be a very long, drawn out ecological disaster which will kill off plant, animal, and insect life from the Atlantic Ocean and the Gulf of Mexico to the west coasts of North and South America.

"Those who are able to locate water and survive the direct effects of Wormwood should ration food as strictly as possible. It could be years before healthy crops can be produced again in North America. GREMA said that it is unlikely that any plant life will grow in the six month period following the impact. Crops produced in the following year may contain high levels of arsenic and will not be safe for human consumption. Some foods retain arsenic more readily than others, with rice being the worst offender. This is particularly bad news as rice production has been the primary source of nutrition for Central and South America since the global economy melted down more than three years ago.

"For those of you who are just tuning in, New Atlantis has been totally devastated by the bombardment of the meteorites. His Majesty and all top-level officials were in Jerusalem for the dedication of the Temple at the time the earth collided with the debris field. The eastern hemisphere saw minimal effects from the meteorites, so they were all unharmed by the event.

Global Republic advisors and those who run day-to-day operations in the capitol sheltered in subterranean bunkers far below the surface of New Atlantis, so citizens can breathe a sigh of relief, knowing that we have the leadership we'll need to rebuild."

Sarah rolled her eyes. "Oh, well! That's a relief. I wouldn't have been able to stand it if the antichrist had been hurt."

The staticky transmission continued. "Very large meteorites, many the size of cars and some larger than a house fell in and around the New Atlantis metropolitan area. The new Ministry of Religion Building was completely destroyed. The old US Treasury Building was demolished as well as the Federal Reserve and the Lincoln Memorial.

"The Global Republic General Assembly Building was damaged to such a degree that it has been deemed unsafe for occupancy necessitating the Global Republic Government to relocate for the time being. The Global Republic Palace built on the site of the old US White House was also destroyed.

"His Most Prepotent Majesty Angelo Luz and his top advisors will be setting up temporary offices in Jerusalem since the largest Global Republic Consulate in the eastern hemisphere is in that city.

"Unfortunately, the widespread destruction of the capitol city will greatly hinder the GR's ability to provide disaster aid in the Americas. Those requiring assistance from the government should expect a longer response time than originally estimated."

"You don't say!" Everett said sarcastically.

"Then I guess Luz isn't going to come dig us out." Kevin looked at Everett with a silly grin.

"I guess we better get back to work then," Everett said.

"Five more minutes. I'd like to enjoy my treat." Kevin took a bite from his last latke.

Everett finished his plate. "Elijah and Sarah, what a great meal. Thank you, both. I was running on empty."

"Thank you for trying to get us out of here. I'll have to admit; it's making me more than a little antsy to think about being trapped in here." Sarah took his plate.

"We're going to get out. Don't fret about that." Everett gave another of his reaffirming nods, even though his own confidence was beginning to crack.

"That rock ain't gonna split itself." Kevin stood up and stretched. "Thanks for lunch."

Everett led the way back to the work area and took the first round of working the chisel and hammer. Courtney joined the two men and resumed her task of extracting the metal wedges from the top of the ax handle. Once the dishes were cleaned up, Elijah and Sarah came back to the work area. Sarah entered the rotation of pounding on the boulder and Elijah maintained the edge on the chisel.

The team continued working in unison for the next six hours. Courtney was able to extract the wedges, and with a little help from Everett and Kevin, she got the ax head off of the handle. The chisel team cut a slit that was long enough and deep enough to wedge the ax head into it.

Everett shimmed the ax head into the channel using the Allen wrenches and the steel punches. "This job will take some serious pounding if we're gonna split that rock. I've been swinging that hammer all day. I don't think I have it in me to keep going."

Kevin shook his head. "Let's call it a day and start fresh in the morning."

"Sounds good to me." Sarah rubbed her shoulder. "I couldn't take one more swing."

"I'll make dinner and then we can all get a good night's sleep." Elijah left to the cathedral.

After dinner, the team settled into their respective sleeping bags. No one had the energy for cards, and the amount of static on the radio made listening to it just plain painful.

Even with the apprehension of being trapped in the cave, Everett slept better than the prior night. The lack of the booming assault from meteorites created an atmosphere which was much more soothing and conducive to slumber.

He awoke at five o'clock. Everett prayed silently, asking, begging God to grant him success with splitting the boulder and digging out of the cave. Everett made his coffee as quietly as possible. He ate a granola bar which was well past its expiration date. It still tasted okay, but it had crumbled apart and was closer to cereal in texture than a bar. "Most folks on the planet would kill for a crumbly granola bar. I've got to be grateful for what I have," he whispered to himself.

He didn't want to wake everyone up with the noise of banging on the rock, but he couldn't stand the apprehension much longer. "If we're stuck, I want to know. If we're buried alive, I'll find a way to be okay with it. But the uncertainty is driving me crazy."

He took his coffee, his flashlight, and his Bible and headed to the work area.

As Everett passed Kevin, he heard a faint voice. "Time to go to work, boss?"

Everett smiled and looked down. In a whisper, he said, "No hurry." He continued toward the cave entrance and took a seat on one of the buckets. Using another bucket for a table, he placed his metal canteen cup of coffee upon it. Everett read through the Psalms seeking peace and comfort. He'd admitted to God that he was nervous and afraid that they might never get out of the cave, but in front of Courtney and the others, he maintained a confident and stalwart demeanor.

Twenty minutes later, Kevin arrived, also sipping his coffee.

Everett folded his Bible. "Is everyone else up?"

"They will be once we start banging on that rock."

Everett gave a lopsided grin. "That's what I was trying to avoid."

"Elijah and Courtney were both awake. And I'm guessing Sarah is awake also, she just doesn't want to get out of the warm sleeping bag."

"I'm anxious to get started." Everett glanced up at the ax head wedged in the slit of the stone.

"I'm feeling good, rested." Kevin stretched. "Ready to go."

"Yeah, me too. I was beat last night." Everett stood up and grabbed the hammer. Once again, his body had to get the feel for swinging a hammer upside down. He took a few practice swings, building up to increasingly harder strikes against the ax head. After ten good wallops, Everett was back in the zone. Swinging the hammer with his back tilted slightly. TINK! TINK! TINK! He continued in his rhythm for fifteen minutes.

"My turn." Kevin held out his hand until Everett passed him the hammer. He too needed a few warm up swings but soon stepped into his flow.

The two men traded off every few minutes. The rest of the group gradually joined them, one by one.

Sarah worked into the rotation, striking the boulder with all of her might.

Three hours passed, and Everett could feel himself wearing down already. "I'll be ready to take a break soon."

"Then lunch will be ready when you are." Elijah stood up and excused himself.

Everett was determined to crack the boulder before lunch. A day and a half had been invested in this project, and he wanted it to be over with. Everett slowed his swings, driving the hammer with all of his strength. TINK! TINK! TINK! Everett heard a slight change in the ring of the hammer against the ax head. This fueled his ambition, and he swung with every bit of strength he had. TONK! TUNK! CRACK!

"Get back!" Kevin pulled Everett away from the

stone with both arms. The boulder split, dropping the ax head and shims to the ground.

Courtney and Sarah both stepped out of the way of the falling debris.

Everett dropped the hammer and turned to watch the boulder in the gap between the ceiling and the slab. The two halves dropped roughly two inches and slid into each other, but moved no further.

Kevin stepped forward with a shovel and struck the two pieces of the rock. Nothing happened.

Everett walked up to the boulder and pushed on each side with his hands. "It won't budge." He bent down to retrieve his hammer. He pounded on the individual chunks of rock, but nothing changed. His face lost every trace of hope, and he swallowed the knot in his throat.

No one said a word. They all knew the meaning of what had just happened. The ominous event and what it portended needed no exposition.

Courtney walked to Everett and put her arms around him. "Let's leave it alone for now. We'll have something to eat and come back to the drawing board after lunch."

Everett exhaled deeply. "You and Sarah go give Elijah a hand. Kevin and I will be along in a while."

"Okay, but don't be long." She kissed him. "You did a good job. We all did. We'll come up with something. We'll get out of here."

"Thanks." Everett put on his brave face as she walked away.

Once the girls were gone, Kevin turned to Everett. "We should start rationing the flashlights. Those batteries from the solar array are over four years old. I'm guessing the longest they'll hold a charge is about six weeks. Once they're dead, we'll have no more light."

Everett stared at the stubborn pieces of stone pressed up against each other to form a more impenetrable wall than they had before. "Then we've still got six weeks to dig out before we're completely in the dark. We've got, air, food, and water."

Kevin's forehead creased. "I'm not trying to be a killjoy, but most of our food has to be cooked. We only have a month's worth of wood."

"We've got nearly two years of food that doesn't require cooking. If we're not out by then, I'll be ready to die."

Kevin nodded. "We should start mentally preparing to get by with no light. It's going to be a lot to handle mentally."

"What are you suggesting? We start learning to eat and get by in the dark? Like blind people?"

"It will be easier if we start training now. We can get everything we'll need down from the storage area and begin counting our steps to this, that, and the other thing. We'll have to memorize where we keep everything, and yes, live just like blind people."

Everett shook his head. He wasn't ready to accept that outcome. "No. God has a mission for Elijah. Somehow, some way, he's going to get him out of here."

Kevin put his hand on Everett's shoulder. "Keep in mind; God could whisk Elijah away in a whirlwind, supernaturally. We wouldn't necessarily have to be rescued."

"Let's give it another week before we bring this up to the rest of the group. It sounds too much like giving up. We need hope to keep going, to keep digging and to keep trying to come up with a plan to get us out of here."

Kevin nodded. "Okay. One week, but promise me that if we're no closer to getting out by this time next week, you'll let me take charge of prepping everyone to live in the dark."

Everett reluctantly agreed. "One week."

The days passed and the team tried various strategies, including trying to bust up the large slab of stone which was blocking the exit. Nothing worked. They simply did not have the tools they needed to break it up. The slab was too large and would have required a series of wedges and feathers to bust it up. The morale among everyone trapped in the cave sank lower and lower as they slowly began to accept the inevitable.

Exactly one week from the day Everett had agreed to follow Kevin's plan, the two of them sat alone, with their backs up against the slab.

Kevin sighed. "It's been a week."

Everett nodded softly. "I know."

"I think everyone understands the reality of the situation at this point. I'm going to lay out the plan to begin our transition after dinner tonight."

Everett's heart sank. The spirit of despair and defeat set upon him like a shadow of death. The impending darkness was a tragedy he did not want to accept. "Can we wait until tomorrow?"

"Everett, you act like I'm doing this to try to torture everyone. That's not it. It's reality and the sooner we face it, the sooner we can begin to prepare for the inevitable. I'm trying to help."

Everett looked at him with pleading eyes. "Just one more day. Please."

Kevin exhaled deeply and shook his head. "You're not making this any easier for me. And you're not helping the group, Everett."

"I know. But it's going to sound like a death sentence. Give us one more day to be happy."

Kevin glared at him. "Tomorrow morning. First thing. Don't ask me to delay anymore." Kevin's voice was harsh, borderline angry.

"Okay." Everett didn't care. He'd been granted a stay of execution for a few more hours. He sat silently beside Kevin.

Everett heard Kevin scratching against the slab. He turned and looked at him curiously, but said nothing. The sound continued. Everett's hopelessness and distress were interrupted by Kevin's bizarre behavior. *What is he doing?* Everett wondered silently. *Is he scratching his back against the slab?* Still, he said nothing.

Finally, Kevin stood up. "Bro, that sound you're making is kind of weirding me out. I'm going to go hang out with everyone else. I'll see you in a while." Kevin left the work area.

Everett felt insulted. Why would Kevin be making strange scratching sounds and then blaming it on him? Everett held his tongue. Everyone in the cave was on edge, and nothing good would come of inciting additional conflict. He said nothing as

Kevin walked away.

"There's that sound!" Everett listened closely. It was faint. The noise he'd assumed Kevin was making resembled a soft composition of scraping, rubbing, and scratching. "It wasn't Kevin, and it sure wasn't me." Everett laid his ear against the rock. "It's coming from the other side!"

A rush of hope, thrill, and excitement began in Everett's chest and erupted outward from there. Euphoria flared up to his head, making him feel twenty pounds lighter, then to his extremities, causing him to spring up from his seated position.

Everett's hands shook with exhilaration. He dashed toward the cathedral, being conscious of his elated state so he wouldn't slip and fall on the smooth surface of the cavern floor.

The group looked at Everett with concern. Kevin stood up as if he was worried that Everett may be experiencing a mental breakdown.

Everett gasped for breath. "Someone or something is digging us out!"

"What?" Sarah stood up. Her face betrayed her disbelief. "Who?"

Everett was giddy. "I don't know. Maybe Tommy."

"We never told Tommy where the cave is. And it's impossible to get a call out on the ham. We can't get a signal, Everett." Kevin's eyes were filled with consternation. He looked as if he was sure Everett was losing touch with reality.

"No, Kevin, listen. The noise you thought I was making, it wasn't me. I thought you were making the racket, but it was coming from the other side."

Kevin walked passed Everett without a word.

Everett and the others followed him to the cave entrance.

Courtney believed Everett right away. Her eyes lit up as she skipped to the work area. "We're getting out!"

Kevin held his hand up as he placed his ear against the rock. "Everyone, be quiet!"

All of them became hushed.

Kevin looked at Everett. "I'm sorry, Everett. I don't hear anything. Maybe you just wanted to hear something. We're under a lot of stress. Our minds play tricks on us."

"What?" Everett's mouth hung open. Was Kevin accusing him of making this up? "No! I heard it. Someone is digging us out!"

"Okay, well, if they are, we'll get out. If not, then we're still stuck." Kevin waved his hands in the air and retreated back to the cathedral.

Sarah put her ear against the rock. Seconds later she gave Everett a look of pity. "Sorry, I don't hear anything either." She walked after Kevin.

"You, believe me, right Elijah?"

The old prophet closed his eyes peacefully. "I know God has a plan."

Everett turned to Courtney. "And you?"

She smiled, big and bright. "I believe you, Everett. You're the most sober one of the group." She glanced over to Elijah. "Well, second most, anyway. If you're going nuts, then the rest of us have probably already been insane for some time now."

He hugged her. "We're getting out!"

Courtney laid her ear against the rock and listened. She remained there for several minutes.

"Do you hear it?"

"They could be taking a break." She held her finger to her lips to signal for Everett to be quiet.

Her facial expression changed suddenly. "There it is! I hear it!"

"Praise God!" Elijah lifted his hands to heaven. "Glory to the Almighty in heaven."

Everett grinned from ear to ear. Kevin and Sarah had almost convinced him that the sound was indeed a figment of his imagination. He looked up. "Thank you, Jesus!"

Courtney went to the cathedral and retrieved Kevin and Sarah. The two of them each had a listen and confirmed that they too could hear the noise.

"It does sound like someone digging." Kevin beamed with hope. "I'm sorry that I insinuated you were crazy."

Everett embraced his friend in a hug. "No problem."

Sarah hugged him also. "Me too, Everett. I'm sorry I didn't believe you."

Everett stared at the stone, expecting it to fall away at any moment.

"They could have quite a lot of digging to do." Courtney stood beside him with her arm around him.

"We should let them know we're in here, so they don't give up." Sarah looked around at the others.

Kevin's eyes narrowed. "You know, we left tracks from the creek up the trail to the cave. We've also made enough trips back and forth from Elijah's barn on the ATV to leave a trail. It could be that crew from Woodstock digging us out. They may assume we're dead in here with a boat load of supplies, free for the taking."

Everett considered what Kevin was saying. "So if we let them know we're still alive, they could potentially walk away and come back after they think we've had enough time to die."

"Or worse, they might come in hot." Kevin stroked his beard.

Courtney looked at Elijah. "What do you think?"

Elijah held his hands out, palms facing upward. "I think they are digging us out. That is a blessing from the Lord."

"Yeah, but if they're hostiles, we need to be prepared for it." Sarah crossed her arms.

Everett's brows drew together. "I'm going to get my HK, just in case. They might have five days or five minutes of digging left."

"Good idea." Kevin followed Everett to the corner of the cave where they kept their weapons.

Elijah and the girls followed them to the cathedral. Courtney said, "We need to have a plan for when the entrance is breached. I mean, I don't want to point a gun in the face of someone who is just trying to help, but we have to consider the fact that they may not be rescuing us with the best of intentions."

Everett checked the chamber of his rifle and hit the light attached to the handguard to make sure it worked. "Kevin, that's your department."

Kevin handed a rifle to Sarah. "Courtney, how's that ankle doing?"

"I can walk. I don't know if I can run."

Kevin pointed toward the supplies. "Then we'll set up a fallback position over there. We'll stack up food buckets as a barrier, and you'll hold it down."

Courtney looked at the buckets. "You think they'll stop a bullet?"

"Rice and beans aren't much less dense than sand. The buckets are essentially sand bags. They'll stop handgun and shotgun ammo. We'll double them up. Everett, why don't you crawl up to the storage area and start lowering more buckets.

"I'll stand watch by the entrance for the time being. Elijah, you and Courtney take up a position along the back wall. Everett, you and Sarah get as many supplies as you can to construct a barricade. Once that's finished, the two of you can take up a position near the cathedral entrance."

Everett slung his HK across his back and immediately began climbing the ladder. He lowered the buckets down to Sarah who ferried them to the wall where Elijah and Courtney were positioned with their weapons.

The barricade was completed in thirty minutes then they waited. Hours passed, and nothing happened. Everett walked up to where Kevin was standing. "Do you still hear digging?"

Kevin nodded. "Yep. It's getting louder which probably means they're closer."

"But it could still be hours before they break through."

"It could be days," Kevin replied.

"Maybe we should set up shifts."

Kevin looked back toward the cathedral. "Two

person shifts. Six hours each. Sarah and I will take first shift. You and Courtney take second. We'll work Elijah in after that."

Everett nodded. "We've got a whistle. I'll bring it to you so you can blow it as soon as you see the entrance is about to be breached."

"Sounds good." Kevin nodded.

"Whatever happens, we won't be trapped. And like Elijah said, that is a blessing." Everett patted Kevin on the shoulder and walked away. He found the others and informed them of the watch schedule. Everett brought the whistle to Kevin. Then, he and Courtney placed their sleeping bags behind the barricade and relaxed for a while. Everett tried to sleep, but his body was tense, waiting to jump up at any moment, in response to the whistle. Nothing happened.

Hours later, Everett checked his watch. "Courtney, we're up for guard duty."

She opened her eyes. "I think I slept for about fifteen minutes."

"Elijah will make us a cup of coffee."

"I'm going to need it." Courtney stretched, grabbed her rifle, and followed Everett to their post.

"You stay here. I'll stand watch by the entrance. If I have to fall back, cover me until I get back here." Everett left Courtney behind the cover of the cathedral wall.

"Be safe!" she called to him as he walked away.

Everett took Kevin's position. "Go get some rest. I'll call you if I need you."

Kevin removed the string from around his neck which held the whistle. "I haven't heard anything for a while. I think they're on break." He handed the whistle to Everett.

"I hope they haven't given up." Everett situated a bucket near the slab.

"Me too." Kevin stretched and headed toward the cathedral. "Whoever they are."

Everett sat on the bucket. Knowing the digging had paused allowed him to unwind more than when he'd laid down. He sat silently, waiting for the work to resume. Hours passed, and his eyes grew heavy. His head lowered, and the sudden jerk from his body about to fall off the bucket woke him up. Everett shook his head, took a deep breath, and stood up so he wouldn't fall asleep again.

An hour later, he heard the sound resume. "They haven't given up." He sighed a breath of relief then the apprehension returned. Immediately after the threat of being trapped had passed, the danger of being attacked quickly stepped forward and filled the gap.

Everett could hear the sound growing louder. He motioned for Courtney.

She walked up to his position. "What is it?"

"Go wake everyone up. I can hear the shovel hitting the back side of the slab. Tell Kevin to come up here and everyone else to be ready. The breach is imminent."

Courtney hustled back as quickly as she could, sprinting on her good foot and slowing for the steps with her other.

Kevin joined Everett in less than a minute. "They're coming through?"

Everett nodded. Just then, the slab lurched away

from the cave. Rock and rubble fell from the gap between the ceiling and the slab.

Everett put his arm out and pushed Kevin back. "Watch out. That boulder we split is going to fall."

More dirt and gravel preceded the fall of the two halves of the large boulder. The individual pieces of the giant stone crashed down to the floor.

Kevin passed a pair of sunglasses to Everett. "You haven't seen sunlight in over a week. You better put these on."

Everett quickly put the sunglasses on and held his rifle at a low ready position. The sound of digging grew louder, and the slab edged away from the cave even more. A sliver of daylight followed the next slide of dirt and rock into the cave.

Everett's heart pounded, both from the joy of seeing daylight and the anxiety of a possible assault. "Breathe," he told himself.

Kevin leveled the barrel of his rifle at the opening.

A voice called out from the other side. "Hello! Is anyone there?"

"State your business!" Kevin held his AR-15 steady.

"I'm looking for Elijah." The man had a thick Jewish accent.

Everett turned to see Elijah walking toward the entrance. "Do you recognize that voice?"

Elijah walked steadily toward the beam of daylight. "Yes, I'm here. Is that you, old friend?"

"Indeed, it is I. It seems like it's been eons since I've heard your voice."

Elijah became jubilant. "Step back, step away

from the slab. We'll push it from the inside."

"Yes, I'm clear. Go ahead, then." The voice grew more distant.

Elijah motioned for everyone to join him. "Come. Everyone. Push against the stone!"

Kevin stepped back cautiously still holding his rifle. "Go ahead team. I'll cover you."

Everett placed his rifle on the ground and climbed on the stone which was slowly pitching more and more outward. Courtney and Sarah joined him. Everett pushed the rock with all of his might, and it moved enough to create a three-foot gap between the ceiling and the top of the slab. Everett scaled to the top.

"Stay in the cave. The arsenic dust is still falling from the sky. It isn't good to get it in your lungs." The man peeked inside. His face was wrapped in a Middle Eastern shemagh, with only his eyes visible.

Everett glanced up at the dark sky. The tiny amount of sunlight which was filtering through seemed bright at first, but he soon realized that it was his mole-like existence over the past eight days that had made his eyes sensitive to even the smallest amount of daylight.

Elijah helped the man inside the cave. "Thank you, thank you, my friend."

The man began to unwrap the shemagh from his face, revealing a long gray beard, bushy eyebrows, and shoulder-length gray hair. "Have you any water, Elijah?"

"Yes, of course. Wait here." Elijah scurried off, leaving the man with the others who simply stared at him.

Everett quickly realized how rude they must all seem. He pulled up a bucket. "Please have a seat. You must be tired. You dug us out by yourself?"

"Thank you." The man sat down. "Yes, just me."

"I'm Everett; this is my wife, Courtney. And this is Kevin and his wife, Sarah. Thank you for rescuing us."

"If you have food, water, and shelter from the dust, it will actually be you rescuing me. It's all a matter of perspective I guess." The man turned to Kevin and eyeballed his rifle. "Dangerous in this cave, is it?"

Kevin cracked a smile and removed the sling of the rifle from off of his shoulder. "No. We just haven't had many visitors. Being the Apocalypse and all, you never know who is going to pop around."

The old man chuckled at Kevin's response.

Elijah brought some water and an MRE. "You must be famished. Haven't you any water at all?"

The man took the cup and drank deeply. He shook his head. "I ran out yesterday." He took another drink. "All the water, the streams, lakes, and ponds, it's poison."

Courtney smiled politely at Elijah. "We introduced ourselves, but we didn't catch your friend's name."

Elijah chuckled. "Oh, forgive me. How rude of me. This is Moses."

Everett felt his head getting light and quickly found a bucket to sit on. He'd read enough of the Bible to know exactly who he'd just been introduced to. Courtney took a seat also. Kevin and

Sarah stood with their mouths hanging open. No one said anything.

Everett took a deep breath, regained his composure and extended his hand. "It's a pleasure to meet you, sir."

Moses quickly shook Everett's hand and tore into the MRE. "Yes, likewise. Elijah, might I have another cup of water? It seems I've worked up quite a thirst with all that digging."

"Of course, old friend. And don't fill up on that MRE. We shall have a grand feast tonight. We will celebrate, eat, dance, and talk. We have quite a bit of catching up to do."

Moses continued eating. "That sounds wonderful. Tonight, we will celebrate. But soon, you and I have business which we must attend to."

Courtney and the others snapped out of their initial shock. Each of them shook hands with Moses and thanked him repeatedly for digging them out of the cave.

Everett's face softened, and he smiled gently. The coming of Moses was nothing less than a miracle. They would still have to shelter in the cave until the rest of the arsenic had cleared out of the atmosphere, but knowing that they weren't trapped brought a magnificent feeling of relief.

Everett experienced an extraordinary sense of honor at being granted the opportunity to meet Moses. Yet he also knew the encounter would prove to be bittersweet. Moses was not just stopping by for a visit. He had come to take Elijah to Jerusalem with him. Everett recognized that the clock was ticking. He was spending his final days with the old prophet who had become like a father to him. Elijah had been their spiritual leader for the past three years. And now, when the worst part of the tribulation was just around the corner, on their very doorstep, Elijah would no longer be there.

Everett wondered if he would have the faith to endure the final trumpet judgments and terminal phase of the Great Tribulation, the Vials of Gods Wrath.

DON'T PANIC!

Inevitably, books like this will wake folks up to the need to be prepared, or cause those of us who are already prepared to take inventory of our preparations. New preppers can find the task of getting prepared for an economic collapse, EMP, or societal breakdown to be a source of great anxiety. It shouldn't be. By following an organized plan and setting a goal of getting a little more prepared each day, you can do it.

I always try to include a few prepper tips in my novels, but they're fiction and not a comprehensive plan to get prepared. Now that you're motivated to start prepping, the last thing I want to do is leave you frustrated, not knowing what to do next. So I'd like to offer you a free PDF copy of *The Seven Step Survival Plan.*

For the new prepper, *The Seven Step Survival Plan* provides a blueprint that prioritizes the different aspects of preparedness and breaks them down into achievable goals. For seasoned preppers who often get overweight in one particular area of preparedness, *The Seven Step Survival Plan* provides basic guidelines to help keep their plan in balance, and ensures they're not missing any critical segments of a well-adjusted survival strategy.

To get your **FREE** copy of ***The Seven Step Survival Plan***, go to **PrepperRecon.com** and click the FREE PDF banner, just below the menu bar, at the top of the home page.

Thank you for reading
The Days of Elijah: Book Two
Wormwood

Reviews are the best way to help get the book noticed. If you liked the book, please take a moment to leave a five-star review on Amazon and Goodreads.

I love hearing from readers! So whether it's to say you enjoyed the book, to point out a typo that we missed, or asked to be notified when new books are released, drop me a line.

prepperrecon@gmail.com

Stay tuned to **PrepperRecon.com** for the latest news about my upcoming books, and great interviews on the **Prepper Recon Podcast**.

Keep watch for
The Days of Elijah: Book Three
Angel of the Abyss

If you liked *Wormwood*, you'll love the prequel series,

The Days of Noah

In ***The Days of Noah, Book One: Conspiracy***, You'll see the challenges and events that Everett and Courtney have endured to reach the point in the story that you've just read. You'll read what it was like for the Christians in Kevin and Sarah's group in their final days before the rapture, and how the once-great United States of America lost its sovereignty. You'll have a better understanding of how the old political and monetary system were cleared away, like pieces on a chess board, to make way for the one-world kingdom of the Antichrist.

If you have an affinity for the prophetic don't miss my EMP survival series,
Seven Cows, Ugly and Gaunt

In ***Book One: Behold Darkness and Sorrow***, Daniel Walker begins having prophetic dreams about the judgment coming upon America for rejecting God. Through one of his dreams, Daniel learns of an imminent threat of an EMP attack which will wipe out America's electric grid and most all computerized devices, sending the country into a technological dark age.

Living in a nation where all life-sustaining systems of support are completely dependent on electricity and computers, the odds for survival are dismal. Municipal water services, retail food distribution, police, fire, EMS and all emergency services will come to a screeching halt.

If they want to live, Daniel and his friends must focus on faith, wits and preparation to be ready . . . before the lights go out.

Buy your copy of *Seven Cows, Ugly and Gaunt, Book One: Behold Darkness and Sorrow* in Paperback, Kindle, or Audio Edition from Amazon.com today!

You'll also enjoy my first series, *The Economic Collapse Chronicles*

The series begins with *Book One: American Exit Strategy*. Matt and Karen Bair thought they were prepared for anything, but can they survive a total collapse of the economic system? If they want to live through the crisis, they'll have to think fast and move quickly. In a world where all the rules have changed, and savagery is law, those who hesitate pay with their very lives.

When funds are no longer available for government programs, widespread civil unrest erupts across the country. Matt and Karen are forced to move to a more remote location and their level of preparedness is revealed as being much less adequate than they believed prior to the crisis. Civil instability erupts into civil war and Americans are forced to choose a side. Don't miss this action-packed, post-apocalyptic tale about survival after the total collapse of America.

ABOUT THE AUTHOR

He brought me up also out of an horrible pit, out of the miry clay, and set my feet upon a rock, and established my goings.

Psalm 40:2

Mark Goodwin is a Christian constitutional author and the host of the popular Prepper Recon Podcast which interviews patriots, preppers, and economists each week on PrepperRecon.com to help people prepare for the uncertain times ahead. Mark holds a degree in accounting and monitors macro-economic conditions to stay up-to-date with the ongoing global meltdown.

He is an avid student of the Holy Bible and spends several hours every week devoted to the study of Scripture and the prophecies contained therein. The troubling trends in the moral, social, political, and financial landscapes have prompted Mark to conduct extensive research within the arena of preparedness. He weaves his knowledge of biblical prophecy, economics, politics, prepping, and survival into an action-packed tapestry of post-apocalyptic fiction.

Having been a sinner saved by grace himself, the story of redemption is a prominent theme in all of Mark's writings.

CPSIA information can be obtained
at www.ICGtesting.com
Printed in the USA
BVOW06s0639250817
493084BV00025B/184/P

9 781540 357724